THE
UNEXPECTED
RETURN
OF
JOSEPHINE
FOX

Winner of the 2019 Richard and Judy Search for
a Bestseller competition

'Jo Fox, a very modern woman in wartime England. Getting
to know her was a delight. More please, Claire Gradidge'

RICHARD MADELEY

'Feisty, determined, and brave – I loved Josephine ('Jo') Fox.
What a debut from a marvellous new author'

JUDY FINNIGAN

'A complete delight, the story sings with authenticity . . .
unputdownable'

CAZ FREAR

Claire Gradidge was born and brought up in Romsey. After a career as, among other things, a nurse and a school librarian, she went to the University of Winchester, where she graduated in 2009 with a first class honours BA in Creative Writing. In January 2018, she was awarded a PhD in Creative Writing and *The Unexpected Return of Josephine Fox* was written as the creative element of her PhD study. An early version of the opening 3,000 words was highly commended in the *Good Housekeeping* magazine competition in 2012.

She has taught at the University of Winchester as an Associate Lecturer for six years and has also had some short fictions and poems published in *South*, *Orbis* and *Vortex*. She has been married for 40 years and has two adult sons.

THE
UNEXPECTED
RETURN

OF
JOSEPHINE
FOX

CLAIRE GRADIDGE

ZAFFRE

First published in Great Britain in 2019 by
ZAFFRE
80–81 Wimpole St, London W1G 9RE

A CIP catalogue record for this book is
available from the British Library.

ISBN: 978-1-78576-998-6

Also available as an ebook

3 5 7 9 10 8 6 4 2

Typeset by IDSUK (Data Connection) Ltd
Printed and bound in Great Britain by Clays Ltd, Elcograf S.p.A.

Zaffre is an imprint of Bonnier Books UK
www.bonnierbooks.co.uk

Note from Richard & Judy

Books are booming. Writers are thriving. New voices arrive on the scene all the time, and it's wonderful to be a part of the vibrant success story that is UK literature today. Since launching the Richard and Judy Book Club with WH Smith in 2010 we have been proud to be at the forefront of some of the biggest publishing sensations of recent years.

For us, the Search for a Bestseller competition is one of the most satisfying features of our club. The response from new writers is always overwhelming, and the sheer quality of the entries never fails to hugely impress everyone involved in selecting the eventual winner. There is absolutely no doubt that many of these authors will go on to find success. Yes, publishing is a crowded, bustling market place but there's always room for fresh talent – which brings us to Claire Gradidge.

As we so often tell the authors of books we select to be on a Richard and Judy Book Club list, choosing them isn't difficult: the novels more or less pick themselves. It's usually obvious within the first few dozen pages that we're reading a shoo-in for the club. And Claire's debut novel was absolutely in that category: a blindingly obvious choice.

What a story. It is 1941. Britain is losing the war with Germany. Josephine ('Jo') Fox returns to the small town of Romsey. She was last there two decades ago, an illegitimate child and the source of profound shame to her family. She arrives just after a devastating Luftwaffe bombing raid on the town. The pub has been destroyed and rescue teams are working in the wreckage to find the remains of seven people known to have been inside when the bomb landed.

But there's an eighth body – that of a teenage girl. Who was she? What was she doing in the pub? Crucially, how did she really die? Jo joins forces with the local coroner, an old friend, to seek answers – not just to the girl's death, but her own past.

Fans of Anthony Horowitz will enjoy definite undertones of *Foyle's War* in this novel. Gradidge has created a wonderful character in Jo; surprisingly modern, feisty, gutsy and resolute. Life in wartime England is beautifully drawn and researched and this is one of those books you can read pretty much in one sitting.

Congratulations, Claire. More please.

RICHARD AND JUDY

For Nick, for everything

Prologue

14ᵗʰ/15ᵗʰ April 1941, the skies over southern England

B OMBER'S MOON. FROM TWENTY THOUSAND feet, the Solent shines like a mermaid's tail, showing the way to the city so plainly the blackout is useless. There's no mistaking the boatyards, the aircraft factories, the docks. The first Junkers follow the water, set down their payload as simple as laying eggs.

Targets lose their definition as the fires spread. The city answers back, ack-ack guns pouring defiance into the sky. Caught in a stream of tracer, one bomber jinks wildly, turns for home. Engine stuttering smoke, it jettisons its load ten miles off target, sees a dark spot light up like Christmas.

Unknowing, the aircraft has seven deaths on its tally sheet when a Beaufighter brings it down barely a minute later. But tomorrow, when the Heavy Rescue Crew digs the last casualty out of what's left of the little Hampshire pub on the outskirts of Romsey, there will be an extra body to carry to the makeshift mortuary. Not seven shrouded corpses, but eight: eight unlawful deaths for the town's coroner to investigate.

1

The same night, on the ground

IT'S MIDNIGHT WHEN THE TRAIN leaves London. I'd arrived much too early, had to wait until the carriages filled up and the labyrinthine processes of wartime travel set us on our way. Now, in the blacked-out, blue-lit, third-class compartment my fellow travellers are sleeping, stiff upper lip in the face of danger. *If it ain't got your name on it . . .*

But I can't sleep. It isn't the bombs, I'm used to them. It's the thought of what lies ahead.

Romsey.

So long ago.

I'd promised myself I'd never go back. If they didn't want me, I'd show them. I'd never set foot in the place again. That's how you think at fourteen, when your life's crashing down around you. And though it's ridiculous to feel the same when you're almost forty, I do. I'm nervous, but I don't have a choice. If I want to know the truth, I've got to go back.

I peer out through a crack in the blind. Before the war, this moonlit landscape would have been peaceful, eerily beautiful,

3

but tonight the distant wail of air raid sirens seeps into the carriage, dogging our journey and sending us cross-country, miles out of our way. I watch the repeated flare of incendiaries in the distance, see the dark huddled towns spring to light, watch the slow-motion fall of bombs. Glimpses, like at the pictures; except this is life and death.

Not far now.

As dawn breaks, the train is still stopping more often than it moves. If my suitcase weren't so heavy, I could walk from here.

But I wait, and at last we struggle into Romsey station. It hasn't changed a bit. The stationmaster's still waiting by the exit, alert for tips and fare-dodgers. Old Bunny Burnage studies my ticket, barely glances at my face. I don't think he recognises me, but I can't help remembering all the times he'd caught us playing near the railway tracks.

When we laid pennies on the line for the express to flatten. The whole gang of us, messing about, daring each other to play 'last across'. Looking for trouble and finding it.

'Penny'll derail the express,' Billy says.

'Nah. Him'll get cutten in half.' That's Bert.

'Bollocks. Look here.' Abe pulls something from his pocket, holds it out. We look, because Abe is the leader, and what he says, goes. 'It'll just get flattened, like this. And hot, if it isn't pushed off.'

'That's treason.' Jem fingers the squashed irregular shape. 'My dad says—'

'My dad's a copper, my da-ad is,' we taunt him.

'Dad says you can get yer head chopped off for spoiling a coin. Put in the Tower of London with the spies and shot.'

'Liar, liar, pants on fire,' I chant. 'Can't get shot and beheaded.'

'Can too, Carrotty-head.'

'They can't kill you twice, you bloody chicken.'

Spitting mad, I run to where the rail is singing already with the train on its way. The only girl in the gang, I have to prove myself every time. As I set down my penny, they scarper. Bunny Burnage is pounding towards me, cutting off my escape as the express screams past in a shawl of smoke, the rush of it nearly knocking me over. Just in time, I grab the penny. Shove it in my pocket, fingers tingling with heat, ear stinging with the station-master's blow as I stumble away.

'Josephine Fox!' he shouts. 'Should have known. Serve you right if you'd been killed. I'd tell your father if anyone knew who he was. Hop it, you little bastard, and don't come back.'

So I'd hopped, and while the penny and the slap had cooled before I'd even caught up with the gang, the stationmaster's contempt stung much longer. In a way it still rankles, so now when he touches his cap and calls me madam, I want to laugh, dare him to call me bastard to my grown-up face.

I push my suitcase forward. 'I'd like to leave this here for the time being.'

'No noxious substances, no perishable goods, no livestock.'

'None of those.'

'That'll be thruppence.' He hands me a pink ticket. 'No claim without a ticket.' He licks the back of the counterfoil,

5

sticks it to the corner of the case. 'Southern Railway wishes to make it clear that the company takes no responsibility for loss or damage caused by war operations.'

I can't help smiling. 'Safe enough in Romsey, surely?'

'Begging your pardon, madam, but that's all you know. We had a tip and run raider come over last night, flattened the Cricketers' Arms. Still digging them out last I heard, dead as doornails, the whole lot.'

'The old place in Green Lane? That's bad.'

'You know it?' He peers closely at me as I turn away. 'Hang on a minute. You got the look of—'

I pretend not to hear, keep on walking.

2

15th April, Romsey

*In all cases of sudden death . . . it is the duty of those who
are about the deceased to give immediate notice to the
coroner. If possible, notice should be given while the body
is fresh, and while it remains in the same situation as
when the death occurred (Jervis on Coroners, 1927:24).*

THE CRICKETERS' ARMS HAD NEVER been one of those
picturesque country inns mentioned in guidebooks.
Brick-built and ugly, it stood alone on the lane for
almost a century, a taproom bar where farm labourers went
to drink at the end of the day. A place with a reputation – a
mind-your-own-business kind of a place where a man could
drink undisturbed, so long as he paid his score.

Now, the bright morning sunlight shows where the bomb
sheared through the building. Though most of the pub has
been demolished, one corner stands almost to roof height.
An iron-frame bedstead balances precariously; scraps of wall-
paper flutter in the breeze. At the foot of the wall, amongst

the heaps of rubble and scattered timbers, a narrow crack pitches into the void beneath.

Sidelined by the Heavy Rescue Crew, Romsey's coroner stands waiting. Bram Nash knows how lucky he is, even if he doesn't feel it. He might have been under the rubble himself. Less than twelve hours ago, he was sitting in the bar, spinning out a whisky, watching the faces come and go.

He'd known them all. Old Ma Bryall, ferret-faced and vulgar. Fred, never-say-boo-to-a-goose Fred, long-suffering worshipper at Ma's shrine. Henry and Bob with their dominoes, poor daft May on her knees by the fire, brushing out the hearth.

Young Stan Hoskin had received his call-up papers that morning. He'd been proud and scared, full of the glory of war. Nash could remember how that felt. He'd watched as Stan picked up Sal, or maybe it was Sally, picking up Stan. She'd been old enough to be the boy's mother, but no lad had to go to war a virgin while Sal was around. She'd always do a soldier a favour, no matter what. Young, old, maimed, it'd all been the same to her.

Despite the sunlight, the persistent breeze, Nash feels suffocated by the thought of them, buried beneath the press of earth and debris. No sounds from below, no chat from the rescue crew. They work methodically, stopping now and again to listen. To call.

'Anyone there?'

Nothing.

'Anyone?'

He rubs his face, tries not to remember how it feels to be buried alive. Tries not to think about the buried dead.

By lunchtime, they're ready to let Alf down on a rope. He's the smallest, the lightest, nerveless with youth.

A voice lifts across the rubble, trying to argue him out of it.

'Leave it, mate, there's no hope. No point risking it.'

But Alf won't be moved. Everyone waits while he scrabbles over the edge. A flash of torchlight shows against the dark. Then, his voice.

'A girl, just here. Not buried nor nothing.' A pause. 'Nah. She's gone. Cold.'

As a child, I'd dreamed of walking into Romsey's most respectable hotel. Taking tea and cucumber sandwiches like a lady. But the wartime reality this afternoon is Camp coffee and a dry biscuit.

The lounge is gloomy, practically deserted, lamps unlit. The only brightness falls where I sit, close to a window overlooking Market Place. At a safe, English distance, an elderly lawyer type in a navy pinstripe suit is plumped down, head buried in a newspaper. Beyond him, two stalwarts in Harris tweed are engaged in conversation. I can hear the rumble of words, but I'm too far away to make out what they're saying.

I recognise the one facing me. Stout, obnoxious, balding, Mr Maitland used to be our family dentist. As a child, I'd loathed him for the way he appeared to delight in giving pain. He'd seemed older than God to me then, but he can't be more than sixty-something now. The other man's unfamiliar,

9

but I take a good look anyway. Much as I hate to think it, both are the right kind of age for my search. Either could be my father.

Disgust sweeps over me as I sip the sweet coffee substitute. I still can't believe it. That he's alive, somewhere in this town.

All my life, I'd thought my father was dead. That he'd died before I was born, leaving my mother to face the disgrace of my birth alone. Nell had been banished from the town like a girl in a Victorian novel, while I was left for my grandparents to bring up. I suppose I might have discovered the truth if I'd been allowed to stay in Romsey, if I'd lived there as an adult. But when I was almost fourteen, my grandmother died. Without her buffering presence, my grandfather saw no reason to keep me. I'd always known that he was ashamed of me, that he hated the fact I was illegitimate; but once my grandmother was gone, I discovered it wasn't just my birth he hated. It was me, too.

'Where are we going?'

Grandfather doesn't reply. It feels daring to question him, but if he loses his temper at least he'll have to say something. *He hasn't spoken to me for days, ever since Granny died. Not even yesterday, at her funeral.*

This morning, first thing, my Aunt Mags had come in and told me to put a change of clothes in a bag. She'd been crying, but so have we all, except Grandfather. He's been like a stone man. At the funeral, he was the only one who didn't need a handkerchief.

'Please, Grandfather?'

I'm frightened. Mags wouldn't look at me at breakfast, and after we'd finished washing up she'd cried when she told me my grandfather wanted me to go with him.

He speaks without turning, without stopping.

'No use begging me,' he says. 'My mind's made up.'

We're coming to the tunnel under the railway. A horrible, dank place. I hate it. I always run through as fast as I can when I'm on my own, but today I drag my feet. I'm sick with dread so even when we come out into the sunshine beyond the tunnel, I feel cold.

Grandfather marches up the slope to the station, through the deserted booking office and onto the platform. He walks to the farthest end, looks around. Looks at me.

There's no one else about, and the expression on his face scares me. He thrusts out his hand, and instinctively I step away, back from the platform edge.

'Don't put ideas in my head,' he says. 'I want to get rid of you, but not like that.'

'I don't understand.'

'Nothing to understand. I only kept you because your grandmother insisted. Now she's gone, you're out.'

'But . . . what have I done?'

'Don't have to do anything. You're a bastard, that's enough. You bring shame on the family. Well, now it's over.'

'You're throwing me out? What am I going to do?'

'Get a job. You're fourteen in a couple of weeks. Plenty old enough to work.'

'I can find a job in Romsey.'

'Not while I'm alive, you can't.'

Tears come to my eyes. Not so much for him – there's never been love between us – but there's Tom and Jim and David, Mike and Mags and Lizzie. My uncles and aunts. We've been brought up together, more like brothers and sisters. Mike's only a couple of years older than me.

'No point turning on the waterworks,' he says. 'Don't make any difference to me. And don't you go snivelling to the family, either. I've told 'em all. They won't help you.'

The idea of them all agreeing dries my tears. I feel like I've been turned to stone myself. Tom's already in France, he might not even know, and Jim'll be leaving for the war before long, but surely the others could have stood up for me?

'Where am I supposed to go?'

He opens his hand, pushes it towards me again.

'That's a ticket for London,' he says. 'Third class. And five bob so you won't starve. Your mother works at a place in Pimlico. Longmoor House.' He spits. 'See what she makes of you.'

I take the coins, sweaty from his palm. The ticket.

'Grandfather . . .'

He's moving away already, he doesn't even turn to speak.

'Train's due in ten minutes,' he tells me. 'Get on it, Josephine, and don't come back. No one wants you here.'

So I'd gone. For a girl who'd never been out of Romsey before, London was terrifying that hot July afternoon. And when I managed to find my way to where my mother was working, she couldn't take me in. She was employed as a parlourmaid in a respectable household, they would've sacked her if they'd known she had an illegitimate daughter. But I'd seen a poster at Waterloo station, recruiting girls for the munitions factories, so I went and signed up, started straight away. The factories were working non-stop by then, taking on practically anyone. They didn't even check my age.

While I was working in London, I saw my mother once or twice a year, though we were never all that close. But it was through her I learned that Uncle Jim had lost an arm in the war, and David and Mike had been killed. Tom had come home safe, brought a French wife, Sylvie, with him. It was she who'd got in touch with my mother, who stayed in touch with her despite my grandfather's ban.

After I moved away, we'd write occasionally, Christmas and birthdays. But it wasn't until the last few months of her life that we had any real contact. When I heard she was dying, alone and frail, it had seemed the right thing to do to offer help. I was on my own again by then; there was nothing to stop me spending time with her.

It had been late August when I moved into her cramped little flat in Southwark, and by September the Blitz had begun. Between her illness and the bombs, we'd been too busy trying to survive to worry about the past. I didn't realise there was anything I should know, questions I ought to ask.

She was in hospital when it happened. They were giving her morphia by then, and because she was so ill they put her in a side ward, let me visit whenever I liked. When she was awake, I'd help her wash or eat, read to her. Talk about ordinary things: the neighbour's cat; how difficult it was to find elastic in the shops. That day, I'd taken in a paper, the local Romsey rag Aunt Sylvie sent each week. I left my mother leafing through it while I went to get fresh water for her flowers. When I came back, she was hysterical, the paper crumpled on the floor.

Weak as she was, she wouldn't tell me what had upset her so much. All I could understand before the nurse shooed me out was that my father was alive. And I saw she was frightened, heard it in the way she kept saying *he's there, he's there*, over and over. I rescued the paper, took it home with me, but I never got the chance to ask her about it again. Less than two days later, she was dead.

I thought I might find some clue about my father when I cleared her flat, but there was nothing. If it hadn't been for her reaction to the paper, I'd never have known he was alive. But now I did, I promised myself I'd find him. I wanted to know what he'd done to her. Why seeing his name was enough to make her give up the fight, slide into death as if she were glad to go, to escape her memories.

I began by listing all the men whose names had been in the paper. Mourners at funerals, sellers of prize pigs. Appearances in court. There were a lot, but I didn't think it would be too difficult to weed them out.

But now I'm here, it doesn't seem so simple. All I know is that he's got to be old enough to have fathered me. He must have had power, some kind of influence, to have used my mother the way he did and not had to pay for it. He has to have it still, if his name alone can frighten her. He must be entrenched in town, an upright citizen or a complete rogue.

I *will* find out. And there's one thing I know for sure. I shan't turn out to be the only bastard in this.

There are peculiar duties ascribed to the coroner, more particularly to inquire into the manner in which persons have come to their deaths where there is any reason to suppose that they may not have been by natural means (Jervis on Coroners, 1927:13).

The parish hall is always cold. Stone built, north facing, it's a grim place for wedding breakfasts and christenings, but it's perfect as a temporary mortuary.

Nash keeps his coat on as he moves between the trestles. He's seen his fair share of death. In France in the first war, and since, as coroner. He's been called upon to inquire into accidents and suicides, sudden fatalities, even a murder or two. He tries to do his job to the best of his ability, give every death a true bill.

He pauses as he reaches the head of each trestle. Lifts the covering to identify, to confirm, to show respect. It ought to be simple enough, but he's puzzled.

Eight dead.

Seven, he knows. Names he anticipated. Faces – what's left of them – he watched last night, called to mind this morning. Yet now the seven have been tallied, one more remains.

The girl they'd brought out first has been put on the far side of the room. Laid apart from the others. He turns the sheet back. This one's different from the rest, and not only because no one, so far, has been able to identify her.

So young. A stranger. And there's no sign on her of the bomb's blast. She's not been butchered, turned into a blackened tangle of flesh and bone like the rest. She's bloodless, neat, clean. She could almost be a waxwork. Her skin's still soft, pearl and pink. There's a scrape on her temple, and her skull's dented, just a little, on the left-hand side. She looks like a doll, played with by a careless child, and abandoned.

Nash frowns, bends closer. Brighter than the bottle blond of her hair, a thread of orange silk is tangled round the gold stud in her right ear. He loosens it carefully. Tearing a blank sheet from his pocket diary, he folds the paper into a make-shift envelope for the thread.

Seven from the Cricketers' Arms. Known, identified. Seven certificates, a formality. *Death by War Operations.*

But the eighth, that's not so simple.

Who is she, this stranger? How did she die?

Silent, he makes her a promise. She may be one death amongst many, but every death matters, or Hitler's blitz is just slum clearance and some bastard Nash knows – some smart alec – thinks they can use the grave of seven innocent people to hide a crime.

It isn't going to happen. He will find out.

*

I sit daydreaming, looking out over Market Place. It seems so peaceful after London. Although I feel like a stranger, the town is much as I remember. A couple of shops have got new owners, but I could still buy a bucket from the ironmongers or a lipstick from the chemist across the square if I wanted to. The women with their shopping bags have half-familiar faces, and I feel like a child again, observing from the fringe of things.

I'm looking back towards The Hundred, the main street into the square, when a man comes hurrying along. He's purposeful, middle-aged and sturdy, wearing a dark coat and grey trilby. I catch a glimpse of the heavy glasses masking his face as he crosses towards the Town Hall.

Bram Nash.

It's my cue. Time to move on. I go across the room to where the two men sit talking. Maitland looks up, hostile at the interruption.

'Can I help you?'

'Good afternoon, Mr Maitland. I don't know if you remember me? Jo Lester. Josy Fox that was. Joseph's granddaughter.'

As he stands up, I catch the faint urine tang of tweed, the antiseptic overload of mouthwash.

'Ah, yes, Josy Fox. It must be thirty years.'

'Not quite that long.'

I smile, a polite nothing to include both men, though Maitland's companion doesn't bother to look up.

'I hope your grandfather's well?'

'I've no idea.' I hope my tone makes it clear I've no interest, either. 'Are you still in practice?'

'Indeed I am. Do you need an appointment?'

'Thankfully not.' He can take that how he chooses. 'I just wanted to make myself known since I'm back in town. You might remember my mother, Nell? She died a few weeks ago.'

He shakes his head. 'I'm sorry to hear it.' But there's nothing of sympathy in his face. If he has a conscience about her, I haven't caught it yet.

'It's why I'm here,' I say. 'There are things she told me . . . things I need to sort out.'

There's a flicker of a look between the two men. Perhaps I've touched a nerve after all. I'm glad. It may not have been the best exit line in the world, but it'll do.

3

The same day, afternoon

NOTHING LIKE IT HAS HAPPENED here in years. The town has had its share of violence: a drunken temper, a hasty blow, instant regret. Of sudden death: a tramp slipped over the mill, a soldier, a grandmother, a blitzed-out friend in Pompey or London or down in the huddle of Southampton's streets. But this is different. This is murder.

The streets buzz with the murmur of lowered voices. People draw together, peering over their shoulders to see who's listening, itching to hear the latest. The only ones who hold aloof are batty old Dave on the corner, cap out for pennies, and Miss Waverley, hurrying past the Town Hall, too snooty to gossip with the hoi polloi.

A stranger, dead, at the Cricketers'.

A girl.

No one knows who she is.

It wasn't the bomb, Tin Chops says, it wasn't that old fucker Hitler. It wasn't bad luck, or mischance, or sheer bloody accident.

It was murder.

A girl, alone in that pub?

She can't have been respectable.

Who could have done it?

Someone we know?

Not in Romsey.

Who, then? Who?

An outsider.

A gyppo, a tinker, a townie.

It can't be one of our own.

I knew one of the most difficult things about coming back to Romsey would be seeing Nash again. And now I'm here, it's even harder than I thought. But it's got to be done.

I stroll into the square, trying to look as if I haven't a care in the world. It'll be difficult if his business keeps him in the Town Hall for long, but I'm lucky, because barely five minutes after I saw him go in, he comes out again. He doesn't notice me at first, turns into Church Street. I hurry to intercept him.

'Mr Nash?'

He tips his hat. Though I know he recognises me, it's the merest gesture. He sidesteps, ready to walk on.

I put out my hand, not quite touching his sleeve. 'We need to talk.'

'Nothing to say.'

'It's not personal. I have to be here. I want to explain.'

'No need.'

'*Bram!*'

'If you must.' He glances around. 'Better get off the street. Standing here's just jam for the gossips.'

It doesn't bother me, I'm ready for people to know I'm back. But I need Nash's goodwill. And something more.

'Where shall we go?'

'The Wheatsheaf will still be open,' he says, checking his watch. 'It's not three o'clock yet. I'll buy you a drink.'

There's a brewery in town, and so many pubs there's a saying, *So drunk he must have been to Romsey*. They reckon a thirsty man can drink himself into a stupor any time he likes. Cross the right counter with silver and there'll be a pint of the best under it.

I feel like a fool, trailing behind Nash in silence. The Wheatsheaf's a miserable dive, but I'm glad to get inside. We settle in the dingy back bar, two chairs and a table in front of an unlit fire. The pub's empty, the room shadowy, the only window blacked out. Apart from the gin Nash fetches from the bar, it's a very different meeting from last time.

London, October 1940. The Blitz

Outside, sirens wail. Inside, the bar is crowded. Touts and tarts, drunken sailors, Brylcreem boys scarcely out of short trousers. But no one bothers to move. The bombers have come every night for more than a month, the alarm has worn off. The fear remains, but there's no point in shifting when you know it doesn't matter where you go. Everyone's heard the stories: shelters being hit, people inside getting trapped – crushed, or burned, or boiled alive. Might as well stay and finish our drinks.

The bar's lit with a sickly yellow glimmer. My throat's ragged with smoking; my eyes sting as I light up another cigarette. The gin's too weak to have much effect, and I'm sick of myself, of everything. I'd almost welcome a bomb.

I'm ready to quit when my attention's caught by a man in the corner. The briefest glimpse, but recognition jolts. I angle for a better look. A sketch of jaw and mouth, yet I could swear I can smell coal tar soap.

There's a moment of instant recall. Of sitting on a sun-warmed bank, hoping the boys would let me join their gang. Watching their leader's profile sidelong, thrilled to be close to my hero. Smelling the clean scent of Wright's Coal Tar Soap on his skin; aware of my own stink, ashamed of it, one bath a week in water everyone's used, the must and dust of the cottage clinging.

Abe. Leader of the gang. When he was away from the rest of us at his posh school, we'd hang around aimlessly, getting into trouble. But when he was home, the adventures began. Bolder, braver, more inventive than the rest of us, he was Captain Abe, and we were his crew.

It is him, I'm sure of it. So far out of place and time, yet I'm convinced. I get up, stub out my cigarette. I can't let the moment pass.

I'm almost too late. A blonde moves close to his table. Her raucous greeting carries across the room.

'Hello, darling! Looking for a good time?'

I don't catch his reply. Whatever he's said, the woman huffs away. His head lifts and the shadows slide back, revealing heavy, black-framed spectacles, thick tinted lenses that obscure his eyes.

I hesitate. I don't remember him needing glasses. But recognition's as strong as sunlight on my skin. Bold with memories, I pull out a chair, sit down across the table from him.

'Hello, Abe,' I say. 'Remember me? Josy Fox.'

A pause. He leans into the shadows.

'Hello, Josy.'

There's something not right about his voice. A kind of slur, but he can't be drunk, not on the gin they serve here. And now I'm close, I can see there's something wrong with his face, too: the left side's blurred, somehow indistinct. I'm so nervous I blurt out the first thing that comes into my head.

'What did you say to that woman?'

'I beg your pardon?'

'The tart. You frightened her off.'

'Ah.' A pause. 'Tell me, when were you last in Romsey?'

'What?'

'You heard. When were you last in Romsey?'

'You know as well as I do. July '15, when my grandfather kicked me out.'

'A lot's happened since then. Are you sure you want to pursue it?'

'Are you telling me to bugger off?'

He makes a sound that might be laughter. 'Same old Josy.'

'Same old Abe. But I prefer Jo, these days.'

'And I was never that keen on Abe. It's Bram.'

'Still no answer, same old Bram.'

'I would have been seventeen when you went away. The next year, I enlisted. The Rifle Brigade. Got sent straight out to France.' He moves forward into the light, lifts his hand to the wrong side of his face. Outlines what seems at first to be a deep crease on his cheek, but now I can see it's a margin. A place where his flesh stops and something artificial begins. He taps, and the sound is metallic. 'The year after that, I got this.'

Now he's moved closer, I can see the strange demarcation continues above his glasses, bisecting his forehead, vanishing under his hair. The eye beneath the left-hand lens doesn't blink. He's wearing a mask, hiding who knows what.

'In Romsey,' he says conversationally, 'they call me Tin Chops.'

'She wouldn't go with you because of that?'

'It's not exactly a first.'

'But you were looking for someone?'

He looks away. 'Perhaps.'

'So was I.'

There's a silence between us, a well of stillness. I watch his face, refuse to be ashamed. In times like these, even strangers do it. In the street, in air raid shelters, in full view of other strangers. Life asserts itself, as physical, as unstoppable as a sneeze.

'How about it then? Will I do?'

'I suppose . . .' He shrugs, meets my gaze. 'Why not?'

We pass the blonde as we thread our way out of the bar. The woman mutters 'freak', and laughs.

Anger flashes through me. Then there's an overwhelming sense of tenderness. Never mind the ugly way we've met. Tonight's not just strangers on a pick-up. It's the past, a girl who didn't belong. A boy who let her join the gang.

Out in the street, the air raid is in full swing. The sky's bright with searchlights and falling incendiaries. Almost overhead, anti-aircraft guns open fire. A skein of tracer rises lazily into the night, at odds with the continuous hammering of the battery, the crackle of spent shells falling back to earth.

'I ought to warn you,' I say. 'My room's on the top floor. You wouldn't rather take shelter?'

I can't make out his reply till he shouts in my ear, the touch of his breath making me shiver.

'Changed your mind?'

'Not at all.'

I take his hand, pull him into a run.

The city around us blazes with light and noise. It's only a few hundred yards to the shabby front door that leads to my mother's flat, but we're laughing, breathless, by the time we arrive.

I sense his hesitancy as I open the door, usher him into the darkened stairwell.

'No one's home,' I say, glad for the first time that Nell's in hospital for a few days. 'Cold feet?'

He doesn't need to reply. There's nothing cold about the way he kisses me. I put my arms around his neck. Despite our past, it's the first time we've kissed, though I used to dream about it long ago. I drown in the taste of him, the scent. The beat of my blood obliterates the sound of battle outside until the sudden close detonation of a bomb and the lurch of the stairs under our feet makes me pull away. Plaster dust sifts onto my face.

'Getting close.'

'Yes,' he mutters. 'Where's your room?'

I lead him in. The blackout isn't up, and the room's bright with light, painted with diamond shadows from the taped windows. He kisses me again, and I can't tell, after that, who's using who. Who gives, and who takes. It's flame and the crackle of burning. It's the shriek of bombs and the rock of the city deep on its axis.

It's so much more than I bargained for.

Feelings I'd buried deep. So much less than I want.

Then it's over.

The night has turned silent when I feel his weight shift as he gets out of bed.

'Jo,' he murmurs, so quiet it wouldn't have woken me if I'd been sleeping.

'Mmm?'

'I don't want you to think . . .'

His tone warns me he's regretting it already. I sit up.

'What shouldn't I think?'

'This isn't, I can't . . .'

It hurts, but I know what I have to do.

'If you're trying to tell me this was just about sex, don't bother. I know.'

Light from burning London illuminates his face, a tricky amalgam of red gold and shadow.

'Ships that pass in the night?' he says.

'Of course. We're never going to see each other again, Bram. I'm never coming back to Romsey.'

'Good. I'm sorry, Jo, but I don't do tomorrow.'

'You know what they say. Tomorrow never comes.'

But it does. And here we are. The meeting in London was a coincidence, but this one isn't. I've engineered it, and I knew how much Nash would hate it. But there's nothing I can do. I have to be here.

The silence between us is barbed. I don't blame him for it. Or for making me speak first.

'What happened,' I say. 'Can't we forget it?'

'I thought I had.' He drains his glass in one.

'I didn't mean to come back, you know that. But then my mother died.'

'Ah.' He rubs his face. 'I'm sorry to hear it.'

Despite everything, when he says it I can believe him.

'I knew what you'd think when you heard I was here. I wanted to explain. There are things I've got to do.'

'I see.'

But he doesn't, not yet. I take a deep breath.

'I may need to be here some time. I have to find a job, somewhere to live.'

'Your family won't help?'

One small sentence. If my coming back has hurt him, he's had his revenge in full with that. I can't forget the way Grandfather said my family wouldn't help all those years ago, because he'd told them not to. And I hadn't asked then and I won't, now. Because as far as I know, none of them except for Sylvie – and she's not even a blood relation – had ever tried to find out what had happened to my mother or me.

'Not likely. You know I can't ask Grandfather for anything.'

He shrugs, won't meet my eye.

'I called in at the Labour Exchange first thing this morning. They said they didn't have anything suitable. Then I went round to your office to look for you, to tell you why I'd had to come back. That's when I saw the card in your window. *Assistant wanted.*'

'You want me to give you a job?' He sounds incredulous, looks as if he wishes he hadn't already finished his drink.

'Why not?'

'You don't think it might be awkward, working together?'

'Of course I think it'll be bloody awkward, but I don't seem to have any choice.'

'I see,' he says again. But the thick glasses hide his expression, and I can't tell what he's thinking.

'It says, *Confidential work, must be able to type.* I can do that. I was a doctor's secretary before.' I pause, wondering how to put it. 'I know how to keep secrets.'

He makes a movement of his head, like someone shaking off a fly.

'It's not only that. It's not a secretary I need, there are girls in the office who can do all that. I'm looking for an assistant for my work as coroner.'

'So what would I need to do?'

'It's not just sitting in an office, typing. The work can be . . . distressing.'

'You mean I'd have to see dead bodies? You can't think that would worry me after London. You saw what it's like. After a raid, the ARP have to go round picking up the bits in baskets.'

'It's always been a man who's done the work.'

'There's a war on, you know.'

'So they tell me.' His tone is dry. But he hasn't said no yet.

'That card in your window looked pretty old. Have you had many applicants?'

'Not even one.'

'And you must be busy now, because of the Cricketers' Arms.'

He's fierce, suddenly. 'What do you know about that?'

I'm taken aback, try not to show it.

'Only what Bunny Burnage told me when I got here. He said there'd been a raid, a lot of deaths.'

'Nothing else?'

'There were people talking about it in the street, but I didn't get close enough to hear what they were saying. You know what it's like when you don't belong.'

'Yes.' That seems to have struck a chord. 'It's not easy, Jo. I don't know what to say.'

'How about, *I'll give you a trial, Mrs Lester*?'

I can see him calculating it. Risk against benefit. I feel as if I should cross my fingers, hold my breath. But at last he looks at me straight.

'All right. A month's trial, then. But I'm not promising anything.'

'When do you want me to start?'

'How about tomorrow, eight thirty? There's a post mortem, one of the dead from the pub. We haven't identified her yet. Meet me at the hospital and we'll see how you get on.'

'OK.'

He gets up to go. 'The hospital isn't on Greatbridge Road any more. They built us a new one, up on Mile Hill. You can't miss it.'

Mile Hill. The cottage where I was brought up, that went with Grandfather's job as a farm labourer, is on Mile Hill. I don't know whether he still lives there, but I'd rather not find out. Nash would probably know, but I'm not going to ask him. I'm not going to fail at the first test he sets me.

'I'll be there.'

4

The same day, late afternoon and evening

I CHECK THE SCRAP OF PAPER I've been given. *Closeacre, Tadburn Road. May have room to rent.* I remember all this as open farmland, but now there's a road with a neat row of semi-detached houses on one side. On the other, there's a fenced-in site that seems almost industrial with its rows of huge glasshouses. A couple of girls in Land Army uniforms are working on the far side of the site under a sign that reads WILLS' NURSERIES. ESTABLISHED 1926. FINEST TOMATOES IN THE SOUTH.

I find Closeacre at the top of the road. It's meticulously kept, painfully neat: the gravel path is raked and weedless, the net curtains starchy white. It doesn't look promising as a prospective lodging house, but it's not as if I have any choice. I'll have to give it a try. I'm reaching to open the gate when a voice from behind makes me jump.

'What's up, Doc?'

CLAIRE GRADIDGE

Turning, I see a skinny young man in dusty overalls and a cloth cap.

'You startled me.'

'Sign of a guilty conscience, Dot says.'

His teasing takes me back, familiar as Billy or Jem.

'Cheeky devil.'

''S right.' He eyes me up and down. 'Have you come about working at the nursery?'

'No.' I'm puzzled. Is this another job I might have been able to try for? 'I've been told I might find lodgings at this address.'

He laughs. 'Someone's been pulling your leg. Miss Bailey that lives here does the hiring for the nursery. That's why I thought you might be looking for her. But her old mum, she's a proper tartar. Can't see her taking in lodgers. From what I hear, she don't so much as let fresh air indoors in case it disturbs the cushions.'

'Damn.'

Seems like someone's got their wires crossed, and I don't think it's me. First the Labour Exchange, now the Billeting Office. Anyone would think they wanted to get rid of me. *Stranger? Heave half a brick at 'im* has always been the town's attitude.

'Have you got somewhere else to try?'

'Not at the moment.'

'No promises, mind, but Dot might be able to help.'

'Who's Dot?'

'Sort of auntie. I'm staying with her while I'm working at the nursery.'

'That's a bit different from taking in a stranger.'

'Oh, Dot's all right. Take in the world, she would. And she's got a spare room since Rosie went home.'

'Would she mind me asking?'

'Give me a minute an' I'll pop over and see.'

'You're sure?'

'Course. Who shall I say?'

'My name's Lester, but . . . Has your aunt lived in Romsey long?'

'Born and bred.'

'You'd better tell her, then. I used to be Josephine Fox.'

'Famous, eh?'

I shrug. 'More like notorious. Wouldn't want to upset her.'

He wipes his hand on his overalls, holds it out.

'Shake, missus. Alf Smith. Pretty well known about the place myself.'

'Good to meet you, Alf.' He shakes my hand so hard all the muscles in my arm protest. 'What ever do you do over there? Lift weights?'

'Stoking in the boiler house. Got a duff foot, they won't let me join up.' He flexes his biceps at me. 'Arms are OK though.'

'I'm impressed.'

'Get on.' But he seems pleased. 'We're down the end, the one with red tiles. Nothing fancy, but plenty of grub. Look as if you could do with it.'

'You're a fine one to talk.'

'Burn it up,' he says. 'What about you?'

'Something like that.'

Alf's 'sort of auntie' is a soft-featured woman in her sixties who takes me in without a murmur. We settle on terms, and if she recognises me, she doesn't say. Nor does she ask for references once I tell her I'll be working for Nash. Good scents of cooking are coming from the kitchen, and I'm grateful for her easy acceptance. Alf's crack about food has reminded me how long it is since I last ate.

At supper, we sit six to the table. Alf, who's fetched my suitcase from the station in a wheelbarrow; Dot, watchful at the head. The two Land Girls I saw earlier are introduced as Joan and Betty, inseparable as Laurel and Hardy. They sleep in a dormitory over at the nursery, Alf says, get their evening meal at Dot's by arrangement. Last is Pa Gray, Dot's ancient father, with the hair and beard of an Old Testament prophet, and so deaf that Dot has to communicate with him by chalking messages on a slate.

They put a chair next to Alf for me, and Dot brings in three big bowls: rabbit stew, cabbage, and potatoes boiled in their skins. Pa doesn't need any prompting to bend his head and rattle through a grace.

'For this good grub we thank thee, Lord.'

'Amen.'

As desperate as if they've been starving through an hour-long sermon, the Land Girls and Alf grab for the dishes, begin heaping food onto their plates. Joan, the thin one, giggles, casts a sly look my way.

'Not so much the Lord be thankit,' she says. 'Our Alfie with his snares.'

Dot gives the Land Girl a cold look. 'Careless talk, Joan. Eat up and shut up. Mrs Lester?' She passes the bowl of potatoes across. 'Help yourself. There's plenty.'

After that, no one says much until the rabbit is replaced by stewed rhubarb and evaporated milk, and a great brown teapot is put on the table to brew.

'You'll have to make do with the evap for your tea, Mrs Lester, till I can register your ration book.'

'I drink tea black, thanks. Won't you call me Jo?'

'I'll call you a little miracle if I can have your milk for cooking.'

'Of course.'

'Your teeth'll drop out,' Betty says. It's the first time she's spoken, a surprising mousy whisper coming from her heavy frame. 'Still, prob'ly don't need to worry when you're old.'

I try not to laugh. I don't feel as old as all that.

'Probably not.'

'You haven't been called up, like?'

'She's Missus, stupid,' Joan says. 'They don't call up married women.'

'Yet,' says Betty. 'Anyway, if she's married, where's—?'

'Had a bit of an odd do this morning,' Alf breaks in. He's been quiet till now, and I bless him for drawing the girls' attention away from me.

'How's that, then, Alf?' Dot asks.

He pushes his pudding dish away, settles his elbows on the table.

'I went up to the Cricketers' with the ARP to help with the digging. There was a lot of rubble and stuff, a great pile all anyhow, you'd hardly credit there'd ever been a building there. We didn't think there was a hope, you know, of getting anyone out alive, but we had to give it a try. There was this hole went right down into the cellar. We couldn't hear anything, but I said I'd go in on a rope and have a look.'

Joan shivers. 'Ooohh, Alfie.'

'They was all dead, I heard,' the mouse whispers.

''S right. Eight of them in the end. They never stood a chance. There was all the regulars, Ma Bryall and the old boys, poor little May. Funny thing was—'

'Funny?' Dot says.

'Strange, then. You know what I mean. There was this one girl, looked like she was asleep. Hardly a mark on her. But the others—' He breaks off, swallowing hard. 'Better not say any more about that.'

Dot puts a heaping teaspoon of sugar in his cup, pushes it across.

'Never mind, boy. You did what you could.'

'Yep.' His hands are shaking as he lifts the cup, slurps a mouthful of tea. 'Sorry. Just sort of hit me.'

'Off you go, girls,' Dot tells them. 'You've had all you're going to get.'

I take the prompt too, stand up.

'You needn't go, Mrs Lester. But the girls have got an early start, and we don't want them having nightmares.' She puts her hand on Alf's. 'We've been lucky, had a quiet war till now.'

'I will go out for a few minutes, if you don't mind.'

'Come and go as you like, so long as you're careful with the blackout. I lock up at ten, but there's a key on a hook in the scullery. Under the old tin bath.'

My watch says half past eight, but I'm dog-tired.

'I won't be that long.'

Outside, it's glimmering dark. Ahead, the drift of the girls' voices moves away from me, a shrill chatter of sound that breaks the silence, grows fainter as Betty and Joan return to their billet. I follow as far as the field gate, light a cigarette, careful not to let the match flare. I need a smoke. I hadn't reckoned how hard the day would be, once the memories started to come creeping back.

'Hurry up, Josy,' Jem says.

'Gi' us a go.' That's Bert.

We're squatting under the hedge, waiting for Abe to turn up. I'm concentrating on the makings of a cigarette: Rizla paper, a few precious shreds of tobacco. Jem's a whiner who'll take one drag and choke and Bert's a hardened smoker at ten, too mean to share the fags he pinches from his brothers.

''S not for you. I got the baccy, didn't I?'

One of my jobs is making Grandfather's roll-ups, better not come out less than twenty-five to the ounce and a clip round the ear if they aren't filled tight.

'Dad'll skin you if he finds out,' Mike says.

'Don't care. And don't you butt in if he does, neither. It's nothing to do with you.'

I eke out the tobacco into a thin roll. It's taken me a week to save enough for this one cigarette. I'm not going to share it. I lick the edge of the paper carefully, roll the fag paper tight. It's hardly thicker than a match, but it's real fresh tobacco, not dog-ends rerolled. I'm admiring it when Bert leans over and snatches it out of my fingers.

'Hey, that's mine.'

'Finders keepers.' He holds it out of my reach, grinning. A hefty big lad despite the smoking. 'Li'l girls shouldn' smoke.'

'Pig.'

I pull at his arm, trying to make him give it back, but he holds me off easily. Somehow, my nails catch his skin and a bloody scratch appears on his wrist.

'Cat.' He crushes the cigarette in his fingers, a pathetic scrap of paper and tobacco. 'Smoke thatten, then.'

I reach to scrabble the pieces together and try again but he stands up, scrapes his boot over the remains so nothing is left but a muddy smear. I get up, hit out at him, ignoring Mike's efforts to come between us.

'You bloody pig.'

'Fight, fight!' Billy and Jem urge.

'Shoulda shared.' Bert gives me a push that sends me reeling into the brambles. 'Rules of the gang.'

I try not to cry as Mike hauls me out of the thorns, thinking that even if Grandfather doesn't notice I've cheated his fags, he can't miss the tear in my skirt.

'Rules of the gang?' It's Abe. None of us saw him arrive. 'What's going on?'

Bert and I clam up, because telling tales is against the rules too, but Jem can't leave it alone.

'She wouldn't share her ciggy so Bert pinched it.' Jem glances at Bert's face and then at mine, decides in a second whose side he'd rather be on. 'Just a joke, like, but she went loony, boss.'

Abe looks at us too. Bert's smug, sure boys will stick together. Despite myself, snot and tears are running down my face and I have to wipe them off with the back of my hand.

'If it was a joke, you won't mind giving it back,' Abe says, easy.

But Bert can't, because he's squashed it in the dirt. He makes a face, takes one of his own out of his pocket and hands it over. Abe smacks him on the shoulder like grown men do, mates against the world.

And now I'm really going to cry. I run away, cigarette in hand. It'd choke me to smoke it, even if I had a match. Bert's mean, and Jem's a sneak, and whatever I said to Mike, I am scared to go home.

'Heya, Doc.'

I don't need to look round. 'Hello, Alf.'

'Spare me a drag, Mrs Lester?'

'Have one.' I offer him the packet.

'Ta.'

'Light?'

He leans towards me, touching the unlit end of his cigarette to mine.

'Thanks.' He takes a deep lungful of smoke. 'Pfffh. Tipped. Girls' stuff.'

'Beggars can't be choosers.'

'True.'

I catch the gleam of teeth as he grins at me.

'You OK with Dot?'

'I'm grateful, Alf.' Yawning, I stub the cigarette out on the gatepost. 'Didn't want to spend the night in the park.'

'I heard you tell Auntie you're gonna be working for Mr Nash.'

'That's right.'

'You won't say anything to him about tonight? That I got shaky, like.'

'I wouldn't dream of it.'

'I was all right when we were at the pub. They said not to go down, but I knew I could. And she might have been alive. Someone might've.'

'It was a brave thing you did, Alf. Dangerous.'

'Only he was there, see. Watching. 'Cos of being the coroner. He said my evidence would be invaluable.' He stumbles over the last word.

'I'm sure.'

'I wouldn't want him to think I'm a coward.'

'Far from it.'

'Bloke like that, you know. Stuff he's been through. Some of the blokes call him Tin Chops, say if he took the mask off you could see his brain. D'you think that it's true?'

I know what lies under the mask. The hollowed-out spaces and the scars. I made him show me that night, though he hadn't wanted to. It had seemed important at the time, but I can't forget it.

'Mrs Lester? You all right?'

'What? Oh, yes, just tired, Alf. I ought to get to bed.'

'Sorry if I upset you.'

'Not to worry. Are you coming in?'

'Nah. Gotta see a man about a dog.'

'Tomorrow's supper?'

'Bit of foraging. See what I can see. Pigeon pie, if you're lucky.'

5

16ᵗʰ April

I SLEEP, DREAMLESS, FOR MOST OF the night. But towards morning, the images begin.

The shelter's taken a direct hit. The stench is terrible, a raw mixture of dust and the butcher's shop. There's something sticky, dark as treacle, sliding down the wall. A child's foot, still in its shoe, gleams bone-white in the doorway.

There's a man in deep water, calling my name.

Blood runs down the face of a boy who has to be Abe. But beneath the heavy-framed spectacles, he doesn't have eyes, just a pulpy crimson mass.

I wake up swearing. Switch on the light. The clock shows a quarter past five. It's too early to risk waking the household, but there's no hope of more sleep. I lie quiet, trying to shake off the pictures – imagined and remembered – only too glad when I hear someone begin to move around. Putting on my dressing gown and slippers, I creep downstairs.

Dot is dressed, ready for the day. The kettle's humming on the stove.

'Fancy a cuppa?'

'Lovely. Can I do anything to help?'

'Pass me that bowl on the sideboard if you like.'

'This one?'

The yeasty smell of proving bread rises from beneath a folded tea towel.

'That's right.' Dot flumps the dough onto the tabletop, begins kneading it. 'Sleep well?'

'Not too bad.'

'Alf said you wanted me to know your name from before. Josephine Fox.'

'That's right.'

'Sylvie Fox is in my knitting group.'

'Is she?'

Dot splits the dough into three, shapes each piece into a round loaf.

'Close-mouthed, aren't you? A proper little Fox.'

'Not what my grandfather would say.'

'I wondered if you might be Nell's little bit of trouble.'

'I suppose I am. Did you know her?'

'Bit younger than me. Real beauty she was, that dark hair and blue eyes.'

It's an evasion, but I don't know her well enough yet to push it.

'I must take after my father, then. Do you know any pasty redheads with ditchwater eyes?'

She takes a knife, slashes the shaped dough decisively.

'I heard your mum died.'

'Yes. Just after Christmas. She wouldn't tell me anything either.'

'This bloody war.'

'It wasn't the war. She had cancer.'

If I'd said Nell had died of syphilis, Dot couldn't have looked more embarrassed.

'That's bad.'

'All death's bad, isn't it?'

'Sometimes folk welcome it.'

'Nell didn't. She wanted to come home. But she was frightened.'

'Your grandfather's a hard man.'

'He's all of that. But I don't think it was him she was scared of.'

'No?' Dot turns away, sliding the loaves into the oven. 'You'll excuse me if I get on. You can take that kettle for your wash if you like. It's nice and hot.'

I take the hint, go back upstairs. But it leaves me wondering, as I wash and dress, what it is Dot doesn't want to tell me. And how I'm going to find out, make her change her mind.

The coroner may, at any time after he has decided to hold an inquest, request any legally qualified medical practitioner to make a post-mortem examination of the body of the deceased ... with a view to ascertaining how the deceased came by his death (Jervis on Coroners, 1927:145).

*

Nash is early arriving at the hospital mortuary, half expecting Dr Waverley to be in an obstructive mood. He's come prepared to argue his case with the senior man. A post mortem on the girl is a necessity; they need to prove she didn't die in the air raid. But when he arrives, he's surprised to find a young surgeon alone in the department, the post mortem almost complete. The body on the stainless steel table is open, Y-incision gaping. Half a dozen jars are lined up along the bench, filled with the internal organs that have been removed from the girl. Only the brain, a lump of pinky-brown matter like a doubled fist, lies exposed on the scales.

'Mr Nash,' the surgeon greets him cheerfully. 'I was expecting you an hour ago. Job's nearly done.'

'I was told to come at eight thirty.'

'Must be some mistake. The theatre list starts at nine, and I'm assisting.'

'And Dr Waverley? I wanted him to do the PM.'

'He said there was no need. Open and shut case.' He grins, shamefaced. 'Nothing complicated, I mean.'

'I see. So what have you found? Cause of death?'

The surgeon prods a darkened patch on the side of the brain.

'What you'd expect. Bang on the head, bleed in the brain. Lights out.'

His flippant manner sets Nash's teeth on edge.

'Anything else?'

'Perimortem bumps and bruises, no signs of force, no significant injuries apart from the skull fracture. No sign of recent sexual activity. She wasn't a virgin, though. She'd had a baby.'

'A baby? She's scarcely more than a child herself.'

'Not at all. She was sixteen, maybe seventeen. Girls like her start breeding in ankle socks.'

Though he doesn't spell it out, his tone says it all. *Lower class, no better than she should be.*

It sticks in Nash's craw to have her so lightly dismissed, even if her work-worn hands and rough little feet, the cheap finery she was wearing when they pulled her out of the cellar, support the glib assessment.

'Time of death?' He's more abrupt, perhaps, than he needs to be.

'What time did the bomb drop?'

'You think she was killed in the air raid?'

'Seems pretty obvious, surely?'

'Too obvious, perhaps. Have you seen the other bodies?'

'Nothing to do with me.' The surgeon laughs nervously. 'More than my life's worth. Between ourselves, Doc Waverley's pretty fed up with you for insisting on having a PM done on this one.'

'Between ourselves,' Nash says, tightly, 'I couldn't care less.' He pauses, holding on to his temper as best he can. 'Tell me, how many post mortems have you done?'

'Enough.'

'And yet you're not surprised at the state of the body? You haven't mentioned any signs of blast.'

'Because I didn't see any.' The young surgeon picks up the brain, slides it into the remaining empty jar. 'The lungs are clear, and there's no blown debris in the wound.'

'Precisely. Then she can hardly be a bomb casualty, can she?'

'Maybe not.' He shrugs. 'Perhaps she was a looter, wandering about in the ruins in the dark. She could have fallen in by accident.'

'Your findings don't seem to support that thesis either. No other significant injuries, you said. Isn't it more likely she was killed elsewhere and brought to the site, dumped there to be found?' For some fool to make easy assumptions, he thinks. For some killer to get off scot-free. He takes a breath, presses down the anger. 'You must see why I'm asking for an approximate time of death. Or don't you feel competent to assess it?'

'There was full rigor at midday when you got her out.' The surgeon's resentful, on his dignity now. 'That's eight hours, minimum. Up to sixteen, maximum. No one thought to take a temperature for comparison, so I can't be more precise.'

'That would mean she died sometime between eight on Monday night and four yesterday morning?'

'If you insist.'

'What I insist on is doing my duty. Finding out who she was, and how she came by her death.'

'I wish you joy of it.' The surgeon turns his back, pulls off his gloves. 'I suppose you want me to tell Doc Waverley the body has to be kept?'

'I do. When will I get your report?'

'Tomorrow?'

'Make it today. Tell Waverley I'll sign the other certificates. Those deaths are straightforward enough. But this one . . .' He touches the stiff, icy hand. 'I won't sweep her under the table for anyone's convenience.'

This morning it feels as if Romsey is claiming me back. Not the people, because this is no prodigal's return. I'm not likely to be taken into the bosom of my family, I'm more of a viper in its breast. But the place knows me, or I know it, and my feet still find the way without conscious direction. Even the scatter of new houses along roads that didn't exist when I was a child doesn't put me off. I follow my nose to the fields, find my way across the stream on stepping stones that have been there since the Saxons came.

No one sees me. At the railway line I avoid the farm gate, duck under the wire, listening for the clack of the signal before I cross the track. A few yards more and the cottage where I was born comes into view. The place looks shabbier than I remember, and there's no sign of anyone around. The door's firmly closed, the curtains drawn, but I go warily, breathe more easily once I'm safely past. The new hospital buildings, raw red brick, loom from the hillside where I remember picking blackberries and making daisy chains. I feel a stranger for the first time today.

I'm early for my meeting with Nash. There's no sign of him, but the porter's lodge has a hatch in the door and a notice which says VISITING 2–3 P.M. WEDNESDAYS AND SUNDAYS, NO CHILDREN, FATHERS ONLY FOR MATERNITY. And in smaller lettering underneath: RING FOR ASSISTANCE.

I ring. The hatch snaps open, and my grandfather is standing on the other side. I'm stunned to see him. Despite the war, it never occurred to me he might be back in his old job at his age. But I have to concede that at almost eighty, he doesn't look it. He's hardly changed from how I remember him. Stretched a bit thinner, perhaps; a little man as tough as old boot leather with a face like an axe, and an expression to match. For a moment I want to run.

'Josephine.' My grandfather finds his voice quicker than I do. His tone is not so much surprised as outraged.

'How are you, Grandfather?'

'Much the worse for seeing you. What are you doing here?'

'I'm working for Mr Nash. I'm his new assistant.'

'Tsss. What's your game?'

'My game? I don't know what you mean.'

'You always were sweet on that Jew-boy.'

'It's a job, Grandfather.'

'Lost your man, or so I heard.'

Aunt Sylvie must have told him about Richard. But he's not the only one who can play dumb.

'And then my mother died.'

No response.

'Your daughter.'

Still nothing.

'Nell.'

'I lost my daughter, *Ellen,* let me see. How old are you?'

'Surely you remember?' I pretend surprise. 'I'll be forty in July.'

'Forty years ago, then. You think a man can grieve for ever?'

'I think he might have regrets.'

He sneers. 'About you?'

'I was talking about my mother.'

'You should never have been born. *Spawned.*'

'Who are you calling a frog?'

The blood – and it sickens me to think it's his blood too – runs chilly in my veins.

'You, you bastard get of—'

'Go on. Whose get? You know, don't you?'

'And if I do?'

'Why don't you tell me?'

'I'll never tell you.' He's full of scorn, of disgust.

The old injustice sweeps over me.

'You threw me out, but I hadn't done anything wrong.'

'You'd been born.'

'You and Granny brought me up.'

'If it had been left to me I'd have got rid of you at birth.'

'You hated me that much?'

'Don't flatter yourself. I don't care a fig for you either way. But thanks to you I lost my daughter. Thanks to you, your grandmother died before she should have. You were born in sin, you brought shame on our family name.'

'What about my father? What about his sin?'

He shrugs. 'A man does what a man must.'

'And Nell?'

'I taught her right from wrong. She knew what she'd done.'

'And you don't blame him? Couldn't he have married her?'

'None of your business. Get out.'

'I'm not going anywhere. I told you, I'm here to meet Mr Nash. Where will I find him?'

He spits at my feet. I can't help it, I step back. It puts the ghost of a smile on his face.

'Nash don't run this hospital, whatever he thinks. I take my orders from Dr Waverley.'

'I'll wait here, then, shall I? Where anyone passing will see me. The red hair's quite distinctive, I'm told. Who knows who might recognise me?'

'Mortuary,' he says, sour. 'Big black door round the back. Sooner you get in there, the better.'

I make myself smile, though there's no mistaking what he means.

'Thank you, Grandfather. I'm sure we'll meet again.'

The hatch slams shut in my face. I'm shaking as I walk away. It's not only the shock of finding him there, the intensity of his reaction. It's knowing he could have told me about my father any time he chose.

What is this secret? How bad can it be?

And there's something else clawing away in my mind. Nash made sure I knew the hospital had moved. So why didn't he tell me my grandfather would be there?

6

The same day, late morning

NASH HAS BEEN WRONG-FOOTED all morning. It began with arriving at the post mortem too late. And then, as soon as he'd dealt with the self-important young doctor, he'd run straight into Jo.

You bastard, she'd launched at him, eyes glittering. *Why didn't you warn me about my grandfather?*

If he'd had a reply for her, he didn't get a chance to offer it before Waverley had come striding down the hall, confrontational as ever.

Still fussing about that girl? Nothing but a little tramp.

Even if that's true, Waverley, she deserves the truth. Her death should be investigated.

Waste of time. This talk about murder, it's a mare's nest, man. You're imagining things.

But Nash hadn't imagined the haughty way Waverley had inspected Jo when he'd introduced her as his assistant, nor the hostile way she'd reacted. And he hadn't imagined the open challenge to his authority from Waverley's parting shot.

I'll have a word with Superintendent Bell. We're in the same lodge.

So it's a matter now of setting an investigation in motion before the old boy network can block it. When Nash arrives at the police station to make his case it seems as if things are going his way at last. He's shown straight into Sergeant Tilling's office.

'Take a seat, Mr Nash. What can I do for you?'

'I've come from the post mortem on that girl in the pub.'

The policeman shakes his head. 'Bad business, a kid like that.'

'We still don't know who she is?'

'No one's come forward to identify her. I reckon she must have been a trekker come up from Southampton, trying to get away from the bombs. Would have been safer if she'd stayed at home.'

'It wasn't the air raid that killed her, Sergeant.'

'Is that what the doctor says?'

'The doctor, bone-headed idiot that he is, assumed she died in the blast. I soon disabused him of that idea.'

'Pardon me, sir, but wouldn't he be the expert?'

'Have you seen the bodies of the seven we know were in the pub?' Nash takes the sergeant's wince as confirmation. 'Well, then. You understand. The condition her body was in, she can't have been anywhere near that explosion.'

'You hear stories,' Tilling says. 'People being found dead after a raid with not a scratch on them.'

'You do, but then you find their lungs are blown to smithereens when you look inside. And hers weren't. There would have been debris in her windpipe if she'd been there, if she'd been breathing as the bomb hit.'

'You can't be sure of that, Mr Nash. It's not as if we've seen anything like it before.'

'Oh, but I have, Sergeant. Don't forget, I was two years on the Western Front.'

'You've got the advantage of me there, sir. But surely . . . the shells, that was all part of what you might call the military machine. The trenches must have been poles apart from a village pub.'

The advantage . . . It's not how Nash has ever thought of it before.

As patiently as he can, he says, 'High explosive doesn't differentiate, Sergeant. Civilian or soldier, you get too close to an explosion and you're dead meat. Ask Ma Bryall and the rest.'

'No need to be coarse, sir. It's bad enough.'

'I apologise, Tilling, but it's true. I'll stake my reputation that the girl died unlawfully, and it wasn't because of a stray bomb. You need to investigate.'

'It's not as easy as that. My boss seems to think—'

'Your boss?'

'Superintendent Bell. He was on the blower to me just before you came in.'

It's only taken Nash a few minutes to get from the hospital, and it seems he's already too late.

'What did he say?'

'I'm sorry, Mr Nash. He told me it wouldn't be an effective use of police time to mount an investigation.'

'No investigation?'

'No, sir.' Tilling shifts uneasily in his seat, blunders on. 'He says your judgement may be affected by the circumstances.'

'Meaning?'

'You said you were there, Mr Nash. Earlier in the evening. And Sally, everyone knows what she . . . Why a bloke like you might be in a place like that.'

He stands. 'I see. Well, you can tell *everyone* that I won't be deterred by what they think. And I won't give a certificate for that girl's death until I'm satisfied I know what happened to her.'

Before he goes back to the office, Nash takes time to calm down. It won't do to let his secretary see he's annoyed, and there's Jo still to face.

He'd known her grandfather might be on duty at the hospital. Joseph Fox had wormed his way on to the staff there the minute war was declared. *Freeing the fit and able for service,* he'd said, when Nash had questioned it. The words *you poor cripple* had hung in the air, as plain on the old man's face as if he'd shouted them.

He should have warned her. Nash knows what the old bugger's like. Fox is Waverley's toady through and through, mouthing the same small-town prejudices, the same vile attitudes. It's no excuse that he was hacked off because she'd backed him into a corner, persuaded him to take her on. He could have said no.

He should have said no last year. If he hadn't slept with her then, he wouldn't be in this tangle of obligation and emotion now.

He's a fool. A bloody fool, but he can't let personal feelings get in the way. If Jo will stay, he'll use that bulldog determination of hers. Set her on to finding out who the dead girl was.

'Morning,' he says, as his secretary, Miss Haward, looks up from her desk. 'Any calls for me, Aggie?'

'Nothing of consequence, sir.'

'Good. You'll be glad to hear we've got a replacement for PC Dacre.'

'That is pleasing news. Have the police found us someone after all?'

'Her name's Mrs Lester. She'll be coming in to the office later.'

'*Mrs?*' Miss Haward looks shocked. 'I know we're short-handed, sir, but a woman? Begging your pardon, but that's hardly suitable.'

'She's not a child, Aggie. She's been living in London. Our few deaths won't shock her.'

'Even so. What about Cissie and June? I won't have them upset with gory details.'

'I'm sure she'll be discreet. It's not as if she'll be in the office much. Like Dacre, she'll be out and about most of the time.'

'You've seen her references?'

'I'll leave all that to you. Just give her a chance, eh? I could really do with the help. Be a saint. It's been a long, miserable morning. Rustle me up a cup of tea, would you?'

I might have asked for a lift back into town, but I hadn't wanted to squeeze into the rattletrap taxi with Nash. I'd sworn at him. *You bastard, why didn't you tell me about my grand-father?* but he hadn't had a chance to explain and I hadn't been able to apologise because Dr Waverley had come along just at the wrong minute.

In his posh pinstripe suit, with his thick white hair waved just so, Waverley looks the part: the noble healer in the flesh. But underneath he's just another rude git who thinks he rules this town. It was there in the way he spoke to Nash, the way he inspected me when Nash introduced me as his new assis-tant. It made me feel dirty all over. I was glad to escape into the mortuary with its bright white tiles and echoes, its smell of formalin and rot.

I'd had another surprise when Nash introduced Billy Stewart, the mortuary attendant. The Billy I'd known had his name on the war memorial, I'd seen it yesterday.

His son? I ask, and Nash says yes, though he's nothing like his father. Our Billy was irredeemably scruffy, face unwashed, hair uncombed, backside out of his trousers more often than not. This Billy's glossy and colourless as everything around him: starched white coat, scrubbed fingernails, pale hair and slick silent shoes. He's as stiff and abrupt as a stick insect in a glass tank. When Nash says he'll be grateful if Billy will show me round after he's gone, Billy takes him so precisely at his word that he doesn't move until the sound of Nash's footsteps has died away. Then he rouses himself as if waking, begins to escort me round the premises.

By the time he finishes, I know more than I'd have thought possible about mortuary systems. How everything is logged in and out, how temperature is controlled, the way bodies are tagged and property stored. I've learned the statistics of mortality in my home town: the number of deaths, sudden and otherwise.

'Murders?' I ask him. It's an idle question, born of boredom. I don't expect the answer to be yes.

'One infanticide this year.'

'A baby?' I'm shocked.

'It was left on the doorstep of the old hospital. We assume the mother was a stranger, who didn't realise the sign was out of date. It might have been all right even then if the rats hadn't got to it. Filthy creatures, they are. They'll eat anything, living or dead.'

I've seen some awful things in London, but nothing as bad as rats eating a baby alive.

'That's terrible.'

'Here you are.'

He turns the pages of a big ledger, points to an entry.

24–2–1941: Newborn male. Caucasian, hair reddish, NDM. COD: exposure, dehydration, rat attack. Property: part blanket, wool plaid (stored). MOI: nil. Disposal: B/CG 32, Romsey Cemetery 7–3–1941.

'These abbreviations,' I say, more to distract myself. '*NDM; COD; MOI.* What do they mean?'

'No distinguishing marks, cause of death, means of identification.' He indicates the last, though I haven't asked. '*B/CG.*

Burial, common grave. They put the babies in the coffin of someone being buried that day.'

'That's . . .' I can't say terrible again, although it is. 'Sad. You never found the mother?'

'Not my responsibility.' He closes the ledger, lays his hands on top as if he's afraid the information might escape. 'There are a lot of strangers around these days. Evacuees and trek-kers. It was likely one of them getting rid of an unwanted child.'

It happens, I think. But sometimes we come back.

'Anything else you want to see?' His hands tap restlessly at the book. 'Only I've got to get on.'

'I think I've had enough for now.'

It's been more than enough, but I can't let it show if I'm going to keep my job.

The coroner's officer is unknown to the law, although his functions are very important . . . the position requires more than average tact, discretion, shrewdness (Jervis on Coroners, 1927:28).

The offices of Nash, Simmons & Bing, Solicitors at Law, are tucked away in an alleyway. The firm is well established, even by Romsey standards, and half the town's legal business is done beneath its mossy slate roof. Discreet, ever so respect-able, three brass plates gleam by the black-painted door. Like Goldilocks, a prospective client has plenty of choice.

Will it be Mr. Simmons, Solicitor? Old-fashioned script, smoothed by decades of polishing. He and his plate have been here as far back as I can remember. No doubting his experience in the law.

Or Mr. V. B. Bing, LLB (Cantab)? Plate shiny, sharp-edged, fancy border. A newcomer, full of titles and learning. Not afraid to advertise.

Or A. Nash? Nothing to indicate his role as solicitor and coroner. One would be assured of perfect discretion with him.

Inside, there's a narrow hallway. Two doors on the left, one marked *Waiting Room*, and the other *Miss A. Haward, Senior Secretary*. Ahead, a precipitous stairway, lit by a low-powered bulb, vanishes into the upper regions of the building.

I choose the secretary's door. A woman in a sludge-green jumper is sitting at a desk, typing. She looks up as I go in. Her face is almost clownish, made up in an exaggeration of a fashion that was popular in the twenties: skin powdered pale, hair shingled tight into her neck, harsh red lipstick and black-pencilled eyebrows.

'Yes? Can I help you?'

'I'm Mrs Lester. I believe you're expecting me.'

The secretary flashes her teeth in what passes for a smile.

'Mr Nash did mention it. If you wouldn't mind waiting a few moments? Take a seat.'

I sit in the only available chair. A curly-backed escapee from a dining set, it's as uncomfortable as it looks. She makes a show of opening and shutting the drawers of her desk, collecting up papers.

'I'm afraid Mr Nash isn't altogether *au fait* with recruitment under wartime conditions, Mrs Lester,' she says. 'I presume there are no obstacles to your taking civilian work?'

'I'm not required to enlist, if that's what you mean.'

'You're married?'

Her eyes are on my hands, but I stopped wearing my wedding ring months ago.

'That's right.'

'What about your husband? A job like this – many men would be opposed to their wives doing such work.'

'I haven't asked him.' I wouldn't ask, even if I could.

'Ah.' She flushes an unlovely pink. 'Mmm . . . might that be a little awkward? If he were to object?'

I wish she would just let it lie, but I can see she won't.

'He's hardly likely to get a chance. He's been missing since Dunkirk.'

'Oh, my dear Mrs Lester, I'm so sorry. Our gallant forces . . . Still, there's always hope.'

'He was a civilian. He took a boat across, didn't come back.'

The eager pity on her face makes me want to bite. What Richard did was sheer bloody bravado. Playing the hero, taking a yacht to Dunkirk against all official advice. And such a waste. A doctor, he'd have been so much more use staying home to help the wounded when they were brought back.

'You must be very worried,' she prompts me.

I shrug. I've nothing to say that she'd want to hear.

'I presume the Labour Exchange recommended you to Mr Nash?'

'I saw the card in your window. I happened to meet Mr Nash and asked him about it. We're old acquaintances.'

'Really?' She raises those improbable eyebrows at me. 'You have references?'

I fish out the envelope from my bag and hand it over. She takes out the papers, studies them, sniffing. Perhaps I should have let her exercise sympathy on me after all.

'These references are rather old, Mrs Lester. 1929, 1931. We usually expect something a little more recent.'

'I don't have anything more recent.'

It's not as if there are any references in marriage. And if there were, I doubt Richard would have wanted to give me one.

'You confirm the Miss Fox recommended here is you?'

'My marriage lines.' I snap the document down. 'And my identity card.'

'Thank you.' She inspects the card, poring over the addresses. Makes notes on a shorthand block. '"Silverbank, Isle of Wight; 4 Garden Row SE1". You've moved around rather a lot in the last year or two.'

'I was first registered at my marital home,' I say, barely able to cling to civility. 'Then I was looking after my mother who was ill. She died in January.'

'I see.' She scrawls something on her pad. This time, she doesn't bother with sympathy. 'And now?'

'I'm lodging with Dot Gray. Tadburn Road.'

Miss Haward pushes my papers across the desk towards me. 'You haven't registered your card with the warden.'

'I only got here yesterday.'

Her eyebrows go up again. 'That was quick work.'

I'm saved from having to answer by a voice calling. 'Aggie.' The rattle of footsteps on the stairs. 'Aggie?' The door opens, and Nash appears.

'Ah, Mrs Lester. You're here at last.'

'Miss Haward was checking me over.'

'I was dealing with the formalities,' the secretary corrects me.

'There's work to be done,' he says. 'Don't fuss.'

Miss Haward looks pained. 'I haven't had a chance to talk to Mrs Lester about conditions of service.'

'Draw up a contract, *Assistant to Coroner*. You know the sort of thing. I'll discuss terms with Mrs Lester, fill it in later. Oh, and let the Labour Exchange know.' He turns to me. 'Come up to the office.'

There are a lot of stairs that grow increasingly rickety as we climb to the top floor. I'd have expected Nash's office to be in a better position, not shoved away in the attic. But when we arrive, I can see why he's chosen it. The room is large, filled with a northern, painter's light. A workmanlike desk with a chair on either side of it stands nearest the door, while at the far end there are bookshelves, a low table and a squashy leather armchair. It has a homely, comfortable feel, as if Nash spends time here that has nothing to do with business.

'Sit down,' he says, indicating the client's chair by the desk. His manner is all business as he settles across from me, leans earnestly forward, hands steepled together. 'Let me tell you what's worrying me.'

And he does. He lays out his concerns about the unknown girl whose body was found at the pub, his suspicions about her death, the fact the police don't want to know. He tells me that he's determined to find out who she was, how she came by her death. She won't go nameless into her grave if he can prevent it. It's his job to stand for the dead, and though he doesn't say it, I know it's more than that, too. It's the same fellow feeling for the underdog that made him persuade the others to let me join the gang. And that, more than anything I said yesterday, is why he's hired me.

'And you want me—?'

'To find out anything you can about her. Everything.'

'Just like that.'

'I thought you wanted a job.'

'I do. It'll be a challenge, though. Like getting past that guard dog.'

'What?' He looks startled. 'I hope you don't mean Aggie?'

I can't help laughing. 'No. I meant the Alsatian at the gravel pit. You remember.'

It's a sultry afternoon at the end of the long summer holidays and we're bored. We hang around, trying to decide what to do.

'Birds' nesting?' Billy loves climbing trees.

''S too late. No eggs this time of year.'

'Scrumping?' Bert's always hungry.

'You'll get bellyache again.'

'The pirate game?'

'Yeh! Cap'n Abe, Cap'n Abe.'

Playing pirates means going up to the abandoned gravel pits on the edge of the common. There are pools of deep water where they've taken out the gravel – sinister orange water thick as soup that stains your clothes and skin. There are spoil heaps to dodge round, crumbling sheds to explore. The game's all about dares: walk the plank, climb the main mast, swing on the rigging, board the enemy. It means getting dirty, going home to a thrashing as like as not, but I won't duck out.

It starts to rain, but we don't care. We're swashbucklers, nothing stops us. Until we arrive, and find there's a new chain-link fence around the site, a padlocked gate to keep us out. Someone's put up a flurry of warning notices: DANGER, KEEP OUT. DEEP WATER. BEWARE OF THE DOG.

We circle the fence. It seems deserted, but they've been working here, tidying the site up, bringing in new machinery.

'Coo, look over there,' *Bert says. A big Burrell steam tractor stands in one of the sheds.* 'Wouldn' half like a go on that.'

'Bet I could climb the fence,' *Abe says.*

'Bet you couldn't.' *Bert and Abe face off.*

'Is that a dare?'

'Go on, then.'

Abe takes a running jump at the fence, clings. Climbs. As he's about to let himself down on the other side, a dog appears.

A half-starved looking Alsatian. He comes rushing out of a shed, pulls to an abrupt halt as the chain that holds him tightens.

'Better come back, boss,' Jem says.

'No fear.'

Abe lets himself down, moves warily over to the tractor. The dog can't get close, but he keeps on barking.

'Next!' Abe calls across. 'If you dare.'

Bert goes, then Mike, and then Billy. There's only Jem and me left.

'No fear,' Jem mutters, and turns away.

I'm trying to make up my mind when Bert jeers, 'She won't do it.'

I take off my shoes and socks, tuck my skirt into my knickers. More than my life's worth to go home with scuffed shoes or torn clothes. My feet are tough enough from running around barefoot so the wire doesn't bother me much. But I can't jump as high as the boys so it takes me longer to get over. I'm hanging by my hands, ready to drop, when there's a splintering crack. I can't look round, but the rush of paws tells me the dog is free. The boys are shouting, trying to distract the animal, but there's hot breath on my legs, growling right in my ear.

The dog's teeth pull at my calf. A fierce pain, and I drop, huddle with my arms around my head.

'Don't move.' A man's voice. 'You, boy, stand still. I'll get your mate.'

Dungareed legs come between me and the dog.

'Blimey, it's a girl,' I hear the man say as he lifts me.

He turns, and I see Billy and Bert and Mike frozen like statues on the tractor, Abe standing in the middle of the yard.

'You tried to rescue me,' I say.

'Didn't do any good. We all got a thrashing that day.'

'I remember.'

'So what's your point?'

'You're telling me someone killed the girl. You're asking me to go poking around, stirring things up. Causing trouble. People won't like it.'

'Ah.' He rubs his face, a gesture I'm beginning to recognise. 'When you put it like that, perhaps it isn't such a good idea after all.'

I look him full in the face. Eye to eye.

'I think it's an ace idea. I'm sick of stooging along. I can't think of anything I'd like more than to stir things up.'

'I don't want you taking unnecessary risks.'

'No dog bites, I promise.'

'You'll be discreet?'

'Getting cold feet, Cap'n Abe?'

A pause. The first ghost of a smile. 'No.'

I couldn't have asked for anything better. The job's perfect cover, the danger, a bonus. I feel alive in a way I haven't since the Blitz cooled, and London began to sleep at nights. It's the code of the gang: you never refuse a dare.

7

The same day, afternoon and evening

A coroner or his officer is justified in searching the premises where the body is found, if there is reason to think that the search is likely to lead to the discovery of evidence bearing on the cause of death (Jervis on Coroners, 1927:268).

I GO UP THROUGH THE FIELDS to the Cricketers' Arms. The path used to be narrow, a foot track only, but it's wider now, the ground rutted with tyre marks. The rough pastures on either side have been ploughed and planted, and a haze of new shoots shows Romsey is taking *Dig for Victory* seriously.

At the wreck of the pub, someone's put up a barrier of rope and a shaky-lettered notice. DANGER, KEEP OUT. In the green quiet, the bombed-out building seems more shocking than whole streets of blitzed London.

I don't know what I'm looking for. Clues. Traces, however thin; like walking into a cobweb first thing in the morning, seeing nothing but knowing there's a spider creeping somewhere. Nash and Alf said the girl's body had been found deep in the cellar, dead but unburied, and I can see the opening where Alf must have gone in. I stay well clear, though. I don't much fancy poking about in the shadow of that precariously standing wall.

Here and there, piles of brick and lath show where the Heavy Rescue Crew worked to clear the cellar. There are odd bits of rubbish littered about: a newspaper, an old tin can, the end of a walking stick. Nothing that looks as if it could help identify the girl. They must have taken everything away they thought might belong to the casualties. I'll have to find out where.

The rescue crews have trampled the ground round the bomb site into an anonymous stretch of dirt. A rank crop of nettles and alder stands undisturbed behind, and the cut into Green Lane is rutted too deep to show any signs I can read. I can't help but think I've wasted my time. It was naïve of me to suppose I'd be able to find some vital clue lying around. Even to imagine I'd recognise one if I saw it. The only sensible thing to do is get back to town. If I go the long way round, there might be someone at the cottages who saw something that night.

Green Lane's tunnelled by trees on either side. If the girl came along here alive, she couldn't have been a stranger. It's too obscure, too far off the beaten track. And if her killer brought her, or brought her body, what had he planned? He might have meant to leave her somewhere out on the common. Unless he'd already known about the bombed-out pub.

But who *had* known?

A regular at the pub? Someone from the neighbourhood? Even with the speed of Romsey gossip, I can't imagine how anyone further afield would have known so soon.

I'm reaching for the thought when a dog begins to bark, steady as a metronome.

'Got you, you little—' An irritated whisper comes from a thicket of brambles. 'Hold still.'

The barking stops, but I can hear heavy breathing, some kind of struggle. A muffled yelp, and then a curse.

'No, dammit, Tizzy, leave it!'

A skinny, khaki-clad backside forces its way out of the tangle of briars. It's the rear view of a woman in a make-do-and-mend striped jumper, tugging at a piece of hairy string. It turns out to be attached to the collar of a white lurcher with a scratched and bleeding nose. I half expect it to bark again, but instead it thrashes its tail in greeting.

'What?' The woman on the other end of the string turns. 'What do you want?'

The dog abases itself at my feet, turns belly up for patting. I crouch to oblige.

Speaking more to the dog than its owner, I say, 'Been chasing rabbits?'

'None of your business!' the woman snaps. 'It's nothing to do with you.'

Her aggression is startling.

'I didn't mean—'

'You're not after me about the dogs?'

'Not at all.'

The woman sucks at her hand where the brambles have drawn blood.

'Nosy parkers keep going on about food regulations. Want me to gas 'em. Have to gas me first.'

'I'm not that kind of nosy parker. I've just been up at the Cricketers' Arms.'

'Sightseeing.' She sounds disgusted.

'Coroner's assistant. I'm new.'

The dog woman looks surprised. 'You're working for Bram Nash?'

'That's right.'

'He was bloody lucky to get away with it.'

Get away with what? Before I can ask, she continues.

'Saw him Monday night on his way home. He was really fed up. Suppose Sal was busy. Just as well for him, though. If he'd stayed, he'd have been a goner with the rest.' The dog woman pulls the little lurcher away from my feet. 'Anyway, can't stand here gossiping. Lots to do.'

Stunned, I watch as the woman and dog lollop off along the hedgerow. Nash was at the pub?

Why didn't he tell me? Why didn't he say something? It doesn't make sense. *Unless . . .*

My brain's fizzing with conflict. He can't have had anything to do with her death – I don't believe it. And a guilty man would have covered it up, not insisted on investigating.

The dog woman said he was walking *away* from the pub before the air raid happened. On his own, because Sal was busy. I don't know who Sal was, though I think I can guess what she might have had to offer. But surely he could have told me? After how we'd met in London, he can't think I'd have been shocked to know he'd been there looking for company.

Unless it's deeper than that. If he'd known the girl, cared for her, it might explain why he's so keen to find out how she died.

But why would he have pretended not to know who she was?

She was *sixteen*. I can't believe ... I don't want to think that he might be another like my father, a seducer of young girls. All my instincts are against it, but what do I really know about him after all? A boy who was kind. A man who's afraid of commitment.

One thing I do know. If he thinks he can use me for his own ends, divert me or obstruct me, it isn't going to happen. I will find out.

I have to go back to the mortuary, see the girl's body. I have to try and understand. Till now, I've been thinking of her as a convenience. A smokescreen for my own search. But I owe her more than that.

I have to face her.

I have to find out.

The chill of the tiled room is infinite, sucking at living warmth. There's a smell of Jeyes Fluid and formaldehyde laid over something meatier, more visceral. Billy Stewart, reluctant, opens a drawer, slides out a shrouded shape. Disapproving, he uncovers the body with its long scar.

Her face has a shuttered look, possessed of the ultimate secret. She isn't going to tell me anything after all.

'Can I see the ledger?'

Without acknowledging what I've said, he covers the body again, pushes the drawer back into the cabinet. In the office, he takes off his white coat and hangs it on a peg behind the door, adjusts the folds precisely. I'm ready to slap him before he fetches the ledger down from the shelf.

15–4–1941: Female, approx 16–17 years. Caucasian, bleached hair, brown eyes. NDM. COD: subdural haematoma. Property: white cotton brassiere and knickers, pink rayon slip, red artificial silk dress, red and white patterned wool cardigan (stored). MOI: nil. Disposal: retain at mortuary until released by coroner.

'Have you got some scrap paper?'

He hands me a neatly cut strip. Fishing a pen from my bag, I copy down the information.

'No handbag or jewellery?'

'Everything is listed.'

And no shoes either, but I don't say it aloud.

'What would happen to any property that was found near the body?'

'The ARP warden would have kept it. Unless it was thought to be of value. Sergeant Tilling would take anything like that.'

'Thank you. I know where the police house is, but the ARP post?'

'The Head Warden's usually at the depot in Church Street. You could try there.'

A boy in scout uniform half leans, half squats against a wall outside the ARP post, an old sit-up-and-beg bicycle propped up next to him in the late afternoon sun. There's a canvas satchel slung over the handlebars, and he's wearing a khaki armband that shows he's the shift messenger. He's younger even than Alf, and I'm glad it's Romsey, not London – that he's bored, not frightened, by his duty. With any luck, Hitler's lightning won't strike twice.

'Can I help you, miss?'

'I'm looking for the warden.'

'Miss Waverley's gone home,' he says. 'Feeling poorly. And Mr Fox has popped over to the police station. He won't be long if you wanna wait.'

The name gives me a jolt. I know I'm bound to run up against one or another of my relatives at some stage, but if my grandfather might turn up, I'm not waiting around. I've had more than enough of him today.

'Which Mr Fox is that?'

'Mr Jim Fox,' the boy says. 'He's our second-in-command today.'

Relief washes through me. Not my grandfather. But I'd just as soon not meet Jim now either.

'Is there anyone else I could talk to? I'm in a bit of a hurry.'

'There's Miss Margaret on the telephones.'

Inside, the girl at the telephone switchboard has the anxious features and bony limbs of a racing greyhound.

'Yes?'

'Sorry to disturb you. I'm Mrs Lester, Mr Nash's new assistant. I'm trying to find out a bit more about the casualties at the Cricketers' Arms. I've been told you have the property that was retrieved from the bomb site here.'

'There's nothing much.'

'If I could just see what you've got?'

'You're working for Mr Nash, you say?'

'I started today. I have a card if you want to see it.'

She colours, seems embarrassed. Perhaps she's not used to being left in charge.

'That won't be necessary.' She tries a smile. 'I couldn't let you take anything away without authority from Miss Waverley. But I don't see why you can't have a look, if you think it might help.'

'It would be a great help.'

'Hang on a mo.'

The girl gets up from the telephone, goes to a rickety-looking cupboard. She picks out a cardboard box that has *Horlicks Tablets* stencilled on the outside, and *Cricketers' Arms 14th–15th April* scrawled over the top in purple indelible pencil.

'Here it is.'

She puts the box down on top of a card table, shoving aside the assorted papers. She's started to unfold the flaps when the telephone rings.

'Excuse me a moment. I must answer that.'

'Of course.'

The interruption couldn't be better timed for me.

I pull the box open. There's a litter of trivial bits and pieces inside. A grubby child's handkerchief. Half a dozen dominoes, an almost new Tangee lipstick in film-star scarlet. A broken comb. Three pages out of an onionskin Bible, a crumpled slip of pink paper I recognise at once. There's no time to inspect it, but a glance across at Miss Margaret shows she's intent, copying down a message from the telephone. Fragments of what she's saying float across the room.

'Code PAIGE . . . unidentified cylinder . . .'

Quicker than thinking, I palm the scrap of pink.

'Tuff's Field . . . righto . . .' The girl puts down the telephone. 'Look, I'm sorry, but I'll have to ask you to leave. I have to deal with this and it's confidential. No offence.'

'None taken.' No offence, anyway.

'Would you like me to give a message to Mr Fox?' She practically shoos me towards the door.

'There's no need. There's nothing of significance. But I'll let you know if we need to pursue it further.'

I keep my hand in my pocket as I thank her, make my way out into the street.

Behind me, in the doorway, Miss Margaret engages the messenger boy in earnest conversation. I peel the scrap of pink paper off my palm, tuck it into my bag as the abbey clock strikes six. I need to get my skates on. Dot won't like it if I'm late for tea.

Basswood House has been Nash's home all his life. He's lived elsewhere – at school, at war, in hospital, at university – but it's the place he's always come back to. The tidy Georgian façade fronting The Hundred, the ramble of outbuildings extending behind, are not what they once were, before the last war, but then neither is he.

There's a big walled garden that had begun to run down in his father's time, lawns growing weedy, fruit trees unpruned, fish pond glossy with lily pads. Nash had liked it that way, the wild encroaching beauty of it. Had left it mostly to itself, only keeping the grass cut, the roses at bay. Even semi-wild, it had been productive. Plums and apples from the old trees, black-berries from head-high thickets of bramble. But now, much of it has been tamed into strict utility with rows of carrots and pota-toes, cabbages and onions – as much as he and his housekeeper, Fan Stewart, and her son Billy can look after between them.

As he lets himself in through the front door, Fan pops out of the kitchen. She's as neat and precise as ever, the grey and white she chooses to wear almost as much of a uniform as the nuns down the road: dark skirt, spotless apron, salt-and-pepper hair.

'Evening, Fan.'

'Mr Nash, sir. How was your day?'

'Could be worse.' He takes off his coat, hangs up his hat. 'And you?'

'My boy was very late home. He said your new assistant came in just as he was getting ready to leave.'

Nash winces inwardly. That won't have gone down well.

'Really?'

'Billy says he doesn't think it's right, having a woman look at dead bodies.'

Nash doesn't answer. So many things Billy doesn't think are right, especially if it puts his routine awry.

'He says her grandfather was hopping mad about her being there, too,' Fan persists, following him as he pushes the dining room door open. The room is chilly, but his place is set at the head of the table as usual, glassware and cutlery gleaming. He'd much rather eat in the kitchen where it's warm, but Fan won't hear of it.

He goes to the sideboard, pours himself a whisky. Thinks about putting water with it. Decides not to bother.

'That's because Joseph Fox is . . .'

Nash takes a sip of his drink, lets the burn in his throat edit his comments. He wants to say, *an evil old devil, bollocks to him*, but he'd better not. He starts again.

'You know what he's like, Fan, all hellfire and retribution. He's never been reconciled to her birth. It wouldn't matter what she'd done, he wouldn't approve.'

'I remember what *she* was like. Josy Fox. Proper little tomboy, always in trouble.'

'Mrs Lester, now. She's going to be a help to me in my job. I'm sure she'll soon settle in.'

'Whatever you say, sir. Shall I serve your dinner straight away?'

'What have we got?'

'Macaroni casserole.'

'Right.'

'And a nice little chop,' Fan says, triumphant. 'I've got it under the grill already.'

Nash tries to look enthusiastic. In all the time Fan's been at Basswood, her cooking's been as awful as her housekeeping is exemplary, but he can live with it. The widow of his childhood friend, he feels he owes her. Billy the elder had followed Nash into war as unquestioningly as he'd followed him in their childhood gang. And when Billy died a few months after the Armistice of wounds received, and left his pregnant wife unprovided for, Nash had persuaded his father to take Fan on. He doesn't regret it. It was the right thing to do, the only thing. There's bicarb in the cupboard; a little indigestion is a small price to pay.

The stable at Basswood House has been opened up, the partitions that divided it into stalls removed. But Nash has kept the farrier's raised chimney-hearth at the end, added workbenches down one side. Tonight, he has a small charcoal fire burning, hot enough to work the silver. A single bulb lights the section of bench nearest to the hearth and picks out a jumble of metalwork pieces. A pair of spectacles, dark framed. And one blue eye, unwinking.

He doesn't use the glasses when no one else is around. He can see well enough, though his depth perception is poor. But by the end of the day the mask is an irritation he's glad to be rid of. It isn't vanity that makes him wear it, but a wish not to shock. He'd no more go out in public without his glasses than he would without his trousers.

He learned to work metal in the last war. Cutting shapes from shell cases behind the lines. Twisting salvaged scraps to make things – God help him – in the midst of destruction. Not souvenirs, though he's heard them called that. No one who was there needs help to remember. Not a gentleman's pastime, he'd been told, but it suited him. There in the mud and terror, the craft had fascinated him, offered a distraction. It still did.

Lately, he's been working on a set of animals. He's beaten out the hoarded scraps, soldered on tails and legs made of wire. He's made a cow and a carthorse, a pig with a curly tail. A five-point stag, fantastically antlered. Now he thinks about a fox. A little vixen on high alert, ears pricked and nose in the air.

He can't help remembering what Aggie said about Jo, pouring scorn into his ears however little he wanted to hear it.

In confidence, Mr Nash. As if anything in the office should ever be anything else. *She's a cold one, sir. So hard, the way she talked. Her poor mother dead, her husband lost. A hero, but she never turned a hair. Are you sure you've done the right thing?*

He's sure. He knows she's not cold, but he's banking on her hardihood. That she'll do what she has to – that she won't go soft or sentimental on him. Let Aggie think what she likes, he needs Jo to be tough. It's precisely what he wants her for.

The water's hot, deep. It's the best bath I've had since war broke out. And blessedly guilt-free, because Alf swears the water I'm using is the run-off from the nursery's heating system, and will only go to waste otherwise.

It's late, and the lean-to shed abutting the boiler house isn't exactly glamorous. But the light of my candle flame makes the surface of the water in the zinc tank glitter, choppy reflections silvering the pipework above. The steam rises leisurely, and the fragrance of my last hoarded scrap of English Fern soap blends well with the assorted earth and oil scents of the shed.

A few of the Land Army girls bath here, Alf said. Just hang a towel over the door handle and no one else will come in. He'd been on his way out, another man-and-dog appointment best left unspoken, but he showed me how to turn the water on and how to siphon it out again when I've finished.

Despite the creeping stupor of the hot water, I can't help thinking about Nash.

Why hadn't he told me he'd been at the pub?

I slide down into the water, slowly submerging. It doesn't make sense. He said he wanted me to find out everything about the girl. My heart thumps as pressure builds in my chest. I should surface and breathe, but I stay where I am, eyes open to the fish-eye view, the bright bulging rim of water above me.

Because he'd been there, looking for sex? I think about London. How it was between us. The urgency and passion.

I surface, gasping, lungs aching. There's a pulse deep in my groin. I'm hot with adrenaline and steam, the thought of Nash and sex. I simply can't believe he's hiding guilty knowledge. He wouldn't have set me to investigate if he'd been involved.

But he hadn't told me the truth. And a one-night stand is no guarantee of character.

Shadows leap as my candle gutters. I'm cold, all at once, skin prickling with goose pimples. I step out of the water, dry myself in the flickering dark. I'm as angry as I've ever been, and not just with him.

8

17th April

Possession should not be taken of property . . . unless there is no trustworthy person in whose charge it can be left, but if no such person is available, it is a convenient course for the coroner's officer to take possession of the property, though this is not strictly any part of his duty (Jervis on Coroners, 1927:268).

ANOTHER EARLY MORNING AT ROMSEY station. Not arriving or departing this time, but waiting. I watch as the down train to Portsmouth Harbour comes and goes, followed a few minutes later by the up line train to Salisbury. A couple of women emerge from the wicket gate and trudge away into town. Should be . . . just about now.

The time between the early trains and school had always given the gang the best chance to hang around the station. Regular as clockwork, Mr Burnage would go across to the stationmaster's house for his breakfast. We had all sorts of opportunities then. Grab a few knobs of coal that had fallen on the ground when a train was refuelling – *never take it from the bunker, that's stealing* – pick up a shovelful of horse manure for Grandfather's roses from where Marsh's carts turn round – *Bunny'll have it otherwise, best display of geraniums on the Southern line.*

I'm hoping the stationmaster still takes the same half-hour break. If the war hasn't altered his schedule, it's my best chance to try and redeem the left luggage ticket I pinched out of the ARP box. It won't work if he doesn't leave his post, because he'll remember what I left with him, know it's already been collected. I look at the ticket in my hand again. Number thirty. The one I got for my suitcase was thirty-two. Whatever it is that's been left – whoever left it – it must have been done in the last day or so, and by someone who was at the pub. I have to find out. Footsteps, ponderous, sound from the platform. In sudden panic I dive into the telephone kiosk beside the ticket office. Pretend to be making a call.

Right on cue, Bunny Burnage goes past. He doesn't look my way as he crosses the station yard and disappears inside the green front door. I put down the receiver, press button B without thinking. As children we always used to do it, hoping for a payout that hardly ever came, but today I'm shocked silly when two pennies rattle into the brass cup.

I hesitate before scooping them up. Taking the left luggage ticket was fair game, like gleaning coal from the shunt yard. The pennies are different, more like theft. An impulse from the past. The girl I'd been then wouldn't have thought twice. Josy would've had them in a flash. We all would – any of us, except Abe. He'd never have done it. He'd never needed the money.

He'd been master of the art of lying by omission, though. *We wouldn't dream of picking apples from your trees, Mr Barr, sir. Just a few fallers . . . You don't mind?* Looking clean, and eager, and decent in a way none of the rest of us could manage. And then, when we got round the corner, collapsing in laughter, all of us crowing at his cleverness. Because of course we'd shaken the apples onto the ground by the bucket load.

Maybe he hasn't changed so much after all.

A boy with a railway uniform two sizes too big and the vacant expression of the not-quite-all-there takes the ticket from me. I'm nervous he won't be able to help me, but he seems capable enough in his own domain. He matches up the ticket, hands over a small leather suitcase. I thank him, offload the guilty pennies as a tip. He looks around shiftily, gives me a grin as he pockets the coins. I feel pretty shifty myself as I walk away.

I'm halfway down Station Road when I hear voices, and two women emerge onto the pavement opposite. One of them's the girl from the ARP post. The other, an older woman, has a vaguely familiar air, though I can't quite place her. Miss Margaret waves across at me, and I smile, but I'm glad they don't cross to my side of the road. I'm conscious of the way I tricked the girl yesterday. I don't think I'm up to making polite conversation with the suitcase so conspicuous in my hand.

We're walking in the same direction, but they're ahead, so after that first moment I'm out of their view. The street's very quiet and I don't think they realise how their voices carry. Or perhaps they don't care. Not that I'm listening, until I hear my own name. And then, like all eavesdroppers, I don't hear anything good.

'Josephine Fox.' The older woman's voice is strident. 'Scullery maid's by-blow. Keep well clear, my dear.'

'But, Miss Waverley . . .'

That's who she is. The girl's voice is less distinct and I have to hurry to stay in earshot.

'. . . working for Mr Nash?'

'Cuts no ice with me. Bad blood there too. Mother was an East End Jew.'

The girl casts an agonised look over her shoulder. The older woman's voice drones on.

'As for Fox—'

'. . . Lester?'

'Never mind about that. Send her to me if she comes sniffing around again. I'll soon see her off.'

I come to a halt, feeling winded. So much for the wartime spirit, all pulling together.

Obviously not in Romsey.

The abbey's north garth, with its ancient cemetery, had always been one of my places to hide. Between the jumbled gravestones and tabletop tombs of long-gone Romsey townsfolk the grass grows lush and flower-studded, and any sense of the dead is a faint, benign presence.

I'd been inconspicuous there as a child, but now I stick out, a curiosity. Visiting the long dead. One Jeremiah Hunton, grandly entombed in 1789, has to accommodate my impatience as I set down the suitcase on his mossy slab. I'm not going to risk taking the case into the office without knowing what's in it, making sure I'm on the right track. I feel sweaty, thinking about it. What will I do if it turns out to be a commercial traveller's samples or someone's leftover sandwiches?

There's nothing to be learned from the outside. No helpful labels, just a few odd scratches and worn places, a bit of nondescript string whipping the handle. It's not very big, scarcely enough to hold a change of clothes. I take a breath, try the clasps. I'm not expecting them to work, but they flip up easily and the lid opens, releases a faint, musty smell.

Clothes. A girl's clothes. For a moment I'm relieved, thinking I made the right guess. But as I take them out, pile them up, I start to doubt. It's a meagre collection, quite unlike the clothes the unknown girl was wearing. Everything here is shabby, thin with washing and wear. There's a pair of Aertex knickers, a vest with a darn on the shoulder. A faded nightdress of pink sprigged cotton. The outerwear looks as if it was once school uniform: a blue cotton blouse and grey pleated skirt, a hand-knitted navy cardigan with a moth hole in the sleeve.

My heart sinks, but I press on. The sponge bag holds flannel and soap, a sample size of Soir de Paris. The tiny blue bottle distracts me for a moment, makes me grin. I had one just like it, pinched from Woolworth's when I was twelve. But the memory's short-lived, and I shiver as I put everything back. It feels shameful to be pawing these poor childish scraps. It's not even as if I can be sure they belonged to the girl. And if they don't, I've no idea how I'm going to get them back where they came from.

One last chance. The lid has a ruched satin pocket with an elasticated top that holds it flat. It doesn't look as if there's anything inside, but I slide my hand in anyway. My fingers find something loose, a papery edge. I pull gently, bring whatever it is out into the light. And find I've struck gold. A double fold of flimsy paper encloses two postcard-sized photographs: a young man in sailor's uniform, and a snapshot of a girl, hugging a black-and-white sheepdog. For a moment, it feels as if my heart will stop, because it's our girl in the picture. Our dead girl. She's looking up at whoever's behind the camera, laughing. It's a bit blurred, and I've only seen her in a chilly, mortuary sleep, but there's no mistake. I turn the snapshot over. Read the pencilled, laborious lettering.

Paddy and me.

At eight o'clock, a depressed-looking man answers my ring on the office doorbell.

'You'll have to come back later. No one here but me till half past.'

I explain who I am. Seeming almost more depressed, he lets me in, shows me to a billet at the back of the building.

'It's yours,' he says. 'It isn't much.'

He's right. It isn't. Someone has crammed a table and chair into what is obviously a storage area, a dog-leg corridor that seems to go nowhere in particular. A space has been made between two battered filing cabinets, forming a kind of cubby-hole to work in. Every other square inch is packed with stuff: shelves heaped with ancient-looking manila files; stacks of boxes piled on the floor.

'Got a duster?' I ask.

The wall behind the table is grey with cobwebs. A film of dust covers the table, where a battered old Remington type-writer has been given pride of place.

'Sorry,' he says. 'I was finishing moving the furniture when you rang the bell.' He fishes in the pocket of his brown over-all, brings out a grubby rag. 'This do you?'

'I suppose it'll move the dirt.'

He watches me rub over the table and chair, clean down the ghost shapes on the wall.

'Dry work,' he says. 'Fancy a cuppa?'

'I could murder one.' I turn the duster to find a cleaner section. 'Surely Mr Nash's last assistant didn't work here?'

'He were a copper, worked over the police station. Just used to come in for orders.'

'I must be a bit of a shock, then?'

'That you are.' He sighs. 'I'll get that tea on.'

'Lovely.' I hand back the rag. My hands are filthy. 'I'll need a wash.'

'Cloakroom's next door. You'll find me downstairs.'

After he's gone, I look around, wondering what to do with the little suitcase. I don't want to leave it on show, but I don't want to carry it around either. There's no kind of security in this cramped space, not even a door to shut.

A stack of tin deed boxes pokes out from under the table. Just right to catch my stockings every time I move, but they might make a hiding place. I stoop, work the case into a narrow gap. When I stand up, I'm dustier than ever. But it will do till Nash arrives.

The thought of him, of what I've got to say to him, makes me queasy. I hope the tea's good and strong.

'Your hours are 8.30 until 5.30,' Miss Haward says. 'Half an hour for lunch. Tea is provided at 10 a.m. and 3.30 p.m., one shilling a week for the kitty.' She stares hard at me. 'In advance.'

'OK.' But I'm not offering yet.

'Saccharin only, unless you bring your own sugar. You'll be working under Mr Nash's instruction, but I expect you to maintain office standards. Confidentiality is the watchword. And I won't have Cissie and June distracted with unpleasant details about your work.'

'I wouldn't dream of it. When does Mr Nash come in?'

'That's really none of your business.'

'It's exactly my business.' She's driving me mad already, with her petty rules and power struggle. 'Since I'll be working directly for him. I can't imagine you'll want to be bothered every time I need to speak to him.'

I watch her work it out.

'He's usually here by 9.00 a.m. if he doesn't have an appointment on his way in.'

'And has he got one today?'

'I don't know.' It's reluctant, resentful, but at least I've won the first round.

'OK. Have you got a Kelly's Directory tucked away somewhere?'

The abbey clock strikes nine, and then half past, and there's still no sign of Nash, though I've been sized up by almost all the rest of the office staff. Miss Haward obviously hasn't told them not to distract me. I know about the caretaker's bad back, Cissie's invalid husband, June's hopes that her boyfriend will propose. Even Mr Simmons, who turns out to be the elderly lawyer type I saw at the hotel, has dropped by to welcome me to the firm.

Such a poppet, June told me. *Should have retired ages ago, but for this beastly war. Mr Nash keeps himself to himself, but you want to watch our Mr Bing. Hands everywhere, and him married with three young kiddies.*

Though it isn't hands when Mr Bing comes in, but sitting on the table, leaning over me; asking if I'm not fed up to be stuck in a dead-and-alive hole like Romsey, and would I like to go for a drink one evening? A proper shark. I didn't need June's warning to refuse him.

By quarter to ten, I've tracked down the address I wanted in Kelly's Directory, paid over my shilling, talked a notebook out of Miss Haward's stationery stash, typed a report for Nash, and still he hasn't arrived. Bloody man. Why can't he get to work on time? I've got places to go, things to do. A conversation to have. And a sailor to find.

But it's past ten o'clock before I stand in the bright north light of Nash's office, lift the suitcase on to his desk.

'I found this.'

I'm expecting him to ask where I got it from straight away, but he doesn't say anything. Doesn't do anything at first, simply stands, hands laid quietly on either side of the scratched leather case. I can't help noticing how many scars and scrapes he has on his hands. Tiny red marks, like fresh burns. I think about what the dog woman said, can't help wondering how he got them.

It startles me when he suddenly slips the catches with a snap and opens the case. He empties it, stacking each item methodically on the desk. I can't read his face as he examines the sad cache, lingering longest over the photographs.

'It's her,' I say. 'The girl.'

'Yes.' He sighs. 'Disappointing there aren't any documents.'

I avoid his eyes. I've a card to play, but I'm not ready yet.

'I expect they would have been in her handbag.'

'No sign of it?'

'There was nothing I could see at the Cricketers'. And I checked with the ARP. I suppose it could be with the police.'

He shakes his head. 'Sergeant Tilling would have told me. You'd better tell me, Jo. How did you get hold of this?'

'The case was in left luggage at the station. I found the ticket in a box they had at the ARP post.'

'They let you take it?'

'Don't ask. Then you can claim ignorance if it comes back to bite me.'

'You think so? Anything else?'

I pretend not to understand.

'Her shoes,' I say. 'She didn't have any. There's nothing logged for her at the hospital, and none lying about at the site, nor in the ARP box. She can't have got to the Cricketers' barefoot.'

'I hadn't thought of it, but ... It's just as I said from the beginning. Someone must have brought her there, dumped her like so much rubbish.'

I flinch, hope he doesn't notice. 'So all we've got to do is find the shoes. Or the bag.'

'He'll have destroyed them the first chance he got.'

'There's the sailor's picture. It was taken at a place in Southampton. I've looked it up. I thought I'd go and see if they've got any records to show who he is.'

'It's a bit of a long shot. Even if they've got something, he'll be at sea.'

'It's worth a try.'

'Where's the studio?'

'College Place.'

'By the Ordnance Survey offices? You'll be lucky. They've had a lot of bombs round there.'

I can't hold back any longer. 'Don't be so bloody defeatist.'

'What?'

'You heard what I said. I'm beginning to think you don't want me to find out about her after all.'

'That's ridiculous.'

'It doesn't feel ridiculous. Not now I know you were at the pub that night.'

'Ah.' A silence. 'You must have run into Ollie.'

'If Ollie's a woman with a dog called Tizzy, then yes, I did. She said you were lucky not to get caught in the air raid.'

'Did she.' It's not a question. But it's not an answer either.

'Why didn't you tell me?'

More silence.

'She said you'd gone to meet someone.'

'I didn't know she was my keeper. Or that you are.' His tone is light, but the words are pitched to sting.

'Don't get all poncy about it. It's not what I meant and you know it. The more you weasel away, the more I wonder what the big secret is.'

'I went to see Sally. The local tart. You know how it is. But she'd got a client already. Though I'm afraid poor Stan probably died a virgin all the same.'

'And the girl?' I try to match his coldness. 'Was she a prostitute too?'

'For all I know. Never saw her before they got her out of that cellar.'

'That's the truth?'

'What is this, some kind of third degree?'

The bright morning light is as cruel as a spotlight. I've got him cornered, on the ropes. Another round to me, but it doesn't feel good.

'I'm just trying to find out what happened. It's what you hired me for.'

'I didn't expect to figure as first suspect.'

'Then don't.'

I can see him thinking it out. Making up his mind.

'I knew it was no go as soon as I got there. With Sally, I mean. So I had a drink, just the one, you know. To save face.' He pauses, makes a derisory noise in his throat. 'Hah. I left about nine, met Ollie in the lane. We chatted for a while, ten minutes perhaps. Then I came home. I didn't see anyone else, though it would have been bright enough if there'd been any-one to see.'

'What time did you get back?'

'You're really getting into the swing of this, aren't you?'

'You should have told me.' I hate the way it sounds, like a nagging wife.

'Perhaps I should. But you must see why I didn't want to.'

'You thought I'd judge you?'

'I'm not exactly proud of it.'

'But the point is, it doesn't matter. It's not about your feel-ings or mine. It's about finding out who killed that girl.'

'Do you seriously believe I might know something about it?'

My turn to be silent.

'You think I'd have been stupid enough to set you on to it if I'd done it myself?'

'I don't know. Would you?'

'OK. An alibi then. If you insist.' There's resignation in his tone, and whatever I've won, I've lost something too. 'I warn you, it's not a very good one. I was on Mile Hill when I heard the bombs. Didn't bother with finding a shelter, just came on home. Got in, I don't know, perhaps ten to ten? Something like that. Fan might know, she was still up. But after that I've no corroboration. No witnesses. The telephone rang about midnight, woke me up. The ARP warden, to say the pub had been bombed, that there had been fatalities. They told me there was nothing we could do overnight, we had to wait for the Heavy Rescue Crew to come up from Southampton. So I went back to bed. No witnesses to that, either.'

He's right. It's not much of an alibi. But there's no point in alienating him by asking any more questions, since I don't really believe he had anything to do with the girl's death. I was angry with him for all the wrong reasons, let my feelings cloud my judgement.

'I've got a confession to make, too.'

'Yes?' The single syllable is hostile, clipped.

'There was a note. With the photograph. It doesn't say much but . . .'

I pull the fold of paper from my pocket, hold it out to him. The tension as he takes it from my hand is palpable. I watch him unfold it, read. I know what it says by heart.

Dear Sis

I cant stand this nomore I'm getting out. I got shore leave tomorrow but after I wont go back. Sis, you got to help me. I'll be at Snappy's till the 16th. Dont let me down.

Frank.

'A brother,' Nash says at last. 'A brother who was expecting her. Yesterday.'

'I thought, if I could find him . . .'

'It's the seventeenth already, Jo. He could be anywhere by now. This *Snappy* could be anyone.'

Though his tone is still austere, I take heart from his use of my name.

'It could be a photographer, though, don't you think? A nickname for someone who takes snaps? The picture was taken locally. It's got to be a chance.'

'I suppose so. But even if they do know . . . don't go haring off after him on your own. If he's done what he said in the letter, the man's AWOL. It could be dangerous.'

I hate being told what to do. And I'm not going to promise anything. But I don't want to start another fight. I just want to get on, to follow my hunch.

'All right.'

After she's gone, Nash can't settle. He paces his room. He's so angry with himself, with her. He wants to yell, swear, slam his fist into the wall. He's not ashamed of going to the pub that night. Sal was a decent sort, didn't make a secret of what she did. Kept it simple, an honest trade, sex for money instead of mucking everything up with emotion. But he can't deny it's humiliating to be caught out in the lie.

Found out. Out for a duck. Out for a fuck. Nash nil while Lester sweeps the board. Perhaps he'll have to go celibate. The irony – unmanned by Josy Fox. Shrapnel couldn't manage it, but she's found him out. Should have kept to his own rules in the first place. No pity fucks, no sympathy. Pay and stay free.

Once, only once. Once too bloody often. Now she thinks she owns him.

Plenty of reasons to kick himself.

9

The same day, late morning and afternoon, Southampton

I GET OFF THE BUS AT Stag Gates. The conductor says a Heinkel was brought down in Padwell Road on Saturday, and like Nash said, the offices at the top of Asylum Green have been badly hit. It's a relief to see that College Place seems to be relatively untouched, the businesses open. Bank, furrier, accountant. And there's the photographer's. Not looking so good. A dusty red curtain obscures the window, and there's a notice on the shop door. GONE TO LUNCH. BACK IN FIVE MINUTES. The faded script and curling edges of paper suggest the writer has been gone much longer than that, months rather than minutes. I try the handle, but the door is firmly shut.

Frank's been on the lookout since first light, even when there was nothing to see through the grimy glass but grey shadows. The bedroom window is loose in its frame and draughts whistle round his ears, but there's a good view up and down the street. He keeps as still as he can, despite the discomfort.

The room's empty, bare boards underfoot. The walls are thin, and every blasted move makes a sound. Mustn't twitch the tatty net curtain, shuffle his feet. Just keep watching.

His leave is over, and she still hasn't come. He must have been stupid to think Ruth would want to help him, to believe she'd turn up. His sister has always been a fly one, first sign of trouble and she's off.

He should never have risked coming here. He's been wasting his time, waiting for her. He should have got away, legged it the minute he could.

From today, he's AWOL.

They'll crucify him.

It doesn't matter what they do, he won't go back. He can still hear the screams, see the blokes drowning in oil, burning in the water. They can do what they like – court-martial him, stick him in the brig – anything's better than that.

It's bright now, but the day hasn't brought any luck. She's scuppered him, the silly cow. Without her, he's had it. No money, no cover. They'll pick him up the minute he puts his nose outdoors.

What the *hell* is he going to do? It's hard to keep on the alert. All the same, he can't quite bring himself to give up, to move on.

He's seen them all come and go. Milkman. Postie. A bloke in a blue suit and brown shoes, walking to work. A hard-faced blonde, opening up the shop next door. Looks like a tart, and he can smell her cheap scent a mile off.

Two old women, slow as shit. Empty shopping bags, looking for a queue. Coming back slower, bags lumpy, cabbages, a bottle wrapped in newspaper.

Watching. Can't afford to rest.

Nothing to see.

Nothing.

Wait a minute, though. Who's this?

He sees a woman cross the road. Tracks her walk, the sway of her hips. Tidy figure, bit on the skinny side. No tits, nothing to get hold of up top. Red hair. Now she's closer, he can see she's middle-aged. He loses interest. There's nothing for him there.

But she doesn't pass by like the others. She's coming straight for the shop, like she knows what she wants. Now she's in the doorway, out of sight. He hears the rattle of the door. What's the nosy bitch doing? Can't she read?

Back in view. She's looking up and down the road. On surveillance, like him. He nearly laughs, but he's too fucking scared.

Official. She looks official. Something on her mind. Does she know about him?

She moves, brisk; out of sight again.

He hears the ting of the fur shop bell. He crouches, ear to the bare floorboards. The voices come through, the blonde and the other one. Muffled. No words he can hear.

Chit-chat.

Chit-chat.

The bell again. He stands, quick, sees Ginger cross in front of the shop.

Piss off, you nosy cow. Nothing to see.

She's off at a clip, turning towards the side alley, not going away. Footsteps confident, like she'll never give up.

Who does she think she is? Fuckin' cheek, serve her right if . . .

Squeak of the side gate.

Breathing hard, he sidles along the wall, works his way down the stairs. Remembers in time to avoid the ones that creak.

Movement outside, very close. She'll see where he smashed the glass to get in.

He freezes, waiting.

Heart pounding.

He'll kill her before she makes him go back.

The saleswoman in the furrier's says Mr Legge moved out of the studio after the big air raid in November.

'He's got a room over Rownhams way, I think. Some kind of mission place. By what he says, it's not much like dear old home. Straightlaced, you know. Has to mind his p's and q's.' She laughs.

'You don't know the address?'

'Sorry, love, no. But I'll ask him next time I see him if you like.'

'Does he come back often?'

She shrugs. 'Two or three times a week. Got to, see. Place like that, they won't let him have the pa—'

A querulous voice sounds from the back room. 'Norah? Is that a customer?'

'Just an enquiry, Mr Glass.' She shakes her head at me, mouths 'sorry'.

I take the hint and go. If someone is there, it might be my chance. I have to try and find a name.

I can't see inside the photographer's from the front because the red curtain blots out any chance of looking into the shop. But the latch on the side gate lifts easily, lets me into a neglected backyard. Weeds grow up through the paving and a window beside the back door is broken, hastily repaired with a bit of cardboard shoved into the gap. Something about it makes me feel uneasy, and not just because I'm snooping.

I leave the gate ajar, knock on the back door.

It yields to my touch, swings open.

'Hello!' I call. 'Anyone home?'

Deep in the gloom of the house, something moves.

'Hello?'

'Come on, you daft bugger, come on. Come on.'

The raucous greeting takes me aback. I step inside cautiously. It's dark, stinking of disuse and something animal. I hesitate.

'Good girlie.' The voice is wrong, somehow. There's a rattle, a scrape like fingernails on tin. A squawk. 'Daft bugger.'

It's a parrot! That must be what the woman in the shop had been going to say. I let out a shaky breath, move forward more confidently. I'm not afraid of a parrot.

'Fuckin' daft.' This voice is most definitely human. 'Live to regret it, maybe.'

A click as the door behind me shuts and every last vestige of light is cut off. Darkness swirls as a fierce hand grips my wrist, forces it up behind my back.

'Stand still, you bitch,' the man mutters. Something cold presses into the angle of my jaw. Freezes me mid-struggle. 'Tell me quick, what you nosing about for? An' make it quiet.'

I've heard people say *the hair stood up on the back of my neck* though I've never felt it before. I've never had a gun at my throat either, but I know instinctively that's what it is. I've never felt so afraid, not when Grandfather took his belt to me, not when the telegram came about Richard. Not even in the worst of the Blitz.

'I'm looking for the photographer.' My voice shakes. 'I wanted to ask—'

'About me?'

'I don't know who you are.'

The cold digs deeper into my throat.

'Where'd you come from?'

I haven't got time to think of a clever answer, calculate what I should say.

'Romsey.'

'Romsey?' I feel him go still. 'Did Ruth send you?'

I can't even shake my head, the way he's holding me. I'm too scared the gun will go off.

'I did come about a girl.'

'Don't play clever with me.'

'If I could explain?'

'You better bloody explain. And make it quick.'

'Daft bugger,' the bird chimes in. I can't help agreeing.

'I was hoping the photographer might help me. I have a picture, a sailor—'

My breath cuts off. The hand on my wrist tightens, pushing my arm higher up my back. The pressure from the metal at my throat is unbearable. Wise or not, I can't help struggling to free myself, to breathe. My shoulder wrenches painfully and stars explode in my vision; dark curtains flap to extinguish them. I feel myself begin to fall.

'Hold up, you bitch.'

The pressure slackens, but I can't stand. There is time, I don't know how much, when I don't know anything.

When I come to, I can see. The pale outline of a window shows between ragged red curtains, and a dim light filters into the room where I am. I'm half sitting, half sprawled on a scratchy, uneven surface that stinks of dust. And though I'm awake, it seems as if I'm hallucinating. There's a tree, and a bird, watching me. Shifting beadily from foot to foot.

'Good girlie,' the bird voice says. 'Come on.'

The parrot. The tree's his perch, and the smell's strong enough in here to tell me this is no dream. I'm lying awkwardly on the photographer's chaise longue, pain in my sore shoulder and the place on my neck where the gun has bruised me. I've got just enough sense left to lie doggo.

'Here.' A rough hand nudges me and something cold splashes onto my face. 'Wake up. Got you some water.'

I make a pretence of stirring, struggle upright in my seat. My captor's face swims in the dimness. He looks like the sailor in the picture, and I begin to connect it up. I take the water, drink thirstily. Try and work out what to say that won't get me killed.

He squats on his haunches in front of me. Wary, he watches me as intently as the bird. He's thin, unkempt. Stubble shadows his face, and his clothes look hand-me-down, worn into all the wrong shapes for his body. He's made sure he's far enough away that I can't reach him, but he's not holding a gun on me any more. Between us on the floor is my handbag, contents tipped out anyhow. My purse is open, and I guess it's empty, but what takes my attention are the photographs. He's put them centre stage, where we both can see them.

'You do know Ruth,' he says. 'Stupid cow, why didn't you say? What's happened to the little bitch? Why didn't she come herself?'

I don't know where to begin.

'Tell me about her,' I say. 'Tell me about Ruth.'

I don't know why, but tears are already running down my face.

In Romsey, Nash pushes the door to the back room of the Comrades' Club open, and is met by a fog of cigarette smoke and stale beer. Three men in Home Guard uniform look up from their pints. Two more at the snooker table pause in their game.

'Watch out,' one of the players says, sour. 'Careless talk costs lives.'

A pint drinker grins. 'Walls have ears, don't you mean?'

'I mean, we got a spy in the room.'

The bald one with the corporal's stripe speaks. 'Come off it, Fred. You know Captain Nash.'

'No captain of mine. Hadn't heard he was in the Guard.'

Nash ignores the hostility. 'Hello, Fred. Same old, eh? Sorry to intrude. I wanted a quick word with Tom, here.'

'What can I do you for, Captain?' The corporal again.

'Wondered if you could help me with a couple of things.' They move away from the snooker table, leaving a thick silence behind them. 'Fred's right, you know. I've no right to rank.'

'You'll always be Captain to me. Can I get you a drink?'

'I won't, thanks. You'll have heard, I'm bothered about this dead girl. No one seems to know anything about her, but I wondered . . .' He cocks his head to the group behind him, where the mutter of conversation has started up again. 'Is it just me they won't talk to? I know you hear things in the shop.'

Tom Fox laughs. 'You're right about that. Plenty of gossip, not much sense, most of the time. All, where's the bananas? Why can't I get a lemon? Mind you, I did hear—'

'Yes?'

'That you've taken on my niece at your place. They say she's got real posh.'

'Posh? I wouldn't have said that. But it's true, she is working for me.'

'Always was a bright girl. Pity Dad couldn't ever see it. Tell her—'

'Yes?'

'You don't mind? Bit of a cheek.'

'Of course not.'

'Say, Sylvie and me, we'd be glad to see her. Be blowed to Dad, she's welcome to come round to ours any time.'

'I'll tell her. You'll bear in mind what I said? Anything about the dead girl would be a help. Gossip, whatever.'

'Our Sylvie's the one for that. I'll see what she says.' He walks to the door with Nash, steps out into the fresh air. 'That's better. Bit of an atmosphere in there.'

'You mean Fred?' Nash shrugs. 'Can't win them all.'

The hut stands beside the millstream, and they stop, looking down into the water, watching the billow of weed, the spotted flicker of trout.

'You know what I think?' Fox says. 'There's not enough talk for once. Someone's got a-hold of it. Keeping it quiet.'

'I agree.' Nash settles his hat. 'You'll let me know if you hear anything?'

'Course I will, Captain.'

Tom Fox waits while Nash crosses the footbridge over the stream and walks away. His bones ache. Trouble ahead, and he's getting old. Too old, maybe. He spits into the water, watches as a great dark fish darts away.

'What'd old Tin Chops want then? Nosing around when a man's off duty.'

'Doing his job, Fred. Making enquiries about that poor lass who got killed up at the Cricketers'.'

'Poor lass, my arse. Got to be a whore, hanging around in that dump. But he'd know all about that, wouldn't he? Dirty Jew. He'll have to put a knot in it now Sal's gone.'

'You know what, mate? I think you've been listening to that bugger Hitler too much. Captain Nash is all right.'

'Arselick,' Fred sneers. 'Yes, Captain, no, Captain, three bags full, Captain. Man's a conchy.'

'Don't talk daft. You know what's under them glasses. Didn't get that picking his nose.'

'He's a bloody coward, then, isn't he? Not doing his bit this time. Afraid he'll get another dose.'

'If memory serves, Fred Deeds, you never got further than the Remount camp in the last lot. Came home to tea every night. And what's more—' Tom pauses as the abbey clock strikes the hour – '*that* says you'll be late for your shift over the brewery if you don't get a move on. Don't let me hold you up.'

It's midnight, pitch black. No moon yet. The train hardly pauses at the little halt, stopping just long enough for the guard to step off and pick up a mailbag before it sets off again. There's no one waiting to board, no porter, just the empty platform. Frank lets me go when he sees it, pushes me out of the door at the very last minute.

'Remember what you promised.' He whispers it, hoarse, shoves something cold and heavy into my hand.

I stagger with the momentum as the train door swings behind me, bangs, and swings again. Someone on the train calls out, but I shrink into the shadows, hiding instinctively. Turn my face away from the dim glow of the passing guard's van as if I'm the one who's done something criminal.

As now, perhaps, I have. Helping a fugitive to escape capture. And alarmingly, now, in possession of a gun.

Even in the dark, I know. As I did in the stinking kitchen behind the photographer's studio. The object I'd grabbed like a lifeline as I struggled for balance was Frank's gun, pressed into my hand as I fell out of the train. Clever of him to get rid of evidence that would damn him every bit as much as being AWOL, and make it harder for me to report him at the same time. It's going to take an awful lot of explaining if I'm found in possession of a firearm.

Just for a minute, it's almost funny. I can imagine what Nash would say if I were arrested and had to call on him to bail me out.

But I'm sober again just as quick. What am I going to do with it? Wipe my fingerprints off, stash it under the nearest hedge? A child might find it. I can't take that risk. I hate having it in my hand. Everything I know about guns comes from films, and while Bogie might know if the safety is on, I've no idea. Frank had been carrying it in his pocket, so I can probably assume it isn't going to go off by accident. I slide it gingerly into my bag. What now?

Sit and wait on the platform till morning, till someone comes along? I've been forced to wait too long already today. Had to sit passive while Frank decided what to do. And he's cleared out every last penny from my purse so I can't telephone even if I want to.

I could bang on a cottage door, wake up some righteous sleeper. Beg for help.

Never.

I can't face it.

It's not much more than six miles to Romsey. I can walk it in a couple of hours, get some shut-eye before I have to tell my story to Nash in the morning.

The night road is very quiet. In all the time it takes me, only two cars pass, people with a petrol allowance to squander. I hear them in plenty of time to get off the road, the instinct to hide strong in me. I don't want to have to explain to anyone what I'm doing on the road at midnight – and besides, I gave my word to Frank that I wouldn't tell anyone about him until he'd had a chance to get away.

The moon comes up as I walk. The night is fine, and the movement soon warms my muscles. But I'm cold inside, chilled by the hours I've been held captive, the threat of the gun. At least walking eases the feeling of helplessness. I just can't work out whether what I've learned has been worth it.

Ruth. Ruth Taylor. I know her name, some of her story. Frank told me she was almost fifteen when she'd been evacuated to Romsey.

'She shouldn't have gone at all, she was too old to be an evacuee, but she was small, like. She slipped in with the kiddies when they shipped them out. Said it was all such a bloody muddle no one noticed. She was scared silly, see. Hated being in tight places. Reckoned she'd go mad if she had to be shut up somewhere small if there was bombs.'

They hadn't been close, but they'd kept in touch after a fashion. She was all he'd got left, he said. No one else.

'Mum an' Ted got caught in a raid last summer. Thought it had saved her, being scared. There I was, out on the convoys and I thought, lucky bitch, she got away with it. Always thought she'd get away with it.' He'd almost cried, then. I hadn't known how to comfort him. 'Dad did a bunk when Ruth was a baby. It's why I come here. Old Snappy Legge, he's like an uncle, sort of thing. Know what I mean? Mum used to clean for him and that. He had a soft spot for her and I thought he'd be good for a few quid. But there's been no sign of him, just the bloody parrot. Nothing to eat in the cupboards. Can't make it out.'

I told him what the woman in the furrier's had told me. That the photographer only came back a couple of times a week. I said I wouldn't tell anyone if he wanted to wait in the house for Mr Legge. I even offered to go and get him some food to tide him over, but he wasn't having any. He'd been angry about Ruth's death as much as grieving.

'Asked for it, probably. Sly little bitch.'

He hadn't been able to tell me anything much about her after she'd left home. Where she'd been living in Romsey, who she'd been working for.

'Never told me nothing. Had to find out about Mum an' Ted from a telegram. Couldn't hardly be a secret where she was, for Chrissake. But Miss Hoity-toity couldn't let her brother know. Had to write to her care of the post office.'

I'd wondered if it was her pregnancy she'd been concealing. I hadn't had the guts to tell him about that. But I felt sorry for him when he told me how his ship had gone down far out in the Atlantic. How he'd been picked out of the sea, while all around him men drowned if they were lucky, or burned in blazing fuel oil if they weren't. The memories had made him jumpy, more dangerous than ever.

He wanted money, and food. He wanted to get to London. Whatever I might feel about him, working out how to help him was a matter of self-preservation, not sympathy. He'd seen my bank book, wanted fifty pounds, but I persuaded him people would be suspicious, ask too many questions if I tried to draw out everything I had in my account. We bargained, and in the end he settled for thirty. That was bad enough, it was nearly everything I'd saved to be independent of Richard, but it couldn't be helped. If I had to choose between pride and staying alive, I'd choose staying alive every time. I said I'd go to the bank, draw a cheque for cash, give it to him. Though I promised not to betray him, he wouldn't trust me to go alone.

I made him wash, and shave his face with an old blade and cold water. Though he complained, he looked less like a fugitive when he was clean. I brushed him down, combed his hair. Combed mine, and put on fresh lipstick. If he wanted us to get away with this, we both had to look normal. I made him let me have my bag, my empty purse, my documents so I could prove who I was at the bank. He kept the photographs. I'd have liked to think he wanted them as a remembrance of his sister, but when we got to the pub where we killed time till the last train and he drank too much beer, he tore them across and across, set fire to the pieces in the ashtray.

He held me close as a lover all afternoon. In the bank, where the cashier tutted and sighed before releasing my money; in the cafe where he ate and I refused curling fish paste sandwiches; when we got onto the train. I hoped he'd let me go then, but he held me even closer till the train pulled out, the barrel of the gun pressed hard into my side. I didn't know whether he planned to take me all the way to London, or whether he was going to throw me out on the line somewhere in the dark. I tried to be ready, but I was so exhausted I hardly cared which it was, so long as he let me go. Not surprising, then, that I couldn't believe it when he pushed me out at the dark little halt and I realised I wasn't far from home.

10

18ᵗʰ April, Romsey

'**Y**OU SHOULD HAVE CALLED THE police,' Nash says. First thing in the morning, in his office, my confession isn't going well.

'I didn't have any money.'

'Don't play the innocent. You don't need it to dial 999. Or you could have asked the operator to put you through to me. You didn't have to let him get clean away.'

'Don't shout at me.'

I've had less than three hours' sleep, and it feels as if I've got one skin too few to face the world.

'I know he put you in fear.' His voice is gritty with temper. 'But after he let you go, you could have called for help.'

'I don't expect you to understand.'

'Good, because I don't. You must go to the police. I'll come with you now if you like.'

'I don't need your help.'

'Fine.' Cold. 'Just so long as you do go.'

'No.'

'Then I will.'

'You wouldn't?'

I don't really understand why I'm so appalled by the thought.

'Of course I would. It's my civic duty.'

'Oh, don't be such a prick.' I take the half-crown that I borrowed from Dot this morning out of my pocket, slap it down on his desk. 'What if I claim privileged information? If you're my solicitor, you can't tell anyone what I've said to you.'

Hands in his pockets, he stares at the coin.

'You're asking me to act for you?'

'I'm asking you not to tell anyone about Frank.'

It occurs to me that part of this is purely selfish: I don't want to have to parade my embarrassment for all and sundry. So stupid, walking into a trap. A prisoner of my own foolishness.

A pause. Then he reaches out, pushes the coin back across the desk.

'Keep your money. But I wish I understood what's going on in your head.'

I sit down in the client's chair. I'm tired, and my feet hurt.

'I felt sorry for him.' And I did – I *do* – feel sorry for him even though that isn't the only reason. 'He was vile about Ruth, but he was terrified. He's the last of the family, and he's afraid he's going to die too. He says he's doomed if they send him back to sea.'

Nash sits down. I don't know if I've convinced him, but it's an improvement that he's stopped looming over me.

'Had you thought he might be the killer? You say he was angry with his sister.'

'He didn't know where to find her.'

'He says he didn't.'

'I don't believe he's the type to kill. He was angry with me, too. If he'd wanted, he could easily have done me in. But he let me go.'

'He stole your money.'

'The police would say I gave it to him. And I'd be in trouble for that, too.'

'You could at least let them know where he was heading for.'

'I could.'

'But you won't?'

'He could be anywhere. He said he was going to London, but he could have got off the train at the next stop. He might be just down the road.'

'Is that what you're scared of?'

'I'm not scared.' Not of Frank, anyway. 'There's nothing wrong with me except lack of sleep.'

He rubs his face, the familiar gesture of frustration.

'All right. You win. What do you suggest we do now?'

I'd like to go back to bed and sleep for a week, but it wouldn't be very productive.

'Frank said he sent letters *poste restante* for Ruth. I thought I could ask at the post office. See if anyone remembers her picking them up.'

'A pity we haven't still got the photographs.'

'I suppose.' At least he hasn't pointed out it was my fault they'd been lost. 'We've got her name.'

'That's something. If she's been in Romsey since evacuation, she must be on the ARP register somewhere.' He pauses. 'I don't understand why no one had any idea who she was.'

'Perhaps they did. They're just not admitting it.'

'True.'

'And don't forget . . .'

I've had plenty of time to think in the last twenty-four hours.

'What?'

'She'd dyed her hair. And the stuff in the suitcase, it was nothing like the clothes she was wearing. She must have looked quite different ordinarily.'

'It's a point.' He frowns. 'If she'd been going to meet a lover, I could understand it. But why would she glam herself up for her brother?'

'We don't know it was for him. We don't know she was going to meet him. Frank didn't know himself. He was just hoping.'

'I suppose we'll never know. Ah, well, better be grateful for what we've got. I'll speak to the Waverleys. They've got access to the registers.'

'You're welcome to that conversation.'

'They aren't the easiest, it's true. But I'll have a shot at it.'

I stand up. 'I was wondering . . .'

More than wondering. I've been trying to stave off the conviction all night. In the waking dream of my walk, in the dead sleep after, Ruth was on my mind – her secrecy, her apparent readiness for flight.

'What?'

'The baby. The post mortem on Ruth said she'd had a baby. Do you think it could've been her child that was abandoned? The one who died of rat bites?'

'Oh, Christ, of course. Where are my brains?'

For a minute, I think he's going to be sick.

'Are you OK?'

He brushes it off, brusque. 'I'm all right. You get on to the post office. If you find out anything more, let me know.'

Nash has a killer headache coming on. He gets them from time to time, a result of his injury. Anything can start them off. Overwork, lack of sleep, strong emotion. Sometimes they happen for no reason at all.

Now and then, he can stop one in its tracks. The doctor's pills work, if he takes them soon enough. Physical effort may nip it in the bud, digging the garden or chopping logs. Or sex, if he's lucky.

The sickness comes in waves, and the flashing lights. He's got no time for this now. No time for weakness. He's got things to do, people to see. He has to get on.

'I really cannot help you, Miss . . . ?'

'Mrs Lester. I'm here on official business for the coroner. Mr Nash.'

'That's as may be.' The post office official who's been summoned to speak to me puffs himself up to his full five foot nothing. 'But without a police warrant, I cannot release any item. His Majesty's mail is sacrosanct.'

'I'm not asking about the King's mail,' I say, exasperated. 'Just Ruth Taylor's. You know, the girl who was found dead after the Cricketers' was hit. She can't exactly come and get it herself.'

'No need for sarcasm. King or commoner, no one may interfere with the mail.'

'Can you at least tell me if there's anything waiting for her?'

'No.' He turns to go back to his station behind the grille. 'Good day to you, miss.'

'*Mrs.*' It's not the title that bothers me, but his attitude. *Run away and play, little girl.* 'You have to understand. We need to find whatever we can to help us identify her killer.'

He doesn't even pause, cracks the counter down behind him.

'Get your employer to ask Sergeant Tilling. It's police business.'

'And the coroner's.'

But I'm speaking to thin air. I stalk off, hoping I don't look as ridiculous as I feel.

At the bank, a similarly infuriating interview awaits; though at least when it's over I'm in possession of more funds than the half-crown Dot lent me. The bank manager's the post office official's twin for disapproval, though he maintains a politer veneer as he sounds me out about my profligate spending. Grudgingly, he agrees to cash another cheque, but he isn't pleased. By the time he's finished, I'm ready to explode. I can't go back to Nash like this. Nothing to tell him, a morning wasted. He'll only remind me that I lost our lead when I let Frank go.

Across the road, the Palmerston tearoom beckons. A cup of tea and whatever the café can provide in the way of food might give me a chance to think what I'm going to do next. Inside, the chalked-up menu offers Welsh rarebit or beetroot stew. The rarebit turns out to be mostly leeks gone khaki with cooking, in a sauce that might once have been in the same kitchen as a piece of cheese, but it's hot, and the toast's thick, and when I've eaten it and drunk a cup of tea I feel better. I'm beginning to relax when the waitress comes over. She's uneasy, peering about her as if she expects someone to shout.

'I'm sorry to trouble you, miss, but – are you the lady that's working for Mr Nash?'

'What can I do for you?'

'There's a boy round the back. Says he needs to speak to you. Urgent, he says.'

'What's it about, do you know?'

'It's the lad who brings telegrams. It's maybe . . . I hope you're not expecting bad news?'

If I was, it could only be about Richard.

'I hope not too.'

'Please, miss. If you'd just come?' She's practically wring-ing her hands, like a character out of a bad play. 'It's only a step. Won't take a minute.'

I get up, follow her out through a steamed-up kitchen. I can't think what the message might be. Could Frank have tracked me down? But I don't see how or, for that matter, why he would.

An alley runs behind the tea room, a dank narrow passageway that can never get the sun. A boy's waiting, and I recognise him straight away. It's the scout I saw a couple of days ago at the ARP centre. He's excited, or perhaps frightened, I can't tell from his expression in the gloom. He moves eagerly towards me as soon as I come out of the door.

'I've got information,' he says hoarsely. 'You were asking at the post office about that girl?'

'Yes.'

'An' you were at the wardens' the other day.'

'That's right.'

'What's it worth, then?'

'I see. A businessman.' I take out my cigarettes, light one. Offer the pack to him. 'You old enough to smoke?'

'Course,' he scoffs. But he puts the cigarette behind his ear, unlit.

A cold draught is blowing along the alleyway.

'Do we have to talk out here? If you come inside, I'll buy you a cup of tea and a bun.'

'No, ta. If him at the post sees me that's my job gone. It's worth more than a bun.'

I take the hint, take the half-crown out of my bag again. No chance it'll be rejected this time.

'That more like it?'

He grabs for the money but I close my hand.

'Not until you tell me.'

'She used to come in the post office on market day to pick up her letters,' he says resentfully.

'I know that already. So why didn't you say something when the body was found?'

''Cos I didn't know it was her, did I? Talk was the girl up the Cricketers' was a tart. Even her own mum wouldn've known her, then, 'cos when she come in the post office she was dressed up like a nun.'

'What?' Now I am surprised.

'Big blue mac she always had, right down to her ankles. And a scarf thing, covering up her hair. Proper little mouse. Wouldn' never have thought of her, till I heard you asking the boss.'

'OK.' I drop my cigarette end, scuff it out. 'Not sure it's worth half a crown, though.'

'Cor, what a swizz! An' Alf said you was all right.'

'You know Alf Smith?'

'Course I do, he's a good laugh.'

'What's your name?'

'Pete. You ask Alf, he'll tell you—'

'All right. And you're sure there's nothing else you can tell me?'

'Course.' But he looks shifty.

'Pete, it's really important we find out everything we can about this girl.'

'Yeah. They're saying she was done in. That true?'

'You know what they say about careless talk.'

'I want me money.'

I hesitate. I'm pretty certain he knows more than he's said, but I don't want him making something up to get more cash. So I hand the coin over, and he stuffs it in his pocket.

'Give us another fag?'

'Don't push it.' But I hold out the pack anyway. 'What is it, Pete?'

'I did see her a couple of times up the Cut. Mooching about. Never spoke to her nor nothing.'

'Do you think she lived up that way?'

'Dunno. Didn't take much notice.'

The feeling that he's not telling me everything is even stronger now.

'Maybe you could show me?'

He edges away. 'Sorry, miss. Gotta go. Boss'll have my hide.' And then he runs.

There's no point trying to stop him. I can find him again if I want to. Or Alf can.

I wonder about Alf. How much he knows. I'm going to have to have a chat with that young man before long.

Back inside the tea room, I pay my bill. I should go and tell Nash what I've learned, but I'm not ready. I haven't got enough yet to blot out this morning's fiasco.

Edith Waverley is at home this morning. In her role as Officer-in-Command of the local ARP unit, she's the obstacle Nash will have to circumvent in order to get the information he needs. One of those raw-boned, horse-faced women the county set breeds so well, she's a middle-aged spinster who seems more at home with blood sports than knitting. Nash sees her through the veil of jagged, gaudy colours that his migraine imposes.

'Ruth,' he repeats doggedly. 'Ruth Taylor. Are you sure you don't recognise the name?'

Miss Waverley bridles. 'Are you calling me a liar, Mr Nash? I've already told you I don't know.'

'She ought to be on the ARP register,' he says. 'And she had a child recently, someone must have attended her.'

She pulls a face, grotesquely magnified by the swirling colours of his vision.

'As to that, I can't comment. And nor will my brother. You know as well as I do, such matters are confidential.'

'The girl's dead, and I suspect foul play may be involved. I think that trumps any issues of confidentiality. I could probably get a warrant to prove it. But I won't argue the point if we can find out what we need to know from the ARP registers.'

'You don't imagine I keep them in my head?' If anything, she is more unhelpful than ever. 'I'll look at the books the next time I'm on duty.'

'If it's too much trouble, I'm sure my assistant would be happy to help.'

'Your assistant? If you mean Josephine Fox . . . God forbid.'

He ignores the rudeness, ploughs on. 'I'm sure your brother's told you how eager he is that I should resolve the matter.'

She sniffs. 'Ridiculous fuss over a little trollop.'

'You'll look at those records for me, Miss Waverley?' he persists. 'As soon as you can?'

'Tomorrow,' she concedes. 'Or Sunday. Depends how busy we are. I take it you don't expect me to go haring off right away?'

He expects nothing from her, other than this bristling personal hostility that's only partly tempered by her recognition of his office as coroner. It's old news that he offends her. Mostly, it's a matter of his heritage. The corruption, as she sees it, of his father's unimpeachable Hampshire stock by his mother's bohemian Jewishness. She's not alone in that; there are plenty like her who think Hitler's policies have merit. And there's his face. Such bad form on his part, not to have done the decent thing and died.

'Well?' She snaps the word. 'You might have time to waste, Mr Nash, but I'm a busy woman. If there's nothing else, I'll get Mary to see you out.'

He clamps down on rising sickness, the roaring dislocation of his vision.

'I'll expect to hear from you soon, then.'

She nods, though it's more dismissal than co-operation. But much as he'd like to, he can't press the point right now. He needs to get out of here every bit as urgently as she wants to see him go.

11

The same day

WHEN THE NUNS OF ROMSEY were ousted by Henry VIII, the abbey church was sold to the people of the town for £100. From its place overlooking the market square, it sees all there is to see of what goes on. Time passes, and the wheel turns. The nuns are back, though not in the abbey itself.

I skirt the precinct, cross the road. Gravel crunches underfoot as I walk towards the convent's front door. I know it's a long shot, but I have to find out if anyone here knows about a girl who went to collect her post dressed like a nun.

I ring the bell, not sure what to expect. I imagine a grille being opened, like in the films. But it's nothing so dramatic. The door opens in the ordinary way and reveals a woman in a grey habit.

'Can I help you?' Her attitude seems somewhere between welcome and discouragement, neither one thing nor another.

'I need to speak to someone who can tell me about your household,' I say.

She looks me up and down. 'You wish to join us?'

'Not at all. I'm on official business from the coroner's office.'

A frown flits across the smooth forehead.

'You'd better come in.' She shows me to an anteroom just inside the door. 'Wait,' she tells me.

There's the smell of beeswax and damp. A narrow, arched window lets in a greenish light. There are fiercely polished benches against two walls, a hard armchair beside an unlit hearth. It reminds me of a station waiting room, except for an elaborate crucifix which hangs against the dark paintwork.

I find the room oppressive. The sense of being watched is overwhelming, and I can't stop myself pacing restlessly up and down.

'Good day.' Another nun, older than the first but otherwise much the same, appears in the doorway. 'I am Sister Gervase, the almoner. I believe you wish to speak with me?' Her accent is precise, not-quite-English.

'To someone.' Subtlety deserts me. 'To anyone who can tell me if a girl called Ruth Taylor was ever here.'

Unruffled, she takes a seat in the armchair, folds her hands in her lap.

'Won't you sit down?'

'I'd rather not.'

I regret it almost at once. Standing in front of her isn't making me feel more powerful, quite the reverse. It's like being called to the headmistress's study for an appointment with the cane. My hands tingle with the memory.

'So,' she says. 'Who am I speaking to, please? Sister Luke said you were here from the coroner.'

'My name's Lester,' I say, holding out one of the cards Nash has written for me. She makes no move to take it. 'Do you know anything about Ruth?'

'I ask myself why you would wish to know?'

I'm rattled by her air of detachment. It makes me want to bite.

'Yours isn't an enclosed order is it, Sister?'

'No,' she concedes.

'Then you must have heard about the air raid on the pub? That there were casualties? One of them, a young woman, hasn't been officially identified.'

'You think it could be Ruth?'

It feels like an admission. There's colour in her face that wasn't present a moment ago.

'Did you know her?'

She considers for a long moment. Then, 'Why are you here, Miss Lester?'

Why is everyone determined to make me into a spinster?

'The coroner—'

She shakes her head. 'No. Why are *you* here?'

I want to say it's what I'm paid for, but it feels rather cheap.

'I don't like the way someone . . . threw her away.' I'm suddenly aware where my anger's coming from. It's not this nun, however infuriatingly calm. 'Killing her was bad enough. There's too much death already and her family . . .' But that's not my story to tell, and I veer away. 'She was so young. She'd had a baby, did you know that? And they dumped her like rubbish. Got rid of her. They're good at that in Romsey. Good at frightening little girls and getting them pregnant and—'

'You?' she says.

'Not me.' With one part of my brain, I'm sober again, wishing I hadn't said anything. But the words won't stop. 'My mother.'

'She died?'

'Three months ago. But they killed her spirit years ago. When they drove her out, threatened her so she never dared come home.'

Though it's just me being stupid, nothing whatever to do with Ruth, somehow the spate of words seems to have softened her attitude.

'Ruth *was* here,' she admits. 'She came to us ... It was Ash Wednesday, I remember that. Late February. It was the twenty-sixth, I believe. She had recently given birth. She was almost too weak to walk, she should not have been out of bed. We took care of her, of course, but she would not talk about what had happened. Only that her child had been taken away to a good home.'

I think of the entry about the baby in Billy Stewart's mortuary log. Had Ruth lied to the nuns, abandoned it herself? But if she'd been scarcely able to walk on the twenty-sixth, could she possibly have been out of bed on the twenty-fourth? And if she hadn't abandoned it, who had?

'She didn't say where she'd been till she came to you?'

'No.'

'No clues? Did she bring anything with her?'

'She had only the clothes she stood up in.' The nun sighs wearily. 'We believed her to be destitute.'

'We found a case,' I say, sketching the size with my hands. 'There were some things inside. A skirt and blouse, a few underclothes.'

'We provided her with a few garments from our store for decency's sake. Plain things, old things from charity. But a case? I don't know.'

As far as it went, the description of the clothes would certainly fit what we found. But it doesn't explain the rest.

'There was a letter,' I say, aware this is going to be another bombshell. 'From her brother. And some photographs.'

'A letter? But we understood her to be without friends or family.' She frowns. 'Could it be this girl was not our Ruth?'

'I'm sorry, Sister. It's certain that the girl who died owned the case. And her name was Ruth Taylor.'

'I don't understand.' She shakes her head. 'It makes no sense. The description of this girl who was found, it was nothing like her. We had no reason to suppose it could be Ruth, to believe harm had come to her.'

'But you'd missed her by then?'

'Yes.'

'When did you last see her?'

'Monday morning, in the chapel. She was lighting a candle.'

'She was devout?'

'Oh, no, not at all, I would say. But we ask our guests to observe the offices if they are well enough. And by this time, she was. As a matter of fact, I had never seen her alone in the chapel before.' She pauses. '*Mon Dieu*, I wonder . . .'

She falls silent and I wait until I can't bear it any more.

'What?' I prompt her.

'Sunday evening, Easter Sunday, you understand.'

'Yes?'

'We prayed for the souls of those departed. One was a foundling baby, buried the first week of March.'

'Her baby?'

'I suppose she may have thought so.'

She may have *known* so, I think.

'Was she upset?'

'I regret . . . I do not know. I do not remember seeing her that evening after the offices.'

'When did you realise she'd gone?'

'Tuesday morning, we began to wonder. She had not been present at offices, nor at meals. I went to her room, I was afraid she might be ill again. But there was no sign. All was tidy. She had so little I could not tell if she had truly left us.'

'You thought she might come back?'

'I hoped,' she says simply. 'But now . . .'

'Her room?' I'm the one hoping now. 'Did you clear it?'

'There was nothing to clear.'

'She didn't leave anything behind? Not even a note?'

'Nothing,' she says again. 'That is to say . . . there was one strange thing, I suppose. In her wastepaper basket.'

My heart skips a beat. 'What was it?'

'An empty bottle. Hydrogen peroxide. We use it in the dispensary to clean wounds. I was worried she had injured herself.'

'No, Sister,' I say, trying to hide my disappointment. 'She used it to bleach her hair.'

She lets out a deep breath. 'I would like to see her,' she says. 'Is that possible?'

'I don't see why not.'

And I can't deny it would be convenient. Provide the final link in the chain, proof positive we have the right identification for the girl.

They're having a good run for their money in Romsey this week. Plenty to gossip about. The air raid, the deaths. And now a murder. It's all grist to the mill.

There's one of the old French nuns from the convent, stepping up the street with a face pale and harsh as one of her own stone saints. But it's no saint walking along beside her.

Whispers shuffle behind hands, mouth to ear.

Josy Fox. Coroner's assistant. It's a man's job, everybody knows that.

Always was a tomboy.

Hard as nails.

Wonder what she had to give him to get the job? You know what they say, like mother like daughter.

Bit long in the tooth for that.

Nah. I'd be in it for a biscuit. Nothing like dunking a ginger nut.

Dirty devil.

By the time I've said my farewells to Sister Gervase, it's almost six. I feel drained, pulled down by knowing who the dead girl is for sure. I should be pleased we've got a positive identification at last, but somehow it hasn't worked like that.

The nun had recognised the dead girl at once, despite the changes Ruth had made to her appearance: bleached hair and plucked eyebrows, face and nail paint. The flirty red dress was still a mystery, they'd never given Ruth anything like that. If she'd had it before she'd come to them, she must have hidden it away somewhere.

The nun couldn't throw any light on what might have happened to Ruth's documents, either. As far as she knew, the girl hadn't owned a handbag. She'd carried her personal possessions round in a gas mask case covered with a scrap of fabric.

'A pattern,' Sister Gervase said before we parted. 'Cherries, I think. Pretty, but faded. It might have been a dress, once upon a time.'

I promise to look out for it, but we both know it must be long gone. It, and everything in it.

Romsey, Rumsey, Rūm's ēg.
Placename, Rūm, personal name, Old English
Ēg, an island, most often refers to dry ground surrounded
by marsh. In late Old English, a well-watered land.

Fire is a quick destroyer, but water will wear down stone. And Romsey is better supplied with water than fire. Its river, the Test: clear running, lively with trout. Its many braids, darting, meandering, busy with mills. The Barge canal: abandoned, heavy, slow; mud and minnows nibbling. Tadburn, *Toad stream*: rising in bog to the east, cutting downhill by secret ways to the Test. Into this network of waterways many things are subsumed: the careless, the lost, the deliberate. The discarded, the cunningly thrown. Somewhere, in the deep curve pool of a stream, half submerged already in silt, lies a clot of paper, a knot of cloth. The waters fret at the unravelling edges, current fraying the fibres, wearing away words. Fish find nothing to engage them, but a questing leech briefly samples the marks, the smudge of blood. Proof of identity, traces of guilt.

12

Five days earlier, Easter Sunday, 13th April, Romsey

R UTH'S BORED. THE EVENING SERVICE has been going on forever. The Latin washes over her, incomprehensible. She's had to go to church more times since she came here than ever in her life before. And she's damn sure she won't be going again, once she leaves.

Right at the beginning, it'd seemed like she'd been on to a good thing, coming to Romsey. She'd escaped Southampton and the threat of the bombs, and even when they discovered she was too old to be evacuated, they hadn't sent her back. They'd found her a cushy little job out in the sticks. Not much fun, but at least it was safe.

She'd had the old devil wrapped round her little finger. He'd promised all sorts when the war was over: a flat in town, nice clothes. She'd maybe even get a fur coat like the ones she'd seen in Mr Glass's shop, and all for the price of a few photographs. She hadn't minded that – it was nothing to her if he liked odd *stuff – but it all changed, turned into a nightmare once he realised she was up the spout. She'd never thought it was possible, an old bloke like him, but there she was, expecting, and it was too late to get rid of it even if she wanted to. Course, he couldn't marry her, she wouldn't have wanted that in any case, but he promised to find the kid a home, give her enough money to get away. It'd been all right where she'd been, they didn't notice anything even when she got quite big. It was only when the labour started, she had to call for help. And they'd come, him and the other one, and they'd dealt with everything and it hadn't been too bad, but there'd been a moment after they took the baby away when she caught a look she hadn't been meant to see, and she was scared. She knew she'd better get out of there, and quick.*

Since then she's been biding her time. Getting strong. Getting the things she needs together. Just waiting for the right opportunity. When Frank's letter had come it had seemed perfect. They'd be able to help each other escape.

She dabs at her headscarf, making sure it's still in place. Her hair has come out just the way she wanted, a bright white blond that makes her look like Jean Harlow. No more Miss Mouse for her. She'll show them. She thinks of the red dress she's stashed away, the scarlet shoes. It's going to be a kick, walking out of this town all dressed up, looking like a proper woman.

The priest's tone changes as he begins to speak in English. It catches her attention. Perhaps the service is coming to an end. She shifts in her seat, sits up straighter, ready to go. But he's off again, praying for the souls of the dead. She sighs, listens to a list of names she doesn't know, and couldn't care less about.

And then, like a blow, it comes.

'February the twenty-fourth,' the priest intones. 'A boy child, hours old, found abandoned. Known only to God.'

Her heart thumps in her chest, and everything goes black around her. It can't be ... But she remembers that look, and knows it is. Those promises, they must all have been lies. They'd left him somewhere to die ... She feels like screaming. What choice had she had? She might not have wanted him, but she hadn't wanted him dead.

The night plays out so slowly. She can't sleep, she can't cry. Her thoughts keep going back to the one brief glimpse she'd had of the baby: pale skin and a tuft of reddish hair, a streak of her blood on his face.

When morning comes, she goes to the chapel, lights a candle. It's the last time she'll be there, she needs to do it.

It's time to go. Frank will be waiting. The only difference is what she's going to do before she leaves. She's not going to let the old devil get away with it. She's got the evidence. He'll have to pay.

13

18th April, evening and night

I T's NO SURPRISE THAT WHEN I get to the office Miss Haward is coming out, keys in hand, ready to lock up.

'I don't know what you're thinking of, turning up at this time of day,' she says, before I have a chance to say anything. 'I'm closing the office up now. I'm already half an hour late.'

'I'm looking for Mr Nash,' I tell her.

'I gather you had a row with him this morning,' she snaps.

'It wasn't a row. If it's any of your business, he tore me off a strip.'

'Whatever you call it. It won't do, Mrs Lester. I warned him, but he wouldn't listen. Nothing but trouble ever since you came. He didn't even bother to let me know when he left the office. I expect he went home with one of his heads.'

It's probably only because I'm so tired that I get a picture of Nash taking his pick from a cupboard full of heads. It isn't funny, but I can't help smiling. If he had a choice, I know he wouldn't wear the one he does.

'Don't know what you're laughing at,' she says tartly. 'All this upset. I knew it wouldn't work, having a woman for his assistant.'

She turns the key viciously in the lock, clatters down the steps towards me. Just as she reaches pavement level, a lorry backfires in the street beyond, and she startles, stumbles, almost falls. I put out my hand to steady her but she shakes me off, flounces off down the street without a backward glance. She hasn't noticed she's dropped the fob with the office key in her haste. I pick it up, call out to her, but she doesn't hear, or doesn't choose to. My better self thinks I should go after her, but I'm so sick of her supercilious attitude I can't be bothered. And as for tracking Nash down at home, I really can't face it. What I know will have to keep a few hours more.

But the key in my hand is a temptation, despite my tiredness. It gives me a golden opportunity to start looking for clues about my father. Just beyond the door is an office full of records, all impeccably indexed. I've got my list in my bag, and there's no one around to ask me what the hell I'm doing.

I wait a minute, to be sure she's not coming back. But there's no sign of her, no sign of anyone, so I make my way up the steps and open the door unchallenged. Inside, the office is unlit, dusky and warm. The building is silent around me. There's a delicious feeling of trespass as I turn the key in the door to lock myself in.

Habit takes me first to the back corridor and my desk. There are no windows, so there's no blackout to worry about.

It's safe to put the light on down here. I flip the switch and the dim bulb glimmers to life overhead. It's so feeble it scarcely counts as light. I put down my bag, loosen my coat, flop down in the rickety chair. No need to rush, for the first time today I've plenty of time. So nice, not to be moving, talking, trying to work things out. I don't have to deal with Nash or Miss Haward. I don't have to make conversation with Dot and the girls, or worry about what I'm going to say to Alf, though there are definitely things I need to ask him. I'll put my head down for a minute, rest my eyes.

Bram Nash knows if he sits very still, in the dark, in silence, eventually he'll feel better. He'll start to believe he can survive this time. But while it lasts, death would be a blessed relief. The nausea, the dizzy spinning of every sense, the tearing pain is as bad as the shrapnel that sheared away half his face.

Lying in no-man's-land, listening to the groans and screams around him, listening to the whistle of shells overhead, sprayed with earth and blood. Growing dark, vision fading, growing cold. Listening to the sound of his own breathing, the bubble of it, feeling the numbness creep, blessed and fearful, so he curses the brave chaps when they come to fetch what's left of him. He screams at them, 'Take my pal over there.' It's not courage, it's cowardice. He wants to die. But it's too late. The silence tells him. His pals have gone already.

He's empty now, but the retching goes on. Pain blinds him, but he doesn't call out. All he wants is to be left alone.

When I wake, I'm so stiff I'm almost paralysed. My face is smooshed sideways against the desk, and there's dribble on my cheek. As I creak upright, unsure what has woken me, my neck and back protest. I know where I am, but for a moment I can't remember why or how I got here. And then it floods back. The key, the records. How much time have I wasted?

My feet and hands buzz with pins and needles as I move. A glance at my watch shows I've slept a long time. It's after midnight.

I make use of the facilities, splash my face with cold water, begin to revive. I'd no intention of staying so late, but if I go back to Dot's now, I'll miss my chance. Another hour or two can't matter to anyone but me. I begin to prowl, pent-up with a savage kind of energy which seems to seep into me from the fabric of the place. There's a feeling, visceral, not butterflies, something more crude in my guts from being here, in a place I shouldn't be, a place where no one comes outside the working day. It shivers through me, the potential of it, fuels the conspirator in me, the spy.

Time to consult my list.

The list of men I made after Nell died. The ones in the paper. My potential fathers, my mother's seducer. The search for Ruth's identity hasn't made me forget my original search. It's just put it off, and for far too long. Now I need to make good.

Miss Haward's indexing is so thorough I have to forgive all the flounces and snottiness she's treated me to, and send up a silent vote of thanks to her efficiency. Beginning with the names that I can't put a face to, I track down three candidates straight away. Eliminate them just as quickly. A deed of conveyance shows Harry Wilks didn't come to Romsey till after the last war, a blow-in from South Africa in 1926. A partnership agreement reveals Antony Bond, the vet, is no older than I am. And Robert Lisle has had a trust fund since a riding accident put him in a wheelchair, aged twelve.

I start again.

Bing, senior partner here. No papers in the general filing for him, but I'd hardly expect it. Maitland, the dentist. Nothing in the records. He must do business with some other firm. I'll need to make enquiries elsewhere if I want to chase up either of them.

Waverley. A drawer full of stuff, though nothing recent. Oxley of Ramillies Hall, a drawer and a half, but most of that looks ages old. I'll have to move on, come back to it later. I can't wade through that lot now.

George Redfern, water bailiff. He's got a thickish file, but there's nothing that seems helpful in my search until a letter grey with age catches my eye. '. . . *the unfortunate circumstance of a childhood infection with mumps . . . apply to adopt . . .*' Not George, then.

Ted Hudson. Newsagent. Like Redfern, a thick folder. I stop, paper in hand. A paternity order, dated 1923. My heart beats quick in my chest, but it's too late for me. Some other poor bastard.

Joseph Fox. Grandfather. I can't bring myself to look in these records for him. Not that I'd exclude him from shameful behaviour, despite his holier-than-thou attitudes, but I'm pretty sure incest's beyond his scope. Besides, he's far too mean to pay for a lawyer.

Alec Humphries. Lay preacher. A single sheet in his file. *Papers in deed box EAH/Bing/QS05*. I make a note to find out what the annotation means.

Outside, the abbey clock strikes two. It's taken me longer than I thought. I'm shivering, sick with tiredness and cold. I can't do any more tonight. I feel like I'm moving through molasses, some substance much darker, more viscous than air, weighing down movement and thought. I look around, make sure I've left everything tidy. I don't want anyone knowing I've been here.

No sound from outside, Romsey's at peace. I unlock the front door, slip through, lock up again. Hesitate. What to do with the key? Drop it for someone to find, let them assume it's been there all along? Not very responsible, if the someone doesn't happen to be an employee of Nash, Simmons & Bing. I could post it through the door, anonymous. I could use it as an excuse to beard Nash in his den at a respectable hour later today, or give it to Miss Haward on Monday.

I could keep it.

Lucky chances aren't really a matter of chance, and there's plenty I still need to find out. There's that deed box to explore, those drawers of filing. It's no choice, really. I put the key safely away in my bag with the list. I'll decide what to do with it later.

Soft-footed, clear-headed now, Nash comes downstairs. The little cubbyhole is empty, but the dust betrays her. In the dim bulb's light, motes dance as thick as a fall of leaves. There's a shine on drawers that haven't been opened in years, that haven't seen polish since God knows when. There's a fragment of colour, a wisp of frayed red tape on the floor. He opens a drawer and a crumpled slip of paper is dislodged. *Rex v Humphries*. It's nothing to do with the case in hand.

There's only one possible conclusion.

She's been snooping.

The question is, what has she been looking for?

14

19th April

I T ISN'T THE SUN POURING through the window because I've forgotten to draw the blackouts that wakes me. It isn't because I've slept long enough, or I've got to get up and pee. It's because someone's knocking, not particularly loudly, but very persistently, on my bedroom door.

I come reluctantly out of sleep, a sick taste in my mouth.

'What is it?'

'Mrs Lester?' Dot's voice. 'I want a word with you.'

I sit up, struggle to get my thoughts in order.

'Come in.'

As soon as she comes through the door I can see she's offended. A glance at my watch shows it's late, almost ten, but it's Saturday. Surely she can't mind? I don't have to work. I try a smile.

'Good morning, Dot.'

'That's as maybe.'

I feel vulnerable, in my night things, not properly awake, while she's fully armed and waiting to explode.

'Is something wrong?'

'Don't play the innocent with me. What do you think this house is, coming home with the milk twice in a row? I don't think so.'

'Look, Dot—'

'Don't you *look Dot* me. This is a decent household.'

It's too much. This again: this, always. As if I can't be decent because of who I am. All the stresses of the past few days rise up in me, pitch me into a mood as black as Dot's.

'Oh, I see. Too good for the likes of me, I suppose.' I throw the covers back, swing my legs out of bed. 'I'll get out, shall I? Give me half an hour.'

I stand up. The room cavorts around me like the Waltzer at a fair.

'Whoa.'

I have to sit down again. Not even pride can keep me on my feet.

Dot comes further into the room, stands over me.

'Looks like drink,' she says, almost conversationally, but I'm not sure it's me she's talking to. 'Doesn't smell like it though.'

'Not drink.' After Richard, the way he was, it's the last thing I want. 'Just not enough sleep.' Sitting down, the room steadies and I rally a bit. 'But there, you know all about that.'

'No call to be rude,' Dot says. Her attitude seems to have softened a little. 'You look bloomin' rough.'

'I feel it.'

'What's wrong with you? What've you been doing?'

'Didn't think you wanted to hear.'

She frowns. 'Never mind about that. Get on.'

So I tell her. All I can tell her, anyway. And some things I probably shouldn't. By the time I'm finished, she's sitting on the bed, tutting sympathetically.

'Sounds like you'd better get back to sleep then,' she says at last. 'I'm a silly old fool and I never should have believed—' She breaks off, looking embarrassed.

'What?' I ask. 'Who shouldn't you have believed?'

'Never you mind.' But there's no conviction in it.

'Dot?' I say, but she shakes her head. I try again. 'Please?'

She shrugs. Pretends not to care, but it doesn't work.

'Miss Waverley came round. She's not happy about me taking you in.'

A flood of questions rise up in my mind. But the one that comes out of my mouth is, 'What's it got to do with her?'

'Nothing really,' Dot says. 'But you know what it's like. She's got her finger in every pie. President of the WI, Knitting Circle, flower rota at church. Evacuee welfare, Land Girl billeting, the lot. Places I go, stuff I do. She can't actually stop me, but she can make life bloomin' awkward if she doesn't like you.'

'And she doesn't like me?'

'You could say that. Whatever did you do to her?'

'Nothing, as far as I know. Other than being born in the first place. You know what it's like. People like her don't approve of people like me.'

'She certainly doesn't approve of you working for Mr Nash. She wanted to know how you got the job. I never let on about you not coming home but . . . she said maybe you were, well . . .'

'Sleeping with him?'

That night in London has nothing to do with guilt, nothing to do with anyone but ourselves and the war, but I'm painfully conscious of how it would look if anyone in this small-minded town ever found out.

'I shouldn't have taken any notice,' Dot goes on. 'But she said she might have to reconsider about letting Betty and Joan come here for their meals.'

'She could do that?'

'I don't know. Those girls – I get a consideration for feeding them. And there's the extra rations.'

'If it's going to make it difficult for you, I will go.' Not that I've any idea where.

'Never you mind for now,' she says. 'Sleep on it.'

And because I can't keep awake any longer, I do.

It's a beautiful spring morning. After the headaches, Nash always feels purged, threadbare, in urgent need of solitude. He's ferociously thirsty, still. Even his skin seems to drink as he washes. He hurries through his ablutions, eager to get out into the fresh air. He can't bear to frowst indoors another moment.

He needs to be able to think.

No. That's not it. First, he needs *not* to think. He wants to be where the sunlight can burn off the memory of weakness, out in the fresh air where the breeze can carry away the taint of sickness. Somewhere that's quiet, and death is a simple matter of killing to eat. Foxes versus rabbits, no malice intended. No secrets and dust, no shut doors. In his present mood, he'd be happy if he never had to see a human face again. Never had to think about the things people do, why they do them.

He walks for hours, out onto the edge of the New Forest, open heath land that offers a great arc of uninterrupted sky above him, only a pony or two for company. By lunchtime, he's ready for more than spring water to drink, and he finds himself a dour public house where the landlord serves him Strong's bitter and a hunk of bread and cheese with taciturn courtesy. He's not let his mind dwell on anything but the walking: sunshine and birdsong, the breeze through the grass. But now, refreshed, once more fully in command of his own body and its functions, he's ready to reconsider the problem of the dead girl.

When I wake again, it's almost a quarter to three. I can't believe it. I'm out of bed on a reflex before I remember. It's Saturday, and I was up half the night and most of the night before, and I've identified Ruth and had a row with Nash and one with Dot, but it's OK with Dot now so I can relax. Except Dot's in trouble with Miss Waverley because of me so maybe I can't. And I still haven't reported to Nash.

It's afternoon, but my body feels like it's midnight. I wash hastily, get dressed. Go downstairs almost at a run, though I'm not sure why I feel such a need to hurry. Granny would have laughed at me, all behind like a cow's tail.

In the kitchen, Dot and the Land Army girls are getting ready to go out. The girls have their coats on, and Dot's reaching for hers. There's the big teapot in the middle of the table, and three used cups on the draining board, and I feel absurdly disappointed that I've missed the party.

'Back in the land of the living, then?' Dot says. 'You're just in time.'

'I am? What for?'

'The jumble,' Joan tells me. 'There's a sale on at the Parish Rooms. Got to get there when the doors open or all the good stuff'll be gone.'

'Um . . .'

'Come on if you're coming.' Joan's practically dancing with impatience.

Dot hands me my coat. 'Change of scene will do you good.'

Before I know it, I'm hustling down the road with Dot and the girls, listening to Joan's excited chatter. Whatever Betty's saying in return is inaudible, but I get the impression she's not as eager as Joan. Dot tucks her arm through mine, as if to make sure I don't duck out.

'Might be the last chance,' she says to me.

'What?'

I'm still reeling from the after-effects of my daytime sleep and the haste of our departure. My brain doesn't seem to be working at all.

'There's rumours they'll be rationing clothes before long. People won't want to chuck stuff out then. It'll be coupons for everything.'

'I suppose.'

It's a long time since I was last at a jumble sale. That was in Romsey, too.

The Annual Garden Party Fete. Held the first Saturday in June at the Briars, the official residence of the senior doctor at the hospital next door. Gates open at two o'clock sharp, highlight of our summer social life. Hoarding pennies for weeks, anticipating the heady delights of candy floss and guess the name of the doll, sleeping in her cardboard box. She has golden hair, lace on her knickers, bright blue eyes that open when they stand the box up. A mauve dress this year, last year it was yellow, but it could just as easily be the same doll over and over again. I've never known any child win her.

Bowling for the pig – my uncles have a go at that. Sweet little piglet, pink as a doll, screaming in its run. Tom won it once. Fatten it up, don't give it a name 'cos there'll be screaming again come Christmas.

Manicured lawns, roses in serried ranks. Ladies in summer dresses and white gloves, kids tidy as Sunday school, hair plaited tight or slicked down, getting bored, money spent, getting loose, playing tag and goosie goosie behind the asparagus beds.

Over by the greenhouse, the jumble stalls. One for clothes, piled high, women with prams rummaging through. They pack up when there's only a pair of grubby white jodhpurs (who'd ever wear those?) and a couple of odd socks left. The other stall's bric-à-brac. One year my heart sets on a china dog with its ear knocked off, and I wait all afternoon, turning up my nose at Lucky Straws and the fortune-telling fish, hoping against hope that the dog won't sell and being lucky for once, carrying it home to Granny in triumph, reduced to tuppence at the end of the day.

It's a scrimmage in the Parish Rooms. There's the smell of fresh disinfectant and old clothes. Loaded trestles are arranged in a hollow square around the room. Jumpers on one table, shoes on another. Skirts and trousers and hats and bags, a table of washed-out, yellow-grey undies. Joan dives into a billowy heap of cotton that might be summer blouses or frocks. Dot's deep into the woollies, looking for things to unravel and knit up again, while Betty goes fossicking through the shoes and bags. I wander past an array of battered china – cups without saucers, odd plates – to a table where there are boxes of books, scruffy for the most part, but irresistible to someone whose books are all in store. I pick out a thin, leather bound volume of poetry, and a nearly new Allingham, and I'm just paying my sixpence to the woman behind the boxes when a rumpus breaks out over by the shoes.

There's Betty with one red shoe in her hand, while another girl has its obvious pair in hers. I've never heard Betty talk loudly before, but she's hissing like a kettle, sibilant with fury.

'Saw it first,' she says. 'It's mine.'

'Liar,' the other girl says, almost as red in the face as the shoes. 'I got mine first. Just couldn't find the other one.'

''Cos it's *mine*,' Betty semi-whispers.

I look around, but though the girls are drawing a crowd, Dot and Joan are nowhere to be seen. It's nothing to do with me, but somebody's going to have to intervene sharpish or it'll turn into a real fight.

Reluctantly, I go across to them.

'Mrs Lester,' Betty practically shrieks, if it's possible to shriek in a whisper. 'Tell this cow . . .'

'Cow yourself,' the other girl says. 'I'm not the one standing out in the fields all day.'

'All right, that's enough.'

Their childishness makes me feel older than Methuselah's granny.

'I saw them first,' Betty insists. 'They're mine.'

'Not unless you've paid for them,' I say. 'Have you?'

'No.' She pouts. 'Nor's she, though. You ask her.'

I turn to her rival, who's clinging like death to the other shoe. I can see the attraction, they're everything the growing drabness of war and uniforms isn't. Red suede, with a high heel and peep toes.

'Have you?' I ask her.

She shakes her head. 'Not had a chance.'

'Do they fit you?' It seems like a reasonable question.

'Dunno.' The girl shrugs.

Betty looks triumphant. She reaches out to grab at the other shoe again, but I stop her.

'Do they fit you?'

'Course they will.' But she doesn't look sure.

'Try it on,' I say. 'Both of you, try on the one you've got. Whoever it fits gets them. That's fair, surely?'

I don't allow myself to consider the possibility that the shoes will fit them both. To my eyes, they look pretty small, and neither girl is petite. It seems unlikely either of them will turn out to be Cinderella today.

The minute Betty's rival tries to put her shoe on, it's obvious it's too narrow. For all her efforts, her toes won't fit in. But she's not going to give up without a fight.

'I could cut it along the top. Put a bow on, I've got some red ribbon. It wouldn't show.'

'You're not cutting my shoes.' Betty snatches the shoe away from her and slides it on. 'There, you see. Perfect.'

''Cept your clodhopper's hanging an inch off the back,' the other girl says. 'No good to you neither.'

And she's right. Betty's toes go into the shoe, but her foot's too long and she can't cram in her heel. She kicks the shoe off, looking mutinous. I gather it up quickly, before the other girl can grab it. Hold out my hand.

'Give me the other one. It's no good.'

'You just want 'em for yourself,' she mutters, but she hands it over.

'Not me. What is it, a two?' I look inside. 'Two and a half. I take a five.'

Betty makes a face at me. 'If you put them back, she'll have them. Cow.'

'Mare.' The other girl tosses her head. 'Keep the rotten shoes. Wouldn't have them for a gift after they've been on your dirty hooves.'

She stomps off into the crowd.

I have every intention of putting them back, but as the light turns on the inner curve of the leather, something catches my eye. It brings me up short. Though I might not be able to wear them, I'm not about to let them go. I shake my head at Betty, turn to the woman behind the stall who's watched the whole business without saying a word.

'How much?' I ask.

'Shoes like that? Everybody wants them.' She smirks at me. 'Five bob.'

It's daylight robbery, and we both know it, but I stump up the cash, make her give me a paper bag so I can put the shoes away out of sight. If we go on like this, Nash will have to pay me expenses. Because though it's far too late for any kind of evidence a policeman might be able to find, fingerprints or bloodstains, there's a mark inside the shoes that tells me who they might have belonged to. Someone's written in them, like a schoolchild, identifying precious property. Untidy capitals that have been rubbed out, though the indention still shows on the soft inner leather. I make out an *R* and a *T*.

The transaction's made, but I hang on. The crowd moves off, finding better things to do now the fun's over.

'Do you know who donated the shoes?' I ask the stall keeper when we're alone.

She shakes her head. 'Couldn't tell you. They've been collecting stuff all over the place for weeks. Suppose you could try Miss Waverley, the organiser. She might know.'

I'll have to think what to do about that. After what Dot said, I don't think I'll have much luck asking. The stall keeper's watching me, curious. I'm aware I've been standing here too long. Drawing attention to myself.

'Fair enough. Thanks.'

I let myself drift away, as if I'm not that interested. Dot's turned up again, and she comes over with a string bag bulging with old cardigans and jumpers.

'Better be off,' she says.

We round up the girls. Joan's empty-handed, but Betty's consoled herself with a bright blue headsquare printed with horseshoes and riding crops. They're whispering together again as we walk back to Dot's, and from the sideways looks they treat me to, the story's growing fresh embellishments with every step. I don't think I'm very popular with Betty today.

15

Five days earlier, the day of the air raid, Romsey

R UTH'S FIZZING WITH EXCITEMENT *as she walks down the street, loving the idea that inside the nuns' hand-me-downs, she's scarlet and bold. She's got a vision of herself revealed in new glory, pulling off her shabby blue mac, emerging like a butterfly from its dirty old shell. He'll be sorry when he sees what he's losing.*

She had a bit of a cry when she got to the hidey-hole, where no one could hear. The baby was never a part of her plans, but they'll pay for letting him die. She's ready for them, she's got what she needs to confront them.

The tap of her heels on the pavement makes her feel confident, brave. She's almost hoping someone will notice the girl in the red shoes, but no one looks round as she passes. No one seems to see that she's there. But she'll show them, she will.

She hasn't brought all of the pictures, she's not stupid. She's kept some for insurance, for later. They're safe enough where they are.

When she knocks on the door, he's not the one who answers. But she pushes past the figure in the doorway, throws off her mac just the way she meant.

'What are you doing here? I thought you were long gone.'

She won't answer that. 'Where is he?'

'How dare you? Get out.'

The door to the room where he's brought her so often is closed. She pushes it open, but there's no one inside. Only the smell of him.

'Where is he?' she says again.

'Out. Get out.'

'No.' She stands firm. 'I'll wait.'

'You'll do no such thing.' Threatening hands reach towards her.

'Don't touch me. I know what you did with my baby.'

'You think anyone will care? You didn't.'

'That's not true. You promised.'

'You promised . . .'

It's such a savage mimicry, it shakes her. Makes her feel helpless, like a child. It's all going wrong.

'I've got pictures,' she says, trying to sound hard, uncaring. 'You know. The ones he took. What about that?'

'How much do you want?' The voice is full of contempt.

'It's not about money.' But it is. She does need the money.

'Pull the other one. How much?'

Tears come to her eyes and she turns away. She won't let them show. What can she ask for? Fifty pounds? A hundred?

'Two hundred quid for starters.'

Behind her, she hears a door open. There's a rush of air. She begins to turn, but it's too late. There's a blinding moment of pain, and the taste of iron floods her mouth as she falls into blackness.

16

19ᵗʰ April, early evening

D OT'S NOT ONE TO LET the grass grow under her feet. Or to let wool go to waste either. By six o' clock she's got me pressed into service, helping her skein wool from the knitteds she bought at the jumble. She's unravelled a green pullover and made a start on a fluffy shawl while I'm still struggling with a huge cardigan in lurid orange.

'It's very bright,' I venture as I wind my aching hands to and fro across the interminable knit.

'Lovely for ducks,' she says. 'Or teddy bears.'

'You could just cut out the shapes as if was cloth. That'd save time.'

'That's the lazy way. Wastes too much wool.' She looks across at me. 'How are you getting on?'

'Not too bad.'

'You'll need a hand in a minute. That sleeve's got the moth, it'll be all little ends.'

Working together like this feels comfortable. Almost as if we're friends. I take a chance.

'Dot?'

'What?'

'Won't you tell me about Nell?'

The ball of fluffy pink wool jumps out of her hand, unwinds itself onto the hearth.

'Dratted thing.'

'You did know her, didn't you?'

She avoided the question so carefully last time that I'm sure I must be right.

'I can't tell you anything you don't know already.'

It's another evasion, but this time I won't let it go.

'Don't you believe it. Pretty much anything you can tell me is going to be news to me. I didn't know her when I was growing up. First time I remember meeting her was when I was fourteen.'

She stops what she's doing, looks over the top of her glasses at me.

'You're having me on.'

'I'm not. It was Granny and my grandfather who brought me up. Nell was banished. We weren't even supposed to talk about her.' I do that thing, a huff of sound that comes out almost as a laugh, but it's exasperation and sadness, a good bit of anger. 'Oh, my grandfather made sure I knew my birth had brought shame to the family. But as for details, I wasn't told anything.'

'We heard you'd gone to live with her when you left Romsey. That was the story.'

'That's all it was. A story. When my grandfather kicked me out, Nell couldn't look after me. She had a living-in place in London, more than her job was worth to tell them about me.

THE UNEXPECTED RETURN OF JOSEPHINE FOX

I never spent any time with her until the last few months of her life.'

'Blimey, that's rough. How did you manage up in the Smoke all on your own?'

It's supposed to be her, telling me things. I weigh it up. Perhaps it'll help if I tell her.

'It wasn't hard. Like now, with the war, there were plenty of jobs. I got a place in a munitions factory. Bed and board, and the pay was all right. And after, when the men came home, and they didn't want us any more I had enough savings so I could train as a shorthand typist. Got a job, worked my way up.'

She smiles. 'Married the boss?'

'How did you know?

'Romsey rumour. Said you'd done well for yourself.'

I shrug. 'It wasn't a success.'

'Divorced?'

'Not so far. He's been missing since Dunkirk.'

She's silent for a minute, seemingly intent on unravelling a stubborn tangle in the wool.

'Nell and me,' she says at last, 'we worked together. In the same spot, anyway. Like I said, she was younger than me and we never did get to know each other all that well. She was a scullery maid, and I'm sorry to say that in those days I thought I was a cut above. Head nursery maid, I was. Used to give myself such airs. Then when she got caught with you . . .'

'You knew about that?'

'Not to say *knew*. But it was the usual reason a girl had to leave without notice. It was all hushed up, you were supposed to pretend she'd never even been there.'

I can hardly bring myself to ask. 'Did you know . . . ? Were there rumours about who my father was?'

'Ask me no questions and I'll tell you no lies.'

Disappointment is like a weight on my chest.

'But you do know.'

She shakes her head. 'No.'

'Guess?'

'Look, deary, there's always rumours. If you believed them, it could have been anyone from the stable lad to the Prince of Wales. But I'm pretty sure it wasn't either of them.'

'Please, Dot?'

'Someone about the house, I suppose.' She shrugs. 'We had lots of visitors in those days, coming and going. I told you, she was a lovely-looking girl, couldn't help but attract attention. And I'm sorry, but if you must know she had a bit of a reputation. Flirting, that sort of thing. After she went, people started to say she'd been having it off with all sorts.'

It can't have been a visitor, because of my list.

'But she was only fifteen.'

'Doesn't signify,' Dot says darkly. 'You'd be surprised.'

I don't believe it. Oh, I know people change, and I know I didn't really know my mother well. But if she'd been like that, wouldn't she have had somebody in her life after she left Romsey? Several somebodies, even? She was still a beautiful woman, even on her deathbed. All those years in exile, she could have done what she liked, been with whoever she liked. And there was nothing, no one as far as I could tell. I had a more chequered history than she did.

'I'm sorry, Dot.' I stand up, put aside the orange wool. 'Excuse me. I need to get some air. I'll try not to be late.'

I wander a bit. Try to think, try not to think. After a while I find myself close to the Corn Market, not far from my uncle Tom Fox's greengrocer's. Tom is the eldest of my uncles; he'd always seemed remote, grown-up. As a child, I hardly knew him. And I've never met Sylvie, the Frenchwoman he met and married in the first war, but she's the one who kept in touch with my mother all those years, in defiance of my grandfather. On an impulse, I think maybe Tom would know about my mother, my father. Maybe he'd tell me.

I know he lives in a flat above the shop, my mother had the address in her diary. It's barely eight o'clock, it's not too late to call.

But the door takes a bit of finding. The greengrocer's is offset to the street, and this evening, with the shop shut up, the unmarked, matte-black painted door in the narrow snicket which gives access to the upper floor is not so much unobtrusive as positively hidden away. I'm relieved to see there's a bell, and I press it before I can lose my nerve. There's no answering sound audible from this side of the door, so I wait, unsure whether the thing's functioning or not. Shall I ring again, or just thank my lucky stars no one's home and leave?

I wait for what feels like an age, but no one comes. I've either got to try again or walk away. I'm about to take my cowardly retreat when the door opens cautiously.

Uncle Tom is standing on the doorstep, a newspaper in hand, his glasses pushed up on his forehead. The look on his face is pitched somewhere between *I'm sorry, the shop's closed* and *bugger off,* but when he sees me, the look clears and he smiles such a welcome I have to believe it's genuine.

'Josy. We were hoping you'd call.' He throws the door wide open. 'Come on in.'

'If you're sure I'm not interrupting?'

'Don't be daft.' He pulls me inside, closes the door behind me. 'Up you go, up you go. Sylvie'll be delighted.'

I climb the steep stairway into a space glowing with light. Whatever I might have expected from the gloomy lower entrance, it wasn't this. The upper hallway has five or six spot-lights high in the arch of the roof space which shine down on white walls and a black-and-white chequer-tiled floor. In front of me, a scarlet door stands ajar, and as Tom reaches the landing, he calls out.

'It's OK, Syl, no need to hide. It's Josy come to see us.'

He pushes the door open, and ushers me inside.

In daylight, the big windows must let in enough light to rival the hallway outside. Like the hallway, there's no ceiling, only the timbered roof space, white painted, brilliantly lit. Black blinds are pulled down between white curtains with black geometric designs. The floor is highly polished parquet, the furniture angular, all creamy-white upholstery and black lacquered wood. No knick-knacks, nothing cluttered. Three cushions – scarlet, mustard yellow and peacock blue – provide the only splashes of colour. Everything is pared to the minimum, perfectly ordered, like something from a high fashion magazine of the 1920s.

I'm shocked. Anything further from the cottage where Tom and I were brought up is hard to imagine.

'Wow!' The gauche exclamation leaves my mouth before I can stop it.

'Like it?' Tom says.

'I love it.'

'Bet you didn't expect this above a veg shop.'

I shake my head. 'It is surprising.'

'Sit down,' he says. 'Go on, the chairs don't bite. You'll find they're quite comfortable.'

I do as he tells me, discover he's right. Despite its sharp angles, the chair I've chosen is pleasant to sit in, even if it does make me feel as if I've been built to the wrong scale.

He laughs at my confusion. 'Get you a drink? Tea, something stronger?'

I can't imagine drinking tea in this amazing room. It's a space designed for cocktails. And like magic, another voice breaks in, echoing my thoughts.

'I can recommend the martinis.'

Even before I turn round, I know it must be Sylvie, because there's the lilt of her native tongue in her speech. I scramble to my feet, all elbows and angles. The woman who's come into the room is as bright and birdlike as Little Trotty Wagtail in her black skirt and white blouse, her precipitous high-heeled shoes pattering on the polished floor.

'Aunt Sylvie,' I say, holding out my hand to her.

'Just Sylvie,' she answers, drawing me into the French-woman's two-kiss salute. 'I beg of you, don't make me feel any older than I do already.'

I like her straight away. I like her for her sharp, clever eyes and her immaculate coiffure. I like her for the knitting she pulls out from under the peacock blue cushion – coarse, khaki wool for servicemen's socks – and for the way the flash and chatter of her needles punctuates our talk for the rest of the evening.

But most of all I like her for the imagination that conceived of – and the steadiness of purpose which carried out – the gesture of sending the local paper to my mother in her long exile, a woman she'd never met, yet for whom she had compassion. And for good or ill, it's the consequences of that long good deed which have brought me home. Without that paper, I'd never have come back.

I can't imagine what Grandfather must make of her, or she of him. That she's not cowed by him is obvious. She'd never have made the effort to be in touch with Nell if she was. And if Grandfather could see her now, could see them both, welcoming me into their home, he'd be apoplectic.

Tom settles us all with martinis. As Sylvie said, they are excellent, but strong. The alcohol goes straight into my blood and despite the spiky decor of this avant-garde room, I feel more relaxed than I have in ages.

'You got my message then,' Tom says. 'I'm glad Captain Nash remembered to pass it on. He's a good bloke.'

Before I can reply, Sylvie says, 'You could have come to stay with us, you know. No need to turn to strangers.'

That's two difficult responses I owe them. Bram Nash hasn't said anything to me that might be construed as a message from Tom, so I don't know what I can reply to that. And after all this time, both of them, family as they may be, are strangers to me every bit as much as Dot is. Rather than say anything, I smile and hold out my glass for a top-up from the cocktail shaker Tom offers.

'What we are curious about,' Sylvie says, eagerly transparent, 'is why you have come back after so long. It was some last request from Nell, perhaps?'

'Quite the reverse, really. She'd have hated to know I was coming back. But it is because of her all the same.'

I tell them how it was that Nell let slip my father was still alive and living in Romsey. I gloss over her distress when she found his name in the paper, because it wouldn't be fair to upset Sylvie when she'd only meant well. I tell them that until that moment I'd believed my father had died before I was born. I'd always thought that was why he'd never married my mother.

Tom grins uneasily. 'That was Mum. My mum, I mean. Your gran. Dad was a right bugger about it, but Mum, she never wanted you to think bad of *your* mum. Poor little Nell—' He breaks off. 'We were all too frightened of Dad in them days.'

'And you still are,' Sylvie says quietly. 'He has cast a blight on you all.'

Tom shrugs. 'He doesn't have a lot to do with us any more. Doesn't trouble you and me much.'

'That is because I will not stand for his nonsense. If your brother and sisters—'

It seems like the beginning of a well-worn discussion, and I don't feel too guilty for interrupting them. I take a deep breath, ask the question that brought me here.

'Did you ever . . . ? Do you know about my father, Tom? Did you ever hear who he was?'

He shakes his head. 'Our Nell was close as an oyster. Didn't matter how much Dad blustered, she wouldn't say.'

'But he knows,' I say in surprise. 'I'm sure he does. The other day—'

'You've seen him?' Tom asks. 'What happened?

'I ran into him up at the hospital. I didn't know he worked there.'

Another thing good old Captain Nash hadn't told me.

'And yet you see, she survived.' That's Sylvie, making her point to Tom. 'He's not so fearsome after all.'

'I wouldn't go that far. He was . . . horrible.' Inadequate as it is, I can't think of a better word.

'You are mad,' Sylvie says. 'All of you. One old man—'

'Leave it, Syl.' Tom pours the last of the martini into her glass.

'I know, *chéri*. It does no good. But it relieves my feelings. And so, Josy, what do you do next? If your grandfather will not help?'

'I won't ask him to.' If I never speak to him again, it'll be too soon. 'I'll just have to do it the hard way. Eliminate the impossible.'

'And what remains, however improbable, must be the truth.' Sylvie caps my quotation with glee. 'Tom will tell you, I adore detective stories. I shall follow with great interest as you look for the clues. And of course it is not just the one mystery you have to solve.'

'Pardon?'

For a moment, I can't think what she means.

'The murdered girl,' she says. 'You are searching for information about her, too, no?'

'Ye-es.' I'm not sure how much I'm supposed to say about that.

Tom laughs at my expression. 'It's all right, gal. Captain Nash told me all about it. Asked me and Syl to keep our ears open for any gossip going about. Syl here is the one for that. If there's anything to know, she knows it. Nothing gets past her.'

'Now who is horrible? I am not a gossip.'

'But you do get to hear an awful lot.'

His look for her is so affectionate it makes me envious. How tranquil it must be, how comfortable, to be married twenty years, and find yourself still in love.

'And – have you heard anything?' I venture.

This is not a mood that is as easy to break into as their earlier banter.

She shakes her head. 'Unfortunately for me, I have heard nothing but speculation. Who is she, they all ask. But no one knows. Or no one will admit it if they do. They all say, that place, that time, she must be a whore. A blow-in, looking for trade.'

If Sylvie is looking for information from me, I can't oblige. I feel mean, when she has been so generous, but it wouldn't be right to tell her things I haven't yet told Nash. Even if he isn't quite so scrupulous in return.

'No. I can't be explicit, but she wasn't a stranger. Not entirely, anyway.'

Sylvie looks intrigued. 'Ah, you have been the good detective, then. Finding things out. I would love to know more, but I understand you cannot. But I hope you will tell me, when you can.'

It's no hardship to assure her I will. Though I've learned nothing I didn't already know in my search for my father, the idea that I have an invitation to come back to this room and this company is very appealing. But it's getting late, and the martinis are catching up with me. If I don't go now, I shall fall asleep where I sit. Reluctantly, I make my excuses, take my leave. Tom offers to walk me home, but I refuse, despite Sylvie's urging. I need time on my own to make the transition between their glittering showcase and Dot's homely back bedroom.

17

The same evening

BRAM NASH SITS IN HIS study at Basswood House, trying to read. The fire's lit and there's a glass of whisky to hand. He needs it after Fan's fussing. She may have a heart of gold, but he can't stand her mothering when he's ill. It's why he chooses not to go home when the headaches hit. He has to be by himself, safe from pity, tucked away in his office where no one can hear.

Except last night there was Jo. She can't have known he was there. He's no idea what she was doing, but he'll have to find out. He yawns, takes a sip of whisky. The burn wakes him up, but he can't concentrate on the paperwork he's brought home. His thoughts keep wandering.

The girl. The dead girl. The murdered girl.

Could he be wrong? Could she have come there after he left, died in the blast? There have been cases where a victim of a bombing has appeared untouched, with no outward signs of damage.

But he knows it can't be. The PM report shows the girl's lungs were healthy. It was the blow to the head which killed her, not the explosion. It was a person who put her there, and whatever Waverley says, he will find out.

Nash knows he's not entirely rational on the subject of Waverley. The man gets under his skin with his prejudices and his certainty that when he speaks, everyone will jump to his command.

But it's not about being awkward, this time, of resisting for the sake of not doing what the senior man wants. It's a matter of principle, of conscience, of human decency. Nash won't let the dead girl down. He takes another sip of whisky, closes his eyes. Her face is there, behind his eyelids. So young. Unmarked. Ready for a life that's been denied her. He can't, he *won't*, brush her aside.

Ruth. He must call her by her name. There's no room for doubt that's who she is. Not any girl, *this* girl, unique and singular. It makes him sad to think how lonely in death she is. It seems no one cares enough to miss her. Even her brother couldn't be bothered.

He can't understand why Jo was so keen to let Frank get away. He must have been able to tell them something more.

Such a pity.

And pity brings him full circle. To Ruth. Death of the young is a fact of war. He's been there, seen it. But this is different. Not war, a private killing. And it's his job to bring justice to the murdered. It's not about taking the easy way out. He won't look the other way.

It's personal, as if Death is laughing at him.

The bombs, falling minutes after he left.

The girl, practically dropped on his doorstep.

And the baby. He doesn't want to think about that, but he must. What Jo said opened his eyes to the possibility – the probability – that Ruth was the mother of the abandoned baby. They've never found anyone else they could link to him.

She couldn't have known what would happen. She's not the first unsupported girl to take the route of leaving her baby on a doorstep. She wouldn't have meant him to die. With that sign still identifying the redundant building as a hospital, she might have thought it was the best place, the safest. Believed he would be found, and cared for. Except . . . If she had been here since evacuation, she wasn't a stranger. Surely she would have known . . . He drifts. The room's warm and he's tired after his night in the office armchair, his long walk this morning.

He's asleep by the fire when his housekeeper knocks at the study door. The papers he's been trying to read have spilled onto the floor, and it takes him a moment to compose himself. Night looks in through the windows, and apart from the glimmer of the coals, it's dark in the room.

'Come in,' he calls.

Fan Stewart bustles in, tutting at the uncurtained windows. She moves to draw the blackouts, speaks to him over her shoulder.

'You can put that light on, now. It's all shut up tight.'

He turns on the lamp beside his chair.

'Thank you, Fan. What time is it?'

'Nine o'clock, sir. I was on my way upstairs.'

'Fine by me. I shan't want anything more.'

'No, sir, I didn't expect you would. But there's someone wanting to see you.' Her tone expresses deep disapproval.

'Really?' He can't think of anyone who might call at this time of night. 'Who is it?'

'Couple of nippers. That Alf Smith from over the nursery and a messenger boy from the post office. But it's Alf with the mouth and *gotta see him urgent* and *can't wait till morning.*'

'He didn't say—'

'He did not.' She sniffs. 'Says it's highly confidential. Would you credit it? The likes of him. Came to the front door, just like anyone.'

'Show them up, Fan.' He catches the look on her face. 'No, better still, I'll come down. I'll see them in the morning room, and you can get off to bed.'

'I don't mind if you want me to wait till they go.'

'No need.' He ushers her out of the room, shuts the door behind him. 'You get on, I'll lock up when they go.'

The boys are waiting in the hallway, obviously ill at ease. Alf's shamefaced but determined, while the other lad won't look up as Nash comes down, but stands scuffing his boot against the doormat.

'What can I do for you, lads?'

'There's something I've got to show you, sir,' Alf says. 'It's not very nice.' He eyes Fan as she crosses the hall to the kitchen door. 'Not for the ladies.'

Nash is amused at the boy's cloak-and-dagger manner. But he keeps a straight face as he opens the morning room door.

'Come in,' he says. 'Sit down. Make yourselves comfortable.'

They choose to sit at the far end of the table. Alf settles doggedly into his chair while the other boy perches precariously, looking as if he's ready to bolt.

Nash positions himself across from them, where he can see both their faces.

'So,' he says, 'what's it all about?'

'It's like this, sir,' Alf says. 'Pete got hold of something he shouldn't have. He says he didn't think anything about it except the obvious, and then when your Mrs Lester came round asking, he didn't like to say anything about it.'

He casts a bitter look at the other boy, who's worrying at the skin around his thumbnail, avoiding eye contact.

It's news to Nash that Mrs Lester has done anything of the sort, and he thinks, fleetingly, that it sounds as if it's her who should have been knocking at his door with things to say. He'll have to track her down first thing in the morning.

'I see,' he says. 'So what was this something?'

'He claims he got shy,' Alf says with disgust. He takes an oblong of card from his pocket, scoots it across the table to Nash. 'Bit late if you ask me, but there you go. It's a dirty picture, see. Horrible stuff.'

The scrap of pasteboard reaches him face down. Expecting something commonplace, Nash turns it over. He's about to say something, ask what it's got to do with his enquiries, when the picture registers. Steals the words from his mouth and turns his belly sour.

The picture is dog-eared, tatty with handling, and it has a sepia, last-century look. Even so, it's clear enough. It shows a girl on the cusp between child and adult. She lies on a padded couch with one raised end and twisty legs that finish in animal paws. The girl's semi-naked, barefoot and dressed in rags. Her flesh is streaked with dirt, like a child who's been living in the gutter. Her body, the budding breasts and half-developed genitalia are not hidden. With a wantonness that belies her childish looks, she seems to offer herself to the viewer, one knee raised and a hand parting the grubby rags to display her sex.

Nash shivers, but it's nothing to do with the chill of the morning room and its unlit fire.

'What's all this about?' he says harshly, addressing Pete directly for the first time. 'Where did you get this?'

He holds up a hand to stop Alf speaking. He doesn't need an interpreter, he wants the truth.

'It's like Alf says,' the boy whines. 'I found it. Didn't think it'd do any harm.' He gnaws at his thumbnail again. 'Well, I knew it was wrong, but I never thought . . . I never meant . . .'

'Don't bother with excuses,' Nash snaps. 'Tell me what you know. What's it got to do with me or Mrs Lester?'

'It's 'cos of the girl,' Pete says. 'I told the lady what I knew about her, voluntary like, but I couldn't say anything about that to her, now could I?'

'Voluntary,' Alf butts in, 'my eye. Took her money, didn't you? Now just stop mucking about and tell Mr Nash straight or you'll get another clip round the ear.'

Pete cringes. 'She was asking about a girl in the post office, but the boss, he wouldn't tell her nothing. So I followed her and told her about how she used to come an' pick up her post. Like a nun, I told her, 'cos she was. Butter wouldn't hardly melt. But she said she was the same as the tart up at the Cricketers' an' she gave me half a crown. I never asked,' he adds virtuously. 'She offered, said it was business.'

'All right.' Nash is still trying to work out which *she* is which from the muddle of Pete's story. 'So, you told Mrs Lester the girl who picked up the post was dressed like a nun, and Mrs Lester gave you half a crown?'

'That's right,' Pete says. 'An' a couple of ciggies, if you must know.'

'Never mind about that.' Nash glances at the photograph. He doesn't want to have to look at it again, but he must. There's nothing he can see that would definitely identify it or the girl. But he doesn't see how it can be Ruth. The picture's too old for that. He frowns. 'I still don't understand what you think this has got to do with the girl.'

'I was telling you, wasn't I?' Pete says indignantly. 'I told that Mrs Lester, I'd seen the girl up the Cut a few times. She'd kind of slink along like she was trying to hide an' I got to wondering what the big secret was. So I followed her, tracking, you know, like a Red Indian. See if I could find out where she was going. But I never thought, I swear it, I didn't know she was the same as the tart . . .'

He grinds to a halt, and Nash is aware that the heart of the story is close now, hovering behind the boy's reluctance to continue. It's got to be something discreditable, something Pete thinks will get him into even more trouble.

'Don't worry about that for the moment,' Nash says. 'Tell me what happened when you followed her.'

There's a silence. Alf shifts impatiently in his seat.

With an apprehensive glance at his friend, Pete says, 'I found her hidey-hole, didn't I? Went in one evening when she wasn't about. Stuff in there, girl's stuff, didn't take any notice of that. Didn't touch any of it, honest.'

He looks straight at Nash, and there is appeal in his glance.

'I see,' Nash says, and this time, he thinks he does. 'So what *did* you touch?'

'There was a ciggy tin,' Pete bursts out. 'One of the big ones, Gold Flake, fifty cigarettes. Thought maybe if there was a lot I could have one or two, no one would notice. It's not like stealing, everyone knows ciggies are fair game. So I opened the tin but it wasn't fags, it was pictures.' He goes red. 'There was a lot, but I only took the one. And it was ages ago, nothing to do with the air raid. Not 'cos she was dead 'cos I didn't know about that, did I? Not till the lady said.'

'You think they were her photographs?'

'Gotta be. It was her den for certain. I saw her going in and out.'

'And the tin?'

'I put it back where I found it.'

'In full view, was it?'

Pete squirms. 'Not exactly. It was in a sort of cupboard. It wasn't locked or anything.'

'A cupboard?' Nash is astonished. He's been imagining a hole in a hedge somewhere. 'What kind of place is this den?'

'It's a sort of hut. Full of junk an' falling down. Nothing in it but spiders mostly.'

'OK. So where is it?'

'You go up the Cut, nothing wrong in that, anyone can go up to the bridge. There's a path just there, goes into the woods.'

'On to Ramillies' estate?'

Pete looks sheepish. 'Suppose so.'

'There's an old summer house,' Alf breaks in. 'Just about lost in the brambles. It's not far from the big house but the woods haven't been cut back for donkey's years.'

'That's it,' Pete says. 'You been in there?'

Alf shrugs, nonchalant. 'Seen it. All in a night's work. But you gotta watch out for old Mingers.'

Pete shudders.

'Mingers?' Nash asks.

'A big bloke with a ginger beard,' Pete says. 'An' a gun.'

'That's the one,' Alf agrees. 'You don't want to go tangling with him.'

Pete draws a quivering breath, lets it out in a barely coherent flood of words.

'I've bin up there loads of times, never seen him before. But I thought, after what the lady said today, Mrs Lester, I thought I'd . . . Hadn't even gone in when this bloke shows up an' tells me to bugger off quick or he'd shoot me.'

Alf nods. 'That's Mingers. Outdoor man at Ramillies. Proper bastard, he is.'

'Ah.' Nash makes sense of Alf's version of the name Menzies. He's seen Ramillies' gamekeeper around town occasionally, though he's had nothing to do with the man personally. But he can imagine why Pete might have been scared. 'You say you've been to the place often, Pete? What were you doing?'

'Nothing,' Pete says sullenly. 'Just looking.'

'At the pictures?'

'Yeah. Gonna make something of it?'

Nash ignores the comment, picks his words carefully.

'So today, because what Mrs Lester told you meant the girl wouldn't be going back, you thought you'd go and see if the pictures were still there?'

'I thought I could have them. She don't want them any more.'

'Were they all like this, Pete? As . . . rude?'

The boy nods.

'The same girl? Old pictures, like this?'

'Dunno. Wasn't looking at the faces.' A pause, then he says, 'Wasn't many pictures that were brown, like that. Most of them were all right. New, sort of shiny. I took an old one 'cos I thought she wouldn't notice so much. Dunno what a girl wants with pictures like that anyhow.'

It's a question that's occurred to Nash. But it won't be solved by sitting here. He'll have to try and get hold of them himself. Part of him wants to set out now, find the place before anyone else does. But it would be foolish, at night, with the game-keeper prowling. There'd be no excuse if he were caught. The man Menzies would be justified in shooting anyone out on private land so late.

'All right, lads,' he says. 'I want you to promise me that you'll leave it with me.'

Pete nods. 'Sure thing, Mr Nash. I never meant nothing bad. You won't have to tell anyone, will you? My dad would skin me alive if he found out.'

'There's no need to tell your father. But I don't want you going back there again.'

'No fear. Can I go home now? It's getting late.'

Nash glances at the clock. It's almost ten. 'You'd better cut along. Your parents will be worried.'

Nash goes with them to the door. Pete's chatty now, relaxed.

'Not them. They'll be down the Wheatsheaf. Won't even know so long as I'm home by half past.'

He grins at Nash and dashes off into the dark. Alf hesitates at the top of the steps.

'Was there something else?' Nash asks.

'Not exactly.'

'I notice you didn't make any promises.'

'It's not that.' Alf takes a dog-end out of his pocket, lights it with a match swiped against the brickwork beside the door. 'I won't go butting in, I'm not that daft. And I hope you'll go careful yourself, sir. That Mingers is a nasty bit of work.'

'I appreciate your concern. But somehow I don't think that's what's on your mind.'

'Shook me up a bit, that picture. Made me think.'

'You do know something.' Nash makes it a statement, not a question.

The spark of the cigarette glows fiercely as Alf takes a drag on the dog-end.

'You know what it's like. It don't do to jump in.'

'We're talking about murder, Alf. If you think you know something, you must tell someone. If you won't talk to me, you should go to the police.'

The boy spits a fragment of tobacco into the dark. 'I'd tell you, sir, if I reckoned there was anything to tell. I made Pete come and see you, didn't I?'

Nash has to concede that much. He can't force the boy, but he remembers what Jo said about the Alsatian in the scrapyard.

'Look, I'm pretty certain there's somebody out there who's got a lot to lose if we can bring the girl's death home to them. If you go meddling and get too close, don't imagine they won't be prepared to hurt you too. There's no telling what they might do if they think you're a danger to them.'

'I get it, Mr Nash, sir. I do, really. But, well, careless talk, you know. It's not right to go tittle-tattling like a girl.'

'Alf . . .' Nash reaches out but the boy's gone, sliding away into the dark like the expert poacher he's reputed to be. 'Damn.'

18

20ᵗʰ *April*

S INCE THE CALL OF THE abbey bells has been silenced, Sunday mornings seem like any other. Though Nash is not a churchgoer, he misses them. In their absence, it's the quietness of the streets which marks the day as different from the rest of the working week.

It's early when he lets himself out of the side gate. Barely half past seven, but he's impatient to check the information Pete and Alf gave him last night. His first impulse is to go alone, to make a find of his own. Jo's had it all her own way with the ticket and the suitcase, even meeting Frank. But it would be at cost to the relationship between his assistant and himself, and their working partnership, the trust between them, is already stretched uncomfortably thin.

That reckless night in London's to blame. He should have known better. He discovered long ago there's no such thing as *no strings* in human relationships. There's always a bill to pay. If it's not cash for services rendered, then it's emotional entanglement. And he's chosen the road he'd rather travel. The trenches in France taught him all the lessons he ever needed to know about detachment, maimed more than his face. He can't subscribe to the belief that love will conquer all. The truth is, it makes you vulnerable so the ripples of destruction spread wider. For every son or husband or father killed, how many more deaths in the hearts of families who'd loved them? How much more pain? He won't risk that terrible responsibility for someone else's happiness.

Not that he flatters himself that Jo Lester harbours any tenderness for him because of one shared night. If she had, she'd never have turned up on his doorstep demanding a job. He knows he should have turned her down. A strand, insubstantial as cobweb, had tugged at his sense that he owed her something.

The feeling remains. Strand for strand, cobweb is stronger than steel.

He should find Jo. Tell her what Pete told him. Take her with him to investigate Ruth Taylor's reputed hideout. Weave another gossamer strand.

He should go alone.

Instead, he picks up a paper from the newsagent, drops in at the tea room for whatever they can offer by way of breakfast. He'll do the crossword if he can, make up his mind after that.

I'm in the kitchen, peeling potatoes, when there's a knock at the front door. Dot looks up from her task.

'D'you mind answering that?' she says.

She's plucking pigeons, and there are feathers light as thistledown all over the sack she's using as an apron. If she gets up, they'll fly everywhere.

'Of course.'

I wipe my hands, make my way into the hall. The caller must be a stranger. No one who knows Dot uses the front door. The door's bolted top and bottom, and the bolts are stiff.

I call out, 'Just coming, hang on,' but there's no response.

The bottom bolt yields suddenly, catches my thumb. Cursing, I drag the door open.

Bram Nash. I'm amazed. What's he doing here?

He tips his hat. I'm instantly hot with guilt, thinking about the irregularities of what I've done in his name in the last day or so. Then I notice how uncomfortable he looks. Perhaps he's not here to tell me off.

'Is it me you want?' I ask him. 'Or did you come to see Alf or Dot?'

'No, it's you. If it's not inconvenient.'

'Will you come in?'

He shakes his head. 'Can you come out? It's about Ruth. There's something I need to show you.'

I glance down at myself. I'm in my oldest clothes. My slacks and blouse have seen better days, and Romsey's not the sort of place which takes kindly to women in trousers, especially on a Sunday. With nothing on my feet and no make-up on my face, my hair tied up factory-style in a faded old scarf, I'm not fit to be seen.

'I'll have to get changed,' I say, though he can probably see that for himself. 'Will you come in and wait?'

'Show Mr Nash into the parlour!' Dot shouts, making it clear she's been listening.

'No need,' Nash says. 'You can come as you are. Where we're going, no one will see you.'

'I'll put on some shoes.'

Back in the kitchen, I apologise to Dot for leaving her in the lurch. I can't tell her where I'm going or how long I'll be, because I don't know.

She waves me away. 'Just as long as you don't let him inside this kitchen.'

Shoes on, gas mask case over my shoulder, I let myself out of the front door where Nash is waiting. He holds the gate open for me, but as soon as we're in the street, he strides off without a word. He's going so fast I'm soon trailing behind, torn between feeling ridiculous and affronted.

'Wait for me!'

'Got to keep up, Josy!' Mike calls back, the only one with any sense of responsibility towards me, and that only because we're family.

The boys are in front, tearing along the towpath Indian file. The way's overgrown, and as they rush through, the brambles whip back to catch me on the rebound, slashing at my arms and face. Before long we're in the woods, and though I can hear the boys crashing through the trees, I can't see them any more. Soon, I can't hear them either.

I don't like it. I have nightmares about being lost in these woods. Parts of it are all right, where the little trees let in the light and bluebells grow and bees buzz and butterflies bask in the sunlight. But I don't like it where the trees grow tangled together, dark twisty paths threading between them. There are roots that seem to heave up deliberately to trip you, and the gnarly old branches reach down to scrabble and tap.

My aunts Lizzie and Mags tell stories about the goblins who live in here, how they go hunting to catch little girls so they can fatten them up to eat for tea. Once, they showed me the leftover bones. I don't really believe in goblins any more. Not now I'm eight. But I'm still scared. The birds don't sing in this part of the wood, and now the boys have disappeared it's so quiet all I can hear is my own jerky breathing.

I stand still, not sure which way to go. I can't remember how to get home. If they've left me here, I'm lost. But I know I mustn't panic. It's my first time out with the gang, and they won't let me stay if I'm a cry baby.

A voice calls from somewhere up ahead. It's Jem, I think, or it might be Billy.

'Finders, seekers! You first, Josy. You're It.'

'Don't want to be It.'

'Hard cheese, it's the rules. Hide your eyes. Count to a hundred, no cheating.'

I start the count, gabbling through the numbers as fast as I can. I'm grown up enough to play with the boys, I am*, but all I can think about is goblins in their pine cone hats and spiky shoes, with their strong twiggy fingers and sharp pointed teeth.*

By the time I've counted to thirty, I'm shaking. There's a rustle in the leaves, the crack of a stick. I freeze, lose count. I know brittle fingers are reaching for me. A long moment passes. I dare to take a peep through screwed-up eyelids, but there's nothing.

'Can't hear you counting, Josy.' A faraway voice. I think it's Mike this time, and I feel a bit braver. I don't shut my eyes, but I start counting again, this time in chunks. Fifty-one, fifty-two, fifty-six, sixty. Gulping the numbers out, calling them into a silence that isn't quite silence. There are noises all around me now, spiky little footsteps. By the time I get to ninety-nine, a hundred, I can almost feel the teeth.

A crash of sound as I call the last number. Hoots and howls. I turn and turn, this way and that. Blundering like a bug in a jam jar, helpless. No escape from the sting of teasing.

A giggle, running feet. 'Can't catch us.'

A flash of red behind me.

'Bert?'

'Scaredy cat.'

'Jem?'

I fall, graze my knees. There's tree sap sticky on my hands, and mud on the hem of my dress.

'This way.' Cap'n Abe.

'Over here.' Mike again.

'Follow me.'

The voices fade as they run, the sound of their feet deadened by the thick litter of brash beneath the trees.

'Where are we going?' I try not to sound peevish, but I've trailed along behind him all the way to the Cut, and I'm still none the wiser. The towpath's deserted, there's no one about. There's no reason for him not to tell me what's going on. 'Can't you slow down a bit?'

'Sorry.'

He lets me catch up, but he doesn't answer my question.

'What's this all about?'

'Hang on a minute and I'll tell you.'

I bite back an ill-tempered response. While I was curious and a bit irritated before, now I'm really fed up. A minute, I think. That's all I'll give him.

We reach the humpbacked bridge where the towpath crosses, and he stops. I recognise the place. I hadn't thought about it since we were kids. It was one of our regular places for a pow-wow, out of the way of adults and eavesdroppers. Mischief was safely hatched here, exploits were planned and boasted about and spoils shared. Nash hoists himself up on the parapet, the way he always used to, sits with his back to the water. I, a scaredy cat even then about heights, prefer to lean against the rough stone, watch the sluggish flow of the canal beneath in safety.

He seems more at ease in this secluded spot than I've seen him since I came back to Romsey, and I let myself relax too. Not a good move.

'I had a visit from Alf Smith last night,' he says. 'He came with a friend of yours. Pete, he said his name was.'

'I was going to tell you about that on Monday.'

He raises his eyebrow. 'You show me yours . . .' he starts to say.

I stare at him, incredulous.

'Sorry, not a good idea.'

You show me yours and I'll show you mine was playground barter back in the day. Jem was the worst, always pestering me to let him see what a girl was made of. I never would, not because of any particular virtue on my part, but because he was a sneak who'd just as likely peek and tell as keep his bargain. In any case, I knew pretty much all there was to know about the difference between the sexes from living in a two-bedroom cottage with four teenage uncles and two young aunts. My breath takes a hitch. I'm closer to Nash than I've been at any time since that night in the Blitz and the unintended image that his words conjure up unsettles me. What *is* it he wants?

'What's this about?'

'Pete gave you some information about the girl.'

'Yes.'

I sketch out what Pete said, how I went to visit Sister Gervase and what she told me. How she'd identified the body. I can tell he's shocked, though whether it's by the sheer volume of what I've learned, or the fact I didn't come to tell him about it at once, I don't know.

I finish by saying, 'So what did Pete tell you? I thought he was hiding something from me.'

'Yes.' Nash reaches into his inside jacket pocket, takes out a piece of card. He hands it to me. 'It was this. He said he didn't want to shock you.'

What I feel when I see what he's given me goes beyond shock. It's like a blow to the solar plexus, and I barely have time to turn away before I'm vomiting. All I can do is thrust the picture back at Nash and wait for the spasm to pass.

'God, Jo, I'm sorry. I should have warned you.'

Warned me about what? I think. Because I'm pretty sure he can't know the picture's real significance for me.

But the minute I saw it, I knew.

It's my mother.

It wasn't her face I recognised, how could it be? No one's ever shown me a photograph of her as a girl. But when she was ill, I often helped her wash. And the patch on the girl's inner thigh that might almost be dirt, a shape like a dog's head, is unmistakably the same as the birthmark on my mother's leg.

My thoughts go round and round. Dot's voice saying *she had a bit of a reputation . . . flirting . . . having it off with all sorts.*

What am I going to do?

I can't tell Nash.

I'm shaking as I wipe my mouth with the back of my hand.

'Here.' He hands me that gentleman's standby, a clean white handkerchief.

'Thanks.' Though I feel better when I've mopped up, the vile taste in my mouth remains. 'Sorry to make a fool of myself.'

'Not at all.'

199

I look at his handkerchief, cringe inwardly.

'I'll wash it before I give it back,' I say, folding the soiled part over before stuffing into my pocket.

'Just as you like.'

'Did you drag me all the way out here just to show me this?' I say, and I can hear the accusation in my tone. It's not his fault, but somebody's got to take the flak.

'Of course not. I brought you here because of where Pete got the picture. He didn't like to tell you yesterday, but he knew where Ruth was going when she came up here. He tracked her to her hideout one day. He found this there. He told me there was a tin full of them. I thought we'd better take a look.'

'More like this?' I'm horrified.

'He said they were similar.'

What would Ruth be doing with pictures like this? And how could she have come by this humiliating image of my mother? I think about the photographs we found in her case. Frank talking about their sort of uncle, 'Snappy' Legge. Was he the one who'd taken them?

'Can I see it again?' I say.

He hands it over. It's not a standard size, and there's no marking on the back to suggest that it's been produced commercially. No photographer's stamp, nothing so obvious or helpful. I force myself to look closely at the picture. Even with her face averted, I can see what Dot meant. Nell had been a lovely-looking girl.

Had she exploited it? Revelled in the wanton posing? Another thought hits me. Whoever took this picture might be my father, but I can't see any kind of flirtation in her pose. Perhaps I'm fooling myself, but it looks more like resignation.

I don't want to see any more like this, but I have to know. If there are more, I have to know the worst. Bile rises in my throat and I spit to one side. I slide the photograph into my pocket, hope Nash won't think to ask for it back.

'We'd better get on.' My voice is hoarse with vomiting and tears I won't shed. That I can't, not in front of him.

19

The same day, Ramillies estate, Romsey

I T'S MANY YEARS SINCE THERE were ladies at Ramillies who might take a fancy to visit the once-elegant summer house in its artful woodland setting. The days of sketchbooks and chatter, of lapdogs and tiny cakes and silver tea services died with the old Queen. After them, only the young men came with their shotguns and hip flasks, stopping by on cold October mornings, taking a break between drives to count their epic bags of game. Then they too were gone, vanishing into the mud of Flanders.

These days, the old summer house is half lost in brambles. The raised dais it rests on, that once concealed the mechanism which let it turn to follow the sun, has collapsed, and the only movement the place sees now is as it crumbles and falls, piece by piece, into the ground. In its heyday it was painted pale green, with fancy white gingerbread mouldings. These days it blends with the woods that surround it, the mouldings grey with mildew, the walls invaded by lichen and fungi. Almost all the windows have lost their glass, replaced by generations of spiders' webs which veil the openings.

For so many years no one came. A wanderer might pass by now and then: a badger, looking for hedgehogs. A hedgehog, looking for slugs, somewhere safe to hibernate. And there were owls by night, a persistent blackbird by day.

Dr Waverley's come to pay his Sunday morning visit to his uncle. It's a duty call, though anything that brings him to Ramillies is shot through with pleasure, a feeling of home-coming. He and Edith were brought up here, and one day, not too far distant, he hopes he'll live here again.

As he gets out of his car, he sees the gamekeeper approach-ing. Menzies seems uneasy.

'Good morning, sir. Hope you don't mind but there's something I mebbe should report. But I didn't like to worry the master with it, not when he's so poorly.'

'Quite right. My uncle's not to be troubled. What's the problem? Poachers?'

'I don't think so. Wasn't the right time of day for that. But there was this young lad in the woods yesterday. No snares or anything of that on him, but he wasn't just lost like he said. I wouldn't trouble you with it in the general run of things, but the little devil was up to something.'

'And you've no idea what?'

'Well, sir, he was near the old summer house. I had a peep inside after he'd run off. By the look of it, someone's been using it regular like.'

'Using it? Not bloody gyppos, I hope? We can do without their sort.'

'It's not gypsies, sir, I'll take my oath on that. Looked like it was kids, mebbe just the lad. I gave him a good fright, I don't think he'll be coming back.'

'I should hope not. Perhaps I'd better see for myself.'

'The quickest way is across the park, but the grass is awful long. Spoil the polish on those shoes, sir.'

'Never mind about that. Just get on with it, man. I haven't got all day.'

Despite the warning, it's rougher going than Waverley expected. The polish has gone from his shoes, and his trouser legs are damp by the time they arrive.

'This? What would anyone want with a wreck of a place like this?' he says irritably. 'Should have been torn down years ago.'

'I agree with you, sir, it's a danger to life and limb, but the master won't hear of it. Go careful, now, that floor's rotten. It might give way any minute.'

'Nonsense.' But the boards groan ominously beneath his feet. 'You'd better stay outside. It might not take your weight. Now, let's see. What's been going on here? You're right. It must be kids, it's not mucky enough for gyppos.' He kicks some stuff on the floor, connects with something solid. 'What's this? Can't see in here. Have to come out.'

'Looks like an old tin of cigarettes, sir.'

'I can see that.' He pulls off the lid. Shock ripples through him. 'Good God!'

'What is it, sir? Oh – dirty pictures. That's lads for you.'

'Get out of the way, man. Didn't ask you to poke your nose in. Have you got a match?'

'Yes, sir. You don't think we should—?'

'Destroy them, it's the only course. If this should come to my uncle's ears—'

'He wouldn't like it, sir.'

'Good God, man, it would kill him. There. That's got . . . Ow, damn, that's my fingers. Stamp it out now, make sure there's nothing left.'

Every unlawful entry onto another's property is trespass, even if no harm is done to the property. (English Tort Law)

Nash and I skirt the darker parts of the wood, and I'm glad. I don't know where the boundaries of Ramillies land run, but it's obvious that it's a very long time since anyone's done anything to maintain the woodland here. There are fallen branches underfoot and scrubby undergrowth everywhere, all hazards to quiet progress.

'Do you think there'll be anything to find?' I keep my voice low, though there's no sign of anyone about.

'I suppose there should be, if Pete's telling the truth. He said he'd been back to look at the other pictures, but he only took one. And then yesterday, after you'd spoken to him and he knew the girl wouldn't be coming back, he thought he'd take a chance to get hold of the rest. He didn't make it, because he was spotted going through the woods. A man called Menzies, the gamekeeper, chased him off. Threatened him with a gun.'

'That's a bit heavy-handed, surely?'

'Not if he thought he was poaching. But Alf said he was a nasty type.'

'I expect Alf would know.'

'There have been rumours to that effect.' It sounds as if he's smiling.

'He calls it foraging. For personal use only, Dot won't stand for black market. But it's why she didn't want you to see inside the kitchen. It was only pigeons, today, but it could easily have been pheasants or a trout. I haven't eaten so well since the beginning of the war.'

'I'll have to make an excuse to come round at supper time. Fan's an excellent housekeeper, but her cooking's awful. Even without the excuse of rationing. Now—' He stops short, waits till I come level with him. 'We need to go quiet from here on. Just in case Mr Menzies is out with his gun this bright Sunday morning. Follow me, and try and remember what I taught you.'

'What—?'

But he's away, a middle-aged man in an overcoat and hat who ought to be out of place in the wild wood. Yet somehow, the ease of his silent progress through the trees reminds me irresistibly of the boy who was leader of the gang. Time was, he'd have made a good poacher himself.

We arrive at the edge of the wood, where glimpses of parkland show to the left. It's harder to stay under cover now, but if

Pete hasn't sent us on a wild goose chase, we should be getting close. A few paces ahead of me, Nash suddenly gestures *stop*, ducks behind the trunk of an ancient oak. I catch a glimpse of movement through the trees. There are voices ahead, and the faint whiff of smoke carries on the breeze towards us. Mindful of the gamekeeper's gun, I crouch into a tall clump of nettles, wishing I'd chosen a better hiding place. My heart is beating so loud, I'm afraid someone will hear it.

'Not a word to my uncle, now.' A posh, public school voice.

'Sir.'

They must be moving away, because I only catch part of the next sentence.

'. . . rely on you. Keep a good eye . . .'

The men make quite a lot of noise as they move off. Even after the sound of their passage has died away, neither Nash nor I move. At last, I raise myself from my cramped position and sidle towards Nash.

'Who were they?' I whisper.

'Gamekeeper and Waverley.'

'Dr Waverley? What's he doing here?'

'Tell you later.'

'Do you think they'd been in the summer house?'

'Where else?' He points. 'It's just there.'

Then I see that a dense tangle of brambles barely ten yards ahead has a wooden structure at its heart. We've had a closer encounter than I realised.

'Catching Pete yesterday must have alerted Menzies,' Nash says. 'Wait here.'

He moves cautiously out of cover. I lose sight of him as he circles behind the structure. After a moment I hear him call. A low voice, but not a whisper.

'Jo.'

In front of the summer house, the grass is lank, trampled. Nash is stooping over something. He pushes at it with a cautious finger, turns it over so I can see the bright yellow labelling of a Gold Flake cigarette tin.

'Too late,' he says.

Next to the tin there's a black greasy mark where someone has ground his foot into the grass, stamped out the ashes of something made of paper. One tiny unburned scrap confirms it.

'The photographs.'

'Afraid so,' Nash says, getting to his feet. 'Now we'll never know.'

I don't have anything to say to that. Part of me – not the part that is supposed to be solving this mystery about Ruth – is glad.

I step into the summer house. The floorboards creak, and in places they've collapsed completely. Inside, the light is blocked by the overgrowth of brambles and filth, and I have to feel my way with care. As my eyes accustom, I can see the place has been used recently, despite its condition. There's an empty ginger beer bottle in the corner, where a scuffed heap of dry bracken suggests someone might have made a bed. An old fish paste jar holds a few stems of dried-out wild flowers on the windowsill, and a standing metal cupboard which might once have held shotguns leans drunkenly against one wall. I open it, and the faint smell of Soir de Paris wafts out at me. An empty coat hanger's hitched on a hook behind the door, but there's nothing else inside. I crouch down, examine the cupboard floor. I make out some shapes in the dust. A pair of small ovals, side by side, and a larger, scuffed oblong. I stand up.

'She was here,' I say. 'Ruth. The scent . . . This is where she must have kept her clothes, her case.'

'It fits with what Pete said,' Nash agrees.

I push the door to, turn away. The girl feels so close, as if I could reach out and touch her, save her, but it's too late. I sweep away a festoon of cobwebs from the one window that still has glass, peer out through the opening. The first shock is how close across the parkland Ramillies Hall is. The second, that I'm in view of two men standing by the portico. I freeze.

'What is it?' Nash says, close to my ear.

'Over there. Surely they must have seen us.'

'No,' he murmurs. 'We're in the shadows here. Should be all right if we keep still.'

It's like watching a spider in the corner of a room. Much as I might want to, I can't tear my eyes away. I recognise Waverley in his dark suit. The other is taller and bulkier, a big man carrying a shotgun broken over his arm. Even at this distance, he stands out, one of a kind. No hiding away for him. The russet coloured jacket he's wearing is a match for his wild red hair and beard.

Waverley takes something from an inside pocket. Hands it to the big man, who tugs his forelock in respect, a gesture I haven't seen anyone perform since I was a child. Waverley must have given him a stupendous tip.

The doctor disappears into the Hall, but the red man stands staring across the park for a long moment, apparently looking straight at the summer house. It's all I can do not to bolt, convinced he can see me whatever Nash might think. But I hold my nerve until he, too, moves away.

'We'd better get on,' Nash says. 'Before he decides to take a closer look.'

I don't think either of us is soundless, going back through the woods, but no one follows. Even so, I'm relieved when we reach the bridge safely.

'Now what?' I ask, as we pause to catch our breath.

'Back to square one, I suppose. Though perhaps it's not as bad as that. Unpleasant as they might have been, I'm not sure what the pictures could have told us.'

I would have discovered how many more there might have been of my mother, I think. But it's not something I'm going to share with him.

'I don't understand why Ruth would have had something like that in her possession. What was she doing with them, Bram?'

He blinks, and I wonder if I've surprised him by using his name. But he's already called me Jo, and I'm not going to say *Mr Nash* out here.

'I don't know. It wants thinking about.'

'And Waverley? You said you'd tell me what he's doing here.'

'You'll remember Ramillies belongs to the Oxleys? The current owner, Mr Paul Oxley, is Waverley's uncle. He's rumoured to be very ill, so I suppose it's only natural that Waverley should be visiting him.' Nash pauses, as if he's wondering how much more he should say. 'And if gossip's anything to go by, the doctor and his sister are angling to inherit after the old man dies.'

20

The same day

WHEN I GET BACK TO Dot's, there are still the potatoes to peel, and after them, carrots, a whole heap of them. And last, one prized – if rather wizened – parsnip out of the sand clamp in the back-yard to add sweetness to the pie. The clan who eat at Dot's take a lot of feeding.

It's been a relief to get back to domesticity after the morning's tensions. But my brain's as busy as my hands. I can't forget what I've seen. There's one question above all that I need an answer for. And I think Dot can provide it, if she will.

'One thing you didn't tell me last night,' I say, 'is where you and Nell worked.'

'Didn't I?'

'No. So where was it?'

'Does it matter, deary?'

'The more you avoid telling me, the more I think it does.'

'Oh, well, if you're going to be like that. It was Ramillies Hall. Had a big staff in those days, everything beautifully kept. Sad to see it like it is now, everything going to rack and ruin. Old Mr Oxley rattles around in that great place, with only a manservant indoors and that chap Menzies to take care of the estate.'

That chap Menzies. There's the rub. With a name like that, perhaps it's no surprise he has the red hair of the Celts. His is not a polite, almost-subdued auburn, but flaming red, unmissably vulgar. Just like mine.

The question is, did I get it from him? He wasn't on my list of possibles from the paper, though old Mr Oxley was. *As usual, our generous benefactor, Mr Paul Oxley, kindly donated the prizes for the Candlemas Fatstock market.*

'I don't remember a Menzies,' I say. 'Has he been at Ramillies Hall a long time?'

'Oh, donkey's years,' Dot says. 'If I remember rightly, he came just after the war. I think they said he'd known the master somewhere abroad. Mind, he doesn't have a lot to do with the town. Keeps himself to himself, as the saying goes.'

Not my father then, if she *does* remember rightly. But I have to be sure.

After lunch, I return to Ramillies. I've changed into my tidy clothes, put up my hair. Put on lipstick, a hat. Smartened myself up enough for Sunday visiting. No sneaking through the woods this time, but straight up to the main gates. Except when I get there, I discover there aren't any gates any more. The entrance stands gaping wide, unguarded. I suppose the ornate ironwork has been sacrificed for the war effort. The gatehouse is boarded up, and by the look of it, for much longer than current hostilities would account for. I prop the bicycle I borrowed from Dot against the wall, set off up the driveway. There are more changes here. The poplars are gone and now I see it clearly, the park, only glimpsed this morning, shows its true state – no longer a vista of beautifully manicured lawns, but pastureland, rough grazing for cattle and sheep.

Ramillies Hall is a grand Georgian mansion, built of fine red brick, with a Portland stone portico at the front entrance. The same pale stone frames the windows: three on either side of the entrance, seven on the first floor, while above, in the grey slate roof, three dormers peer out. I remember it as a fine, glittering palace when I was a child, but today, it seems almost abandoned: the windows blank, blinds pulled down; the white stone dulled; the grey slates mossy. It's surprising it hasn't been requisitioned for the war. Someone's pulled some strings, saved it from War Office bureaucracy. Dr Waverley, perhaps, with an eye to his inheritance.

In the old days, I'd have gone round the back to the servants' entrance. But despite my nerves, this afternoon I march up to the front door. It starts to rain as I ring the bell, but the grand portico with its Greek pillars keeps me dry while I wait. I stare across the park. The woods' eaves are clumped with brambles, yet I can identify the place where the summer house stands from here. I'm shaken to discover how easy it would have been for Menzies to have seen us this morning.

But perhaps we were lucky. He didn't follow us, or try to intercept us. I'm trying to puzzle it out when the door opens.

I assume it's Oxley's manservant, but I'm surprised how decrepit he seems. Though he's pin neat in a black suit, he's old, gaunt of features. A few sparse strands of sandy hair are brushed across his forehead, and he's breathing hard, as if he's had to come a long way.

'I've come to see Mr Oxley.'

I'm expecting him to fob me off, tell me the master isn't available, but he pulls the door wider, moves to one side.

'Better . . . come in.'

I step inside, follow as he shuffles through the hallway and to a room at the back of the house. The blinds are shut here too, and a table lamp illuminates a patch of floor where there's a wing chair, and a side table piled with books. He lowers himself into the chair. He's not a servant then. This must be the master himself. He looks at me, head cocked, fingers steepled precisely together. He doesn't invite me to sit down.

'I'm . . . Oxley,' he says. His breathing's bad and his words emerge in little jabs. 'What . . . can I do . . . for you?'

'My name's Josephine Lester.' I could beat around the bush, but I don't. 'Born Fox, here in Romsey. My mother wasn't married, so I'm a bastard. I've come looking for my father. He's one too, but a different kind.'

'And . . . this concerns me . . . how?'

My attempt to shock him doesn't seem to have worked.

'I came to ask if it was you.'

'What?' he croaks. It's not clear whether it's his breath or his manners which have failed him.

'She was working here, in this house, when she got pregnant.'

A frown as he looks me up and down. 'Her name?'

'My mother was Ellen. Nell. Nell Fox.'

'Doesn't . . . ring a bell.'

'She was a scullery maid.'

He makes a face. Fastidious disapproval.

'Never . . . had anything . . . to do with . . . scullery maids.'

The reply is everything I hate most about Romsey. Never mind he's half dead, he's still snooty enough to look down his nose at Nell.

'Oh, pardon me. I didn't realise that *droit de seigneur* didn't extend to the lower orders. I suppose even the pretty ones are just too lowly to fuck.'

He blinks. This time, I have shaken his condescending calm.

'Out . . . *rageous*.' He struggles a moment. 'I insist . . . you leave.'

Instead, I go closer. Lean in.

'Insist all you like. I'm not leaving till I know the truth.'

He shrinks into his chair, panting, putting what distance he can between us. Even so, I don't think he's afraid of me. It's more as if he can't bear my common flesh to be so close.

'Godsake . . . sit down. Talk . . . this through.'

He looks so helpless, that despite everything, I feel sorry for him. I step back, my hands shaking. I push them into my pockets, feel the slip of cardboard. The photograph. The thought of it stiffens my spine, nips compassion in the bud.

'I'd just as soon stand, thank you.'

With the distance I've put between us, he relaxes a little in his chair. Not too much, I think. I'm not finished yet.

After a pause, he says, 'Forgive me but . . . when . . . were you born? Some . . . time ago?'

I laugh, I can't help it. With all that's been said, he's too delicate to ask my age?

'I was born in July 1901. My mother was barely fifteen. She'd been working here for a year when she got pregnant.'

'Ah.' He looks strangely relieved. 'In that case . . . if she told you . . . I . . . might be your father . . . she, ah . . . she was . . . spinning . . . a yarn.'

I'm not letting him off the hook as easily as that. He doesn't need to know Nell never told me anything at all about my father.

'Are you calling her a liar?'

'No, but . . . impossible, you see. I was . . . away. Three years . . . Switzerland. TB, '99 to '02.'

Speechless, I stare at him.

'Have you . . . considered . . . the other . . . servants? There were . . . quite a number . . . in those days. Young . . . men, you know.'

'Menzies?'

I pull off my hat so he can see the colour of my hair.

He seems to shrink even more than when I was looming over him. I know red hair is not to everyone's taste, but it seems like an overreaction. His voice, when it comes, is full of regret, though I've no idea why.

'No. Not him . . . He . . . didn't come here . . . till after the war. 1920.'

'If it wasn't him, and it wasn't you, it was someone here or hereabouts. Someone who frightened my mother so she didn't dare to come back to Romsey however much she might have wanted to. It was someone who took disgusting photographs of her.'

I don't know if that's the truth, of course. But it's the only card I have left to play.

I pull the photograph out of my pocket, hold it in front of him. He reaches out a trembling hand, but I draw it back so he can't take it away from me. After one long look he slumps, grey in the face, exhausted. The shock on his face is plain. I slide the picture away, out of sight, safe in my pocket.

'God,' he mutters. 'God . . . God . . .'

Matters of flesh and blood seem more than he can bear to think about.

'I don't know if you've come across my grandfather, but he's a hard man. Yet it isn't my father he blames for my birth. And he knows who it was, he as good as told me so himself. I don't believe it was a servant. Grandfather would have thrashed someone of our class within an inch of his life, made him marry my mother afterwards. It had to be someone Grandfather respected. That's why I thought of you.'

I've been over and over it in my mind, and I'm sure my logic holds. Though now I'm here, confronting the fabled Oxley of Ramillies Hall, I can't believe my grandfather would have felt respect for this timid little man, despite his family name.

'I understand. But I . . . can't help you.' He clears his throat. 'Please, sit down.'

I perch on the edge of the chair opposite, half in gloom. But if I lean forward I can stay within the circle of lamplight. I don't feel angry with him any more. He's too old, too tired, too sick. He possesses the arrogance of his caste, but even if I didn't believe what he says about being away, I can't imagine him seducing anyone. I can't imagine him having enough red blood in him for that, or for frightening Nell enough to keep her in exile for life.

But here I am, so there has to have been someone.

'A minute,' he gasps.

I wait. There's a long pause. He sits with his eyes shut. His breathing is noisy, so I know he's still alive, but so erratic I begin to wonder if something awful has happened to him. I'm trying to decide what to do, wondering if he's slipped into unconsciousness or simply fallen asleep, when he speaks again.

'Ah?'

'What is it?'

'If you would . . . be so kind? Fetch me . . . a little brandy. On the . . . sideboard.'

I make my way through the shadows to where a vast piece of furniture stands, find a half empty decanter and a sticky glass. It should be washed, but I don't like to waste time and he's not in any state to notice. That grey look has got worse. I pour a good three fingers of spirit into the glass, carry it over.

'Here you are.'

He takes the glass in both hands, brings the drink shakily to his mouth.

'Are you alone here?' I ask. 'Surely you need somebody with you?'

'Baxter's . . . half day . . . Since the girl left . . . someone . . . looks in.'

He hands me the glass, goes very still.

'Are you all right?'

I can't help feeling guilty about the way I've tackled him.

'Go . . . please. Find your own . . . way out. Get in touch . . . a day or two. Might have . . . something to tell you.'

I stand for a minute, irresolute. If he's thought of something, of someone, I want him to tell me. But I've gone too far down the road of pity to force him. A little snore of breath, and I see he's asleep. I turn, make for the door. There's no choice but to do what he says, come back another day.

It's a question of timing. The margin between success and failure hangs on a hair: arriving a moment before the train leaves, or being a second too late and watching it pull out of the station. But for Mr Oxley's third visitor of the day, everything falls just right.

In time to see Josephine Fox leave.

Not so early as to be seen themself.

Inside, the visitor finds the old man asleep in his chair, a brandy glass at his elbow. He takes the stuff like medicine, any time he's in pain or upset.

A thought stirs.

The visitor watches the old man sleep. His breathing's bad, irregular. In, a little gasp, so shallow. Out, a sigh, a wheeze, a rattle. A moment of pause. Too long? Not this time. A catch, and the old man's chest rises, he breathes again. Clings to the thread of life.

The visitor sighs. Such a miserable existence. It would be a mercy if he never woke up.

The idea stirs again. It's nothing new. It's been waiting a long time for opportunity and circumstance to come together.

The visitor smiles. For them, it has.

An unexpected visit from Josephine Fox.

Then, a death.

What could be better? A scapegoat, if anyone suspects.

Hateful as it may be to touch the elderly flesh, all it needs is a hand. Palm across dry lips, occluding. Thumb pinching the bony nose closed. Sealing off the little thread.

A moment's struggle, nothing more. No real fight for life. It's a kindness, he'll be glad to give up.

Be patient. Make sure. Hold on long enough. Then—

—release. Step away.

The visitor stands, looks down at the huddled figure in the chair. The rush of power is extraordinary.

All in the timing. Oh, yes, it's all in the timing.

Bram Nash is not happy. It hasn't been a good day. In fact, on the whole, it's been a lousy day. His own fault. He's messed up all along the line. If he hadn't held off from exploring the old summer house, if he'd gone without delay, he might know a lot more now than he does.

He'll have to do the best he can with what he has. The photograph. Sickening as it is, he needs to study it, get what information he can from it. He searches his pockets, comes up empty. What's he done with it? Then he remembers. Jo asked to look at it again, never gave it back.

He curses.

Jo's reaction was so extreme. The picture is vile, it's true, but she's not exactly an innocent abroad. He'd never have guessed it would shock her so much.

He thinks about it. The sepia tint suggests it must be old. Turn of the century, perhaps. It can't be Ruth.

But why else would the girl have had it?

Perhaps he's missing the obvious. Perhaps it's not old, has just been printed like that to meet some warped artistic notion.

Deep in his thoughts, there's a worm of disquiet. Reluctant, he brings it out into the light.

It can't be Jo, can it? He would have recognised her. But he needs to look at the photograph again to be sure.

He never wants to see it again, but he'll have to.

21

21ˢᵗ April

EARLY ON MONDAY MORNING, I know what I must do. I've tried the ugly sisters, now it's time for a macabre Cinderella. It has to be early, before I go into the office and see Nash. If I ask him, he won't let me. But I have to know. Unorthodox as it may be, I'm determined to establish the chain of evidence.

The rhythm of my life has become a thing of shadows. I'm living like a thief or a spy, creeping around in the half-light, never quite legitimate. As I'm circling the hospital, looking for a way in that won't take me past the porters' lodge, the thought makes me grin. Nothing, really, has ever been legitimate about me. I've always been put – or put myself – on the fringes. A bastard. The only girl in Abe's gang. Outcast from my home town, against my will in the first place and then by choice. My affair with Richard. I was so much more successful as his mistress than I ever was as his wife. Long before he set sail for Dunkirk it was over, and we both knew it. I should have expected that what he'd done *with* me to his first wife, he'd soon do *to* me, with someone else. A lot of some-ones, as it turned out. And while he seemed happy to take his distractions in drinking and girls, I could only withdraw, reject everything we'd ever shared. And whether he's dead – though I don't hate him enough to want that – or alive, and a prisoner somewhere, my mind's made up. Even if he comes home, we'll never be a couple again.

Enough. Concentrate.

I come to a place where a snicket of path leads to the rear of the wards. A nurse scurries out of a door, wrestling with a large bag of what looks like laundry. She disappears round a corner, and I follow. It's the right direction for the mortuary. As I turn the corner, I can see an open-sided store where a heap of linen bags is stacked. The nurse heaves the one she's carrying on top of the others. If she comes back this way, she'll see me. I'm trying to think of an excuse for being there when a bell rings somewhere in the front part of the hospital and she hurries towards the sound without looking back.

Beyond the linen store I can see the jut of the mortuary porch. When Grandfather sent me to meet Nash, the door was unlocked, and Billy Stewart was already on duty, but I've no idea what time he comes to work.

I can't afford to hang around. I cross to the black door. Lift the latch. The door's hard to open, but it isn't secured. It yields, and a gust of air rushes to meet me. It's dim inside, the only illumination filtering through a high window in the far wall, but I can't risk switching on the light. I stand still, listening, but there's nothing to suggest there's any presence here but my own.

The insidious smell I noticed before makes me feel queasy. Everywhere's gleaming clean, but there's a disquieting element that won't be denied, a kind of chemical bleed-through that's worse than outright decay.

I know where to find the room where the bodies are stored, which compartment Billy Stewart rolled Ruth's body into the last time I was here. It'll be all right so long as they haven't moved her.

I open the drawer, pull out the stretcher. Turn back the cover. It is Ruth, there's the tag on her toe. I don't have to see her face, I don't have to do anything except try the shoe.

I fumble it out of my bag.

I don't want to do this. But I can't turn back now.

Her feet are icy. I don't think I've felt anything so cold in my life. The corpses I've been acquainted with till now have been soft, still warm, recognisably made of the same flesh as my own. Even meat from the butcher doesn't have this icy chill, this absolute deadness.

The first glancing contact makes me want to draw back, run away. But I won't. I'll play the grim fairy tale through to the end.

This isn't about identity. The shoes, if they are hers, are proof of where she was. Whoever gave them to the jumble sale is linked to her death.

And before I try and track them down, I have to be sure.

I grasp the stony flesh. Her foot is inflexible, the shoe stiff and intractable. At first it seems impossible. And to force her foot would be more wrong than I want to think about. A sacrilege against the dignity of the dead.

One last try, and the shoe slides on. A fit.

I slip it off again. Her foot is so small, so forlorn. It feels like abandonment to cover it over again without trying to chafe it warm, the way Granny used to do for me when I was little. But it's ridiculous to feel like that. The only thing I can do for this girl is find her killer, bring them to justice.

I straighten the sheet. Push the stretcher back.

Outside, relieved to be free and clear in the air again, I turn to shut the door behind me. But my luck's run out. There's someone approaching. Billy.

'Hey, what are you doing there?'

I dive for the path. Race to the corner, bump into a nurse, knock another of those awkward laundry bags out of her arms. It scatters its burden across the path.

'Sorry.'

No time to stop.

I run on to the next corner. Out of her sight, and out of Billy's, if he's following. I pull up to a walk, fast as I can but not running, not screaming my fugitive presence. I reach the outpatients' entrance. Brisk, now, trying to seem unconcerned, not looking behind though I'm desperate to.

I'm past the porters' lodge, and onto the street. Cupernham Lane is on the right and I turn that way. A glance behind now, irresistible.

No one following.

Perhaps I've got away with it.

'Sit down,' Nash snaps.

Blimey, he's looking grim.

'I've had a telephone call from the hospital.'

Ah, that.

'From Billy Stewart. He's very upset.'

He's easily rattled.

'You're not going to ask me why?'

Not going to say anything that might incriminate me.

'He says you were at the hospital this morning. He thinks you may have gone into the mortuary without permission.'

He's not sure, then?

'I defended you. Said it couldn't possibly have been you. Said I knew you wouldn't do anything underhand.'

Underhand? Is that what you think? Mr Magnanimous himself. Specially when I was doing your dirty work.

'But he said he was sure he hadn't been mistaken. He noticed your hair.'

My bloody Judas hair.

'Don't play games with me, Jo. You were there?'

I play games to win. And if that means not talking . . .

'Still nothing to say? That's not like you.'

You'd be surprised.

'What were you doing?'

I was going to tell you, but not like this. I'm not going to be interrogated.

'Very well. Then how about this? You were in the office on Friday night.'

Oh my God.

'You looked at a number of files.'

How can you possibly know?

'I don't know how you got in—'

Aggie hasn't peached, then?

'Though Miss Haward has mislaid her key—'

Misjudged her. She has. Mislaid it, my arse.

'She said she saw you as she left.'

That makes me the obvious suspect?

'Level with me, Jo.'

Incriminate myself?

'Talk to me. We're supposed to be in this together.'

Not in this, we're not.

'You probably didn't realise. On Friday night, I was in the office myself. Had a headache, didn't want to go home to a lot of fuss, so I decided to sleep it off in peace and quiet.'

Oh . . . my . . . God.

'By midnight, I was feeling better. I was thirsty, I came down-stairs to get some water. Imagine my surprise when I found a light was on. And there you were. Sleeping at your desk.'

So that's what woke me.

'I should have woken you then. Don't know why I didn't. I suppose . . .'

Yes, what?

'You could put it down to a kind of fellow feeling. I didn't think it'd do any harm to leave you alone. To let you sleep.'

Big of you.

'And then in the morning . . .'

Yes?

'You'd gone.'

Good job too. If I'd known . . .

'But I could see you'd been looking at the files. The drawers were clean where you'd wiped them.'

A proper Sherlock Holmes.

'You know how seriously we take client confidentiality. It's a breach of trust.'

So's what happened to Nell.

'I trusted you.'

And now you don't? Doesn't take much, does it?

'I need to know, Jo. Why were you there?'

None of your business.

'Was it anything to do with the business I hired you for?'

That'd be telling.

'Tell me.'

Oh, why not. 'Because . . .'

'She speaks. Three cheers.'

'If you're going to be sarky . . .'

'All right. I'm sorry. I shouldn't have said that.'

No.

'Don't go all silent on me again, Jo.'

I don't want to abandon the safety of silence, but I think I must. I take a deep breath. It's going to be hard to explain.

'I was trying to find out about my father—'

I break off. There's a stomp and clatter of feet on the stairs, the sound of raised voices. One is Miss Haward's. The other belongs to a very angry man.

The door bursts open. Dr Waverley.

'Nash.'

Miss Haward edges into the room behind him. 'Mr Nash, I'm sorry . . .'

For a moment I'm almost amused.

Then Waverley's gaze lights on me.

'You, you bitch. Do you know what you've done?'

He starts towards me, but I'm so shocked I can't move.

Miss Haward squawks outrage. 'Dr Waverley!'

Bram Nash moves to block the doctor's path. It's mayhem, but I sit like a lemon, mouth open, not knowing what to do.

'Enough.' Nash's voice is quiet, but it cuts through the bluster and outrage. 'Jo, my chair, now. Miss Haward, tea. Waverley, sit down.'

Like a set of squabbling children responding to teacher, we do as we are told. Miss Haward disappears downstairs. I slide into Nash's chair behind the desk, a protective width of polished mahogany between me and the irate doctor.

Nash stays standing, the position of power. I envy him.

'Now, Waverley, what's all this about? Calmly, please.'

'That bitch—'

'I said, calmly. Without the language.'

'That woman there—' Waverley speaks as if through gritted teeth – 'your assistant, killed my uncle.'

'What?' I can't believe it.

'Shut up, Jo. Not another word.'

My mind skitters inconsequentially. That's a bit much. After the last half hour of him trying to get me to talk, now he's telling me to shut up.

'Now, Waverley, let's be clear. What exactly are you accusing Mrs Lester of?'

Waverley stares at me. 'Late yesterday afternoon, that *woman* there was seen leaving Ramillies Hall. Shortly after, I was called to attend my uncle. I was told he had collapsed, but by the time I arrived it was too late. There was nothing I could do. He was dead.'

I can feel the blood drain from my face. I open my mouth to speak, but Nash holds up his hand in warning.

'No,' he says, and it would take a braver person than I am to challenge him. My hands and feet have gone icy cold, and there's a tremor in my gut.

'I'm sorry to hear that Mr Oxley is dead,' Nash says. 'But what can his death have to do with my assistant? His health has been fragile for years.'

'Fragile in the extreme,' Waverley spits out. 'I had forbidden him to put himself in any situation of stress or anxiety. Then *she* visits and—' He breaks off, begins again, directed at me. 'What did you say to him, you—?'

'Careful.'

I don't know if the warning is for me or Waverley. I look to Nash, get a curt nod. *Permission to speak.* But my brain has kicked in and I'm cautious on my own account now.

'It was a private matter. He was sleeping peacefully in his chair when I left.'

'Where I found him,' Waverley says. 'And by all accounts, scarcely an hour after you left.'

'You're reporting the case to me as coroner, then?' Nash says coolly. 'Sudden unexpected death?'

'Ghoul,' Waverley snaps. Turns the evil eye on Nash. 'Utterly obscene suggestion. You're not getting your claws into my uncle. Not unexpected, it's been on the cards for years. Respiratory failure, cardiac failure. As his physician, I'm within my rights to sign the certificate.'

'So you're not actually accusing Mrs Lester of any crime?'

I don't know who's the more surprised at the mention of crime. Waverley looks as taken aback as I feel. He recovers quickest.

'I hold her morally responsible,' he says. But some of the wind has gone out of his sails. 'I demand that you dismiss her.'

Nash raises his eyebrow. 'But I haven't heard her side of the story.'

'She doesn't deny it, does she? *Private matter. Left him sleeping in his chair.* Look at her. She knows what she did. She frightened an old man to death.'

Nash does look at me. I think my face must be a blank. I hope it is. I'm so numb with what Waverley's said, I haven't had time to work out what I feel. But there is guilt, coiling around somewhere, waiting to surface.

'Peacefully,' Nash reminds him. I bless the lawyer's habit of mind that has kept him logical, despite everything. But his eye on me is thoughtful, almost wary. He's not defending me, simply stating the case. 'She said he was sleeping peacefully. Can your witness say as much?'

Waverley bounces up from the chair. Confronts Nash with renewed belligerence. Though he must be half a generation older, he's a powerful man. There is such a feeling of threat in the room that I find myself rising from my chair, though what I'll be able to do if it comes to blows, I can't imagine. The desk top is unhelpfully bare, there's nothing I can use as a weapon.

Miss Haward saves the day. She comes in with a tray loaded with teapot and cups, milk jug and sugar bowl, a plate of biscuits. I'm surprised she's brought it herself instead of delegating the job to Cissy or June.

'Tea?' she says brightly.

The tension fractures.

Waverley makes a noise of disgust. Breaking the confrontation with Nash, he barges past Miss Haward so the cups rattle in their saucers. He turns at the door.

'I won't forget this in a hurry, Nash. Keep that woman out of my way. And *you*, you'll stay clear too, if you know what's good for you.'

'Well,' Miss Haward says, putting the tray down on Nash's desk. 'How rude. See what he's made me do. The milk's slopped all over the biscuits.'

22

The same day

BRAM NASH IS IN A dilemma. Jo's revelation this morning has shaken him. He'd had no idea she'd come back to Romsey looking for her father. Now he does, what's he going to do?

He opens his private safe, takes out an envelope. It's almost forty years old, but it's never reached the archive. Like a number of other records, it's always been considered too sensitive to allow general access.

He'd inherited it with the business when his father retired in 1929. If he'd thought about it at all in the last ten years, it was only as a sort of curiosity, an oddity of no particular importance. But now he has to reconsider. Though the documents were obviously drawn up naïvely by the parties involved – he can imagine how his father might have deplored the vagueness of the language – he doesn't doubt the letters would stand as proof of paternity in a court of law.

On the outside of the envelope, in his father's beautiful copperplate, is written: *Deposited by Mrs Rose Fox, 25th July 1901. For safekeeping.*

Nash remembers Rose Fox. Jo's grandmother had been the kind of woman for whom family was everything. Somehow, she must have persuaded Joseph Fox to let her keep Jo, bring her up, though he'd banished Nell. And somehow, Rose had engineered this.

Inside the envelope, there are two sheets of paper. Plain, no heading, no salutation. Each is handwritten, but not his father's writing. Each is signed, but it's not the same signature on each, because these are parallel documents, not duplicate copies. The first reads:

> I acknowledge that the female infant born to Ellen Fox on 5th July 1901 is my child. In respect of this (and so long as the matter remains secret between us) I undertake to pay Mrs Rose Fox the sum of £12 per annum until she or the child shall die or the child attains independence.

The signature is illegible, but unmistakable. The second sheet of paper is even briefer in content.

> I swear not to reveal the name of the father of Ellen Fox's baby born 5th July 1901. In return, he will give me £1 a month for the child's upkeep, paid privately to me and to me only.
>
> R. Fox (Mrs)

He wonders about Joseph Fox. Was this why he'd thrown Jo out when Rose Fox died? Because the money dried up, and he couldn't access it any longer? It makes Nash angry on Jo's behalf to think that her care might have been dependent on cold cash. And so little of it. Yet the old man hadn't held a grudge against the father. For men like Joseph Fox it was always the women who were to blame. It was Nell and her daughter who'd had to pay the most.

He looks at the documents again. Should he tell Jo? There'd be no question of it if it had been her father who had deposited the documents. His first duty of confidentiality is always to the client. But the client in this case is Rose, and she's dead. He can't ask her what she'd want him to do now her granddaughter is looking for her father.

Nash slides the letters back into the envelope, locks it safely away. He mustn't act in haste. He'll have to think what would be in Jo's best interest. But right now, he hasn't the faintest idea what that might be.

What had Jo been going to say? Waverley's interruption had put paid to her telling him. And after, he'd been more concerned to hear her story about her visit to Oxley.

She'd been unwise, but he doesn't think she has a case to answer. By signing Oxley's death certificate, Waverley's put himself in a position where he can't accuse Jo of wrongdoing without calling his own professional judgement into question. It would lay him open to a counter-charge of slander.

No. That would definitely be a step too far. But though the lawyer in him is satisfied she's in the clear, it doesn't stop him feeling uneasy. While not everyone in Romsey worships at Waverley's door, the man has it in him to make life very unpleasant for her.

He'll keep her on, of course. It wouldn't be a good idea to dismiss her. That would be a signal that he thinks she's guilty. On the other hand, what's he going to do with her now? How's he going to keep her out of trouble?

When Nash told me to go home after the scene with Waverley I was feeling shaky, and glad to leave. But now, I want something to do. Dot's out, and there's only so much nodding and smiling one can do with deaf old Pa Gray before he drifts off to sleep in the sun. And I don't want to disturb him. I'm feeling pretty sensitive about the comfort of old men right now.

Did I kill Oxley? Not literally, because he was alive when I left, but . . . did I shock him so much his heart gave out? The picture upset him. Now it's too late, I can't help wondering if he knew something about it. Something more than he said.

He could have done. He said he might have something for me in a day or two.

Why didn't I pursue it? Now I'll never know.

But that doesn't mean I'll give up. If one person knew, or could guess, then so can others. Dot, for instance. I'm sure she knows more than she's admitted.

She'd been at Ramillies like Nell. She'd worked for Oxley.

Thinking about him makes me cringe inside. I can't escape some part in the blame. I was there. I upset him and he died.

I can't stay here, guilt and justification winding round and round in my head. I have to get out. I set off without any real aim in mind. I'm not sure where I'm going, although it won't be anywhere near Ramillies.

My thoughts calm as I walk. Though my personal quest is a mess, Nash hasn't fired me yet. I've still got a job to do. So many questions about Ruth remain. Where had she been between the time she was evacuated to Romsey and when she turned up at the convent? And her baby, why had she abandoned him? Had she meant to meet her brother Frank, or had she dressed up for someone else? The baby's father, perhaps. Who was he? Was he the one who'd killed her, brought her body to the wreck of the pub?

That's somewhere to start. Something I can do. I never got round to asking at the cottages along Green Lane about the night of the air raid. It's got to be worth trying. I turn uphill, towards the Cricketers' Arms. Now I've got a goal, I step out with a lighter heart. If I can accomplish something today on Ruth's behalf, I'll feel better.

By the time I've asked everywhere along the lane from Highwood to Crampmoor, the only thing I've found out is that Pete lives in one of the cottages between the level crossing and the village school. He's embarrassed when he sees me, but sixpence soon settles that. When I ask him about that night, he's obviously disappointed he can't help me. He's not hiding anything this time. I have to accept that apart from the excitement of the bombs, no one heard or saw anything.

I'm about to turn back when I hear the distant sound of dogs barking and remember the woman I met the first time I came this way. What did Nash call the woman? The dog was Tizzy, but . . . Ollie, that was her name. I haven't come across her yet, but if she saw Nash that night, she might have seen someone else as well.

Pete's still loitering on the corner. I beckon him over.

'The lady with the dogs. Do you know where she lives, Pete? Is it somewhere round here?'

'It's just down the track, but you don't want to go there. She's got a load of dogs. She'll set them on you if she sees you hanging round.'

'I'll risk it if I can find it. I thought I'd asked everywhere along the lane already.'

'You can easy miss it. 'S tucked right back off the road.'

'So tell me.'

'Don't say I never warned you. You gotta go back along to the corner. There's a turning, just past the farm. There's a box on the gate for post an' that. Says *Private, Keep out,* but you gotta go through there, and then it's about half a mile along the track.'

'OK.'

But my heart sinks at the thought of it. Is it worth the trek if she lives so far from the road?

'There's a short cut.' He grins at me, calculating. 'I could show you.'

'You've had all the cash I can spare, Pete. If you won't tell me, I'll have to go the long way round.'

I start to retrace my steps.

'Nah.' He trots after me. 'Reckon I'll show you anyway. I prob'ly owe you.'

'You probably do.' I pat him on the shoulder, relieved. 'Thanks, Pete.'

I couldn't have found the short cut myself, though once he points it out, there is a faint path leading through the trees that tunnel the lane. Out on the far side, there's open grazing, a field full of cows.

'Go down the field,' he tells me. 'Along the hedge. It's not far. The dogs don't come into the field, but when you get near the cottage, make sure you holler out so she can tie 'em up.'

'I'll remember.'

I skirt along the hedgerow, the way Pete showed me. It's downhill, easy walking, pleasant in the sun. So quiet I can hear the cows munching grass half a field away. Every now and then a dog barks, a bit closer each time but not threatening. I can't see any sign of habitation and I'm beginning to wonder how long this short cut might be, when I come to a place where the slope of the land turns steeper. At the foot of the incline, there's a cottage.

It's not very big, and it sits in the landscape as if it has grown here. Well-weathered red brick and tile, a double, barley-twist chimney. Windows glazed with tiny diamond panes of glass glitter in the sunshine like insect eyes and a narrow, green painted door stands open to the day.

I pause on the field side of the hedge where there's a rickety stile. Call out.

'Hello.'

A fusillade of barks. A pack of dogs come charging round the side of the house towards me. Five or six. No, seven. I recognise the white lurcher, can identify an Alsatian and a terrier type, but the rest are mongrels of various sizes and shapes. Their barking doesn't strike me as particularly threatening, but I stay on my side of the hedge in case.

I call again. 'Hello. Ollie?'

It's a bit of a cheek, because I don't know her well enough to make free with her name, but I'm hoping it will signal that I'm friendly.

The dogs mill about, tails wagging. I take a chance, hold out my hand to the lurcher.

'Good dog, Tizzy. Where's your mistress, then?'

'Hey, you.' A shout. I recognise the voice, the same suspicious tone as when we met before. 'Whatchamacallit. Nash's assistant. What do you want?'

There's the shape of a person in the doorway, but the woman doesn't come any closer. I shade my eyes, see she's holding herself up with one hand on the door frame, while on the other side she's leaning heavily on a stick.

'It's Jo Lester,' I remind her. 'Are you all right?'

'Damn fool question.'

'Can I come through?'

'If you must. Dogs. Leave it.'

They don't rush to obey her, but when I climb over the stile they don't attack me either.

'What happened?' I ask.

She's got her ankle bound up in strips of cloth, and she's not putting any weight on that foot.

'Sprained my blooming ankle. Tripped over Bluebell, silly bitch.'

I'm not sure if she means the dog or herself. But if Bluebell's the terrier winding itself around my feet, I can see how easy it would be.

'Is there anything I can do? Do you need a doctor?'

I think of Waverley. If she says yes, I'll have to get someone else to call him.

'You didn't come to ask me about my health,' she says. 'What do you want?'

'Can't we go indoors? You'd be better sitting down.'

'Long job, is it? All right.'

She hobbles inside, surrounded by a swirl of dogs, and I follow. I find myself in a low-ceilinged, stone-flagged kitchen. The windows don't let in much light and it takes a minute for my eyes to adjust. A big range dominates the room, but it doesn't appear to be lit, because the room's cool to the point of chill. The smell of paraffin from an Aladdin stove competes with the smell of damp and dogs. There are rugs and pieces of sacking on the floor, more hazards to trip over. An airing rack festooned with washing takes up the ceiling space, while a cluttered table, three bentwood chairs and a broken-down armchair next to the range complete the inventory. Ollie lowers herself into the armchair with a groan. The dogs settle on the rugs, leave me stranded uneasily in the middle of the room.

'Sit down,' Ollie says brusquely. 'Chuck something on the floor.'

I take a large basket of cabbages and rhubarb off one of the bentwood chairs, and do as I'm told.

'So what do you want?' Ollie says for the third time.

'I came to ask if there was anything more you could tell us about the night of the air raid.'

She eases herself in her chair, flinching as she shifts her foot.

'Like what?'

'Like, did you see anyone hanging around that evening?'

She grins at me. 'Apart from Mr Nash?'

It's a fair point.

'Apart from him. We wondered if you might have seen or heard something later in the night.'

'Can't say I did. Dogs were a bit jumpy, barking on and off. Had a bit of a go about half past four, five o'clock. Thought it must be a fox or something. The bomb had got them worked up. They're strays from Southampton, most of them. They've been through the raids, can't blame them if they don't like bangs.' She shifts again, and I can see she's in pain.

'Why don't you let me look at that?' I say. 'I might be able to make you a bit more comfortable.'

'Have at it. Don't suppose you can make it any worse.'

I unwind the strips of cloth she's used to bind up the ankle. Underneath, the joint is puffy and swollen, black from her toes to well above the joint.

'I could put a cold compress on it, that might help. But don't you think you ought to see a doctor?'

'No doctors,' she says. 'Don't trust 'em. Do what you can. Appreciate it.'

'Cold water?'

'Pump it up outside. There's a bucket.'

'You've none inside?'

'Only what I bring in. Hadn't got round to it when I crocked the ankle. You could fill the big jug if you like. Dogs probably need water too.'

I take the jug, go outside. There's a paved yard where a bucket stands under a pump. The water that comes up as I work the handle is clear and icy cold. I gulp down a handful and it's pure and sweet. I was a child the last time I tasted water so good, clean out of the gravel. I use the first bucketful to fill a trough which stands near the house wall. The dogs come out as soon as they hear the water being poured, and drink eagerly. I fill the jug, take it indoors.

'When did you last have something to drink?' I ask her.

'Not thirsty. Don't bother about me.'

'Rubbish. Would you like some tea?'

'Have to light the Aladdin. I only have the range going on high days and holidays.'

While the kettle's boiling, I soak the strips of cloth in a bowl of cold water, wring them out and bind her ankle up again. When I'm done, and she's warming her hands on the mug of tea I've made her, I turn the empty wood basket over and make a footstool of it.

'Keep it up all you can,' I tell her. 'You don't need to take the bandages off, just soak them again if they dry out.'

'You've put them on tight, but it does feel better. You a nurse or something?'

'No, but I was married to a doctor once. Well, I suppose I still am. But we're separated.'

'Snap. Me too.'

I'm astonished, and I suppose it shows. I don't know why, but I'd imagined her a spinster with her dogs and her brusque attitudes.

'I haven't always been the mad dog woman.' She laughs, but it's not a happy sound. 'I made a bad choice, picked the wrong man.'

'Me too.' It's my turn to play echo. 'It's easily done.'

'Hard to put right, though. You don't want to hear about that.'

'I'm not in a hurry if you want to tell me.'

'No. But one good turn deserves another. Steer clear of Edward Waverley.'

'You're married to Dr Waverley?'

'Sadly. Won't give me a divorce. Dreadful man.'

'Oh.'

'I can see by your face you know him.'

'Not really.' I can't work it out. 'But I did have a run-in with him this morning.'

'Yes?' She blows on her tea, takes a noisy swallow.

'I went to see his uncle yesterday. Mr Oxley, you know? But . . . he died last night, and Dr Waverley says it was my fault because I upset him.'

'No.' She's white as paper.

'What's wrong? Is your foot worse?'

'No.'

She's not looking at me, not focused on anything in the room. There's pain in her expression that doesn't seem to have anything to do with the injury to her foot.

'Ollie?'

I'm frightened now. I don't know what's going on.

'Mr Oxley?' she says slowly. 'He's my father.'

'Your father?'

My flesh prickles with goose pimples. I'm the last person in the world who should have brought her the news.

'Yes.'

'You didn't know?'

She shakes her head. A tear slides down her cheek, and the lurcher comes rushing up to her, whining. She pats it absent-mindedly.

'I'm sorry.'

I'm not sure what I'm apologising for. For being the one to tell her, for the way I told it. For his death, and my part in it. I stand up, feeling the weight of gravity on my bones.

'You won't want me here,' I say. 'Can I fetch someone to come and stay with you?'

'What?' There's still only one solitary tear tracking down her face. The dog leaps up to lick it off. 'No. It's all right. Don't go.'

'Dr Waverley said Mr Oxley had been ill for a long time.'

'All my life. Had TB as a young man. Never really got over it.'

I don't know what to do. What to say.

'I'm so sorry. I didn't mean . . .'

She reaches out a hand, pats my arm the way she patted the lurcher.

'It's all right,' she says again. 'It's Eddie I'm upset with. He should have let me know.'

In the end, I tell her almost everything about my visit to her father. The only thing I leave out is the photograph. Like Pete, I can't bring myself to show it to a lady. She takes what I say calmly. After that first moment of grief, she seems remarkably resigned.

'I haven't seen much of my father,' she says, 'not for years. He didn't approve of me, of my leaving Eddie. He thought I should stay with my husband no matter what. But after what happened, I couldn't. And I couldn't bear to be at Ramillies, too many memories. He didn't understand. It was all about family for my father, keeping up appearances. He was very traditional, you know? Very straight-laced.'

'He was?' I feel even worse. 'Ollie, I said some things . . . Accused him of seducing my mother. What if the shock was too much?'

'It wasn't words that killed my father. I told you, his lungs were shot. It could have happened any time.'

But it happened just after I'd seen him, I think. I can't forget that.'

'Dr Waverley said . . .'

'Don't believe a word that man says. He's a liar and a cheat. He hasn't even had the decency to come and tell me my father's dead.'

It's getting late, but I don't like leaving her. It's only when she says I'll be more help if I go that I agree. There's the basket of cabbage and rhubarb to take to Uncle Tom's shop. She tells me he sells whatever fruit and vegetables she can produce, and I get the impression that the proceeds are almost her only income. This early in the season, there's so little to be harvested, she can't afford to let the stuff go to waste. She gives me a list, some bits and pieces she wants in town, and there's a message for Nash.

'Ask him to come and see me if he will. I wouldn't expect him to call in the ordinary way, but with this blessed ankle it might be a few days before I can get about. And I think I need his professional advice as soon as possible.'

'I'm sure he'll come straight away.' He will, if I have to drag him.

'No, not tonight. Now you've sorted me and the dogs out,' – a sandwich for her, a supper of sheep's head for the dogs – 'I'll get some shut-eye if I can.'

She won't let me help her to bed.

'I'm comfortable here.'

'Will you be warm enough? Shall I light the range? Or I could get the Aladdin going again.'

CLAIRE GRADIDGE

'No need for that. I don't want to waste the fuel. I'm getting a bit low on paraffin, in any case. Just chuck me a blanket. The afghan over there will do. Now, off you go.'

The basket of vegetables is heavy. As I slog down the road in the last of the afternoon sun, I have to shift it from arm to arm every hundred yards or so. I tell myself, if Ollie can carry this into town, so can I. But though my arms ache, I feel better than I did when I arrived at her door. This woman, who's got every right to be angry with me, isn't. She doesn't blame me for her father's death. Instead, she's . . . absolved me. And we're friends. It's instinctive. I'm like one of her strays, I know I can trust her.

23

22ⁿᵈ April, the outskirts of Romsey

WHILE ROMSEY HAS WOKEN TO fog, Nash is abroad early again today. He knows his way well enough not to let a little weather discourage him. In town, the greyed-out streets turn early risers into ghosts. Sounds distort, voices boom disembodied in the gloom. A door shuts with the noise of a rifle shot as a dark shape plunges into the roiling damp.

His shoes have rubber soles, silent on the slick pavements, though from time to time he seems to hear an echo, a faint patter of feet that tracks his progress. Nudged into suspicion, he pauses under the railway arch. Listens a moment as the tricksy sound runs on. Like water dripping, or soft wings beating, it seems to come from everywhere and nowhere. The fog billows around him but no one emerges. He shakes himself, moves on. He has work to do, an appointment to keep.

He strikes off uphill. Sometimes he regrets his incapacity to drive, but on a morning like this it's no disadvantage. No point in calling a taxi, he wouldn't reach his destination any quicker. What little traffic there is on the road can go no faster than he does on foot.

On the northern side of the railway, the fog grows thinner, more patchy, as his route climbs out of the river valley. Nash begins to pick out landmarks. A cottage, a wall, a public house.

Not far now to the turning into the lane. Almost there. The sound of a dog howling reaches him through the damp air. Feeds the feeling of unease that has accompanied him from the town. He quickens his pace.

I sleep better than I expected. Wake early, but that's OK. I've a job to do, so I beg the loan of Dot's bicycle once more, strap Ollie's basket to the front and set out.

The bicycle wobbles as the wheel hits a stone. It's full light now, but for all I can see, I might as well be riding with my eyes closed. The fog surrounds me, as dense and clinging as wet muslin curtains. For a while, the chatter of the stream lets me know I am still on the path. But as my route brings me out of the valley, I can only feel my way, hope I'm going in the right direction.

Birds are busy in the hedgerows when I reach the lane. The light is growing stronger, though the fog clings on around me. I've seen no one on my travels, but a steaming trail of manure shows where the cows have been let out after milking. Somewhere, a dog is howling. The sound swirls and bellies, refuses to be located. Without being sure why, I pedal faster.

As soon as Nash comes within sight of the cottage, he sees the white dog by the front door. Ollie's lurcher, Tilly or Dizzy, some name like that. It's the one making all the noise, scrabbling at the door, standing up on its hind legs and crying.

He opens the gate, walks to the door. The dog takes no notice of him, but now he's close he can see how distressed it is, shivering in the chilly morning light.

He knocks and calls out, but there's no reply. Knocks again. 'Anyone home?'

No response. Another time, he would have thought nothing of it. Imagined Ollie might be out, or sleeping. But the message Jo relayed last night was clear. Ollie wants to see him about her father's death. Needs his advice. And she can't get in to town because she's hurt her foot. So here he is.

But where is she? Surely she can't have slept through the dog's howling, but if she's awake, why hasn't she called out to him?

His anxiety mounts. She'd never ignore one of her dogs in trouble.

He tries the latch. The door opens readily.

'Hello?'

It's as cold and damp inside the cottage as it is out. There's the smell of dog and something else, oily and pungent. He calls again, but the stillness of the place is absolute.

The dog darts ahead to an inner door. This one is stiff, reluctant, but he wrestles it open, stumbles into the room. The only light comes from behind him, filtering through the open front door. There's the suffocating reek of paraffin, the choke of soot. He coughs, trying to get his breath. The lurcher is whining somewhere in the depths of the room, but he can't deal with it now. He's got to get some fresh air in here. Blundering across the murky room, stumbling against half-seen furniture and tripping on a litter of rugs, he arrives at the back door, pushes it open. Takes a grateful breath of the clean air that rushes in.

The white dog is a pale blur beside the bulky shape of a chair. He thinks someone might be sitting there, but he can't be sure. And if there is someone, they are ominously still.

'Ollie?'

A blanket hangs as a blackout over the window. He tears it down, and the light elbows in, lets him see the hunched-up figure in the chair.

'Ollie.'

He's at her side, fearing the worst. He tries to rouse her, but there's no response. He searches for a pulse at her wrist, in her neck. His hand is unsteady. He can feel nothing.

Her face is flaccid, unhealthily pink, but there's a trace of warmth left in her flesh. He won't believe she's dead. He shakes her roughly, hears the faintest whisper of sound.

The dog renews its whining, and he hushes it impatiently. He's sure it was a breath he heard. The room is stifling – he can hardly breathe himself. He has to get her out into the air.

He throws off his hat and glasses, picks her up in his arms. She's an awkward burden, not heavy but tall, and he struggles to manhandle her through the narrow back door. He sets her down on the paving stones beside the pump, hears another ragged breath.

He knows the theory of artificial respiration. He learned it in the trenches. There'd been a night when four young soldiers barricaded themselves up in a dugout, lit a make-shift stove because it was so cold. In the morning, they'd all been dead. Not a mark on them, only the cherry red of their faces to show they'd suffocated. Such senseless deaths. The medico had shown him the Silvester Method, but it hadn't worked then.

Now, it has to.

He bundles up his coat, pushes it under her shoulders. Begins the manoeuvre. Chest compressions and arm exten-sions. It's hard work, but he doesn't give up, even though he's heard nothing since those two random breaths.

I must be quite close to Ollie's cottage when the dog stops howling. I'm trying to find the gate in the lane Pete told me about, because I can't take Dot's bike across the fields. I grope along, painfully slow, convinced I've missed the place in the fog. Then, suddenly, there it is. The relief gives me wings. I rattle along the track, cursing the potholes. Alarmed, I see the front door of the cottage is wide open, but there's no welcome committee of dogs to inspect me as I prop up Dot's bike and open the gate.

I call out. 'Ollie?'

'Here.' The voice is strained, and it isn't Ollie. 'Come here. Quick.'

I follow the sound through the hallway. Trip over a scuffed-up mat by the door into the kitchen. The smell of paraffin catches my throat.

'Outside.' The voice comes again, and I realise it's Nash.

Outside in the yard, he's down on his knees, working feverishly over a still figure. I recognise the rhythmic effort of artificial respiration, and my heart clenches. Though I can't see her face, I know it's got to be Ollie because of the bandaged foot.

'What . . . ?' My mind is teeming with questions, but now's not the time to ask them. 'What do you want me to do?'

'She's . . . cold,' he says between movements. 'Something . . . to cover her . . . would be good.'

Inside, the blanket I hung up as a blackout for Ollie yesterday is lying on the floor. There's her afghan on the chair and I grab both, head out into the yard. Though I'm only in the room for a split second, details seem to print themselves on my brain. The still shapes of the dogs on their rugs. Two glasses on the table cosied up to the unblinking painted eye that looks out from Nash's discarded spectacles. The paraffin heater by the armchair, a curl of rolled-up sacking by the back door.

Outside, Nash is still working over Ollie's motionless form. The white dog is curled up close to her legs, and when I try to shift her to cover Ollie, she shows her teeth. I hesitate a moment, then tuck the blankets around them both. At least she'll give Ollie some warmth.

Nash is sweating with effort.

'Do you want me to take over? I know what to do.'

'Can . . . if you like.' He sits back on his heels, and I take his place. 'Not sure it's working.'

'Of course it is.' I won't contemplate anything else. 'How long—?

'Ten minutes,' he says. 'Maybe a bit more. She was breathing when I got here.'

'What—?' It's all I've got breath for myself.

'Don't know. Bloody stove, I suppose. No ventilation. It's lethal. She should have known better.'

'It wasn't lit . . . when I left.' Though I had offered to light it. I feel a shiver of something that might be fear. 'She said she was . . . low on fuel.' As I speak, Ollie shifts suddenly under my hands. Gasps, groans. Retches. 'Quick. Help me roll her.'

We turn her on to her side as she brings up a stream of yellow bile.

'Thank Christ for that,' Nash says, though the vomit has run over the coat under her shoulders, which I guess must be his.

Ollie groans again, struggles to sit up.

'Wha–a?'

'You're going to be all right,' Nash tells her. 'Nothing to worry about, Ollie. Let's get you to bed.'

He scoops her up, speaks to me. 'If you could go ahead?'

I go back through the kitchen, kicking aside the snarled-up rugs so he won't trip. The stair opens out of the hallway by the front door, steep steps that wind up to a tiny landing. There's a raised threshold to step over, a low beam to duck under, but somehow Nash manages it.

We slide her between the covers of a bed whose mattress and covers are so soft and puffy they must be goose down. She's already starting to warm up. Her breathing is better too, though her colour is still high.

'Aah,' she says as we settle her. ''S good.'

She's half asleep, but when the dog hops onto the bed, she reaches out to pat it.

'We should get a doctor to look at her,' Nash says.

'No doctor,' she says, with surprising strength.

It doesn't seem right after such a close call. 'But, Ollie—'

'No. No fuss.'

I look at Nash. He shrugs.

'Are you sure?' I ask her.

'Be a'right.' And then, abruptly, she falls asleep.

'Do you think it's safe to let her sleep?'

'No idea,' he says. 'Maybe we'd better open a window.'

He does, and a wraith of fog drifts in through the casement.

As far as I can tell, Ollie's sleep seems natural.

'I suppose it's OK.'

Nash rubs his face. For the first time, he seems to realise that he hasn't got the mask of his spectacles to hide his scars.

'Sorry, I'll . . .'

He ducks out of the room, clatters downstairs. I hear him stumble, curse. I don't know whether to stay here, watching, or to follow him downstairs.

After a moment, Nash calls softly up the stairs. 'Jo. Can you come?'

I step closer to the bed for another look at the sleeping woman. I don't like to leave her, but she seems peaceful enough. The dog raises its head, watchful.

'All right, Tizzy,' I say. 'You look after her for me.'

The kitchen is a charnel house. The smell, the dead dogs on their rugs. But at least Nash has put his glasses on again.

'What do you want?' I say.

'Awkward about a doctor. You know she's Waverley's wife? They don't get on. Suppose that's why she doesn't want him barging in.'

'She told me yesterday. But . . . surely we could get someone else?'

'They're tight as ticks, these medicos. It might do more harm than good if it gets back to him.'

'I could stay with her if you don't want me at work.'

As soon as the words are out of my mouth, I regret them, because I'm not sure he'll want me to work for him ever again, after yesterday. I'll be sorry if I've given him the perfect opening to say I've got to go.

'I daresay we can manage without you today.' His tone is dry, there's no clue to what he's thinking. 'If you're sure you don't mind?'

'We can't leave her alone like this.'

'Jo, do you think she tried to . . . ?'

The words *kill herself* hang in the air between us.

'Why should she?'

'Her father?'

I remember the single tear, but it wasn't despair. She'd been resigned to her father's death.

'No. I'm sure she was all right when I left her.'

He kicks the mat by the door. 'But there was this. And sacks by the back door.'

'I know.' But I'm already wondering. 'I can't believe she'd have done anything to hurt the dogs.'

He looks round, as if for the first time.

'I suppose not. An accident, then?'

My turn to shrug. I don't want to discuss it until I've had time to think.

'What a mess,' he says. 'I don't like to leave you with it.'

'You need to get back.'

He looks at his watch. 'God, yes.'

We go out through the front door together. The bicycle is still propped by the gate.

'You could take Dot's bike.'

'I could?'

'Drop it off for me. I said I wouldn't keep it long.'

'Haven't ridden a bike for ages. Don't know if I still can.'

'They say you never forget.'

'We'll soon see about that.' He hands me Ollie's basket, steps through the frame. 'Just as well it's still foggy. Might cover my blushes.'

I watch as he pushes off. He's got nothing to blush for, because he's away without a wobble. He's almost out of sight in the fog before I realise he's forgotten his coat, but then I remember the vomit. It's probably just as well.

It's mid-morning before the sun breaks through the mist. I'm glad of the light, the lift of spirits it brings. I've lost count of the times I've run up and down the stairs to check on Ollie's breathing. Mostly she sleeps through my anxious visits, but sometimes she stirs, responds to my voice. Once she even asks me for a glass of water, but by the time I bring it, she's asleep again.

Downstairs, I don't need to be idle. The kitchen and yard need a major clean-up. And something will have to be done about the bodies of the dogs. The stiffening corpses make me feel bad enough; I can't let Ollie come downstairs and see them. But at the same time, I mustn't rush in. I shouldn't do anything until I've had a good look round.

I don't think what happened was an accident. And I don't believe it was deliberate on Ollie's part, either. So there's only one conclusion to draw. Someone tried to kill her. If Nash hadn't arrived, she would have died. The question is, why would anyone want to murder Ollie? Were they afraid of what she might have seen on the night of the air raid?

Perhaps I led them to her by coming to the cottage yesterday. With her damaged ankle, she'd been so vulnerable. I should never have left her alone.

The Aladdin stove had been out, I'm sure of that. After I'd boiled the kettle, I'd turned the wick down till the flame died. I'd left it where I'd found it, a long way from her armchair. And when I asked her, she'd been clear. She didn't want it relit.

Now, it's tilted on the rough flagstones next to her chair. Though it's quite cool, I think about fingerprints. Use a cloth to touch it.

As I lift it, set it straight, I hear a faint slosh of paraffin. There must be some still in the reservoir, but a sooty deposit on one side of the chimney shows where the wick burned itself out. Just as well. If every last drop of oil had been used, Ollie would have been dead for sure.

I try to work out what to do for the best.

If I really believe someone tried to kill Ollie, I should call the police. But I can't. Not just because of my fingerprints from yesterday, I could wipe them off in a moment, remove any evidence that might incriminate me. But because they might think what Nash did – that Ollie meant to commit suicide. And then she'd be in trouble herself. At risk of prosecution.

I can't do it.

But that doesn't mean I can't gather evidence for what happened myself.

The rugs. There's a roll of sacking next to the back door, which looks as if it was meant to keep out draughts. The other door, the one from the hall, has a rug by it too. While Nash and I must have kicked it or tripped over it half a dozen times, it's caught fast by one corner. Stuck on the *outside* of the door, the hall side. It must have been put there after the door was closed.

Yesterday, I'd arrived by the back door, left the same way. I can't rule out the possibility that the rug had been there all the time. But what I am sure of is that Ollie wouldn't have gone all the way round to the outside of the door to block the draught last night. Her ankle was sore, and if she'd wanted to kill herself she only had to put the rug on the inside, and spare herself the effort of walking.

The dogs. I make myself look at the sad little shapes on the floor. However unhappy Ollie might have felt, I don't believe she would have hurt the dogs. I remember our first meeting, her hostility when she thought I might have come to complain about them. *Nosy parkers . . . want me to gas them. Have to gas me first.* A woman who'd said that could never have done this.

There are two drinking glasses on the table. Though the tabletop is a muddle of books and papers, jars and bottles and gardening tools, I'm certain they weren't there yesterday, when I left. I'd washed up, made sure I put the crockery and glassware back on the dresser where they belonged.

Both the glasses have been used. I look more closely, sniff without touching. There's a sticky residue of brandy in each, but they're not the same. One glass has a scum of white grains powdering the side. Could be sugar, I suppose, or scale from the kettle if someone made a toddy. But then both should be the same.

Carefully, so as not to smudge the glass, I dip my finger in the powder, taste. It's bitter, not sweet. Could be aspirin. Ollie might have taken some for the pain in her foot. But there's nothing on the table that might have held tablets. No brandy bottle, either. And she wouldn't have needed two glasses.

It's suspicious, but not conclusive. None of it proves anything against anyone. The police could say I'd planted the evidence. I'd been alone with Ollie yesterday, and I'm alone again here this morning. And if they did believe someone had tried to harm her, I could easily find myself chief suspect. It's a horrible thought, and it leaves me shivering. I know I did nothing wrong, but who's going to believe me? Dr Waverley wouldn't. After what he said about me and Mr Oxley, he'd be first in line to accuse me.

24

The same day

'MISS WAVERLEY WANTS TO SEE you, sir. She hasn't got an appointment.'

Miss Haward looks reproachful. Unexpected visitors are not in her line at all.

'Really?' Nash is surprised. Has she come to rant, like her brother? 'Did she say what it was about?'

'Something about a register.'

She sniffs with disapproval, a habit that's beginning to drive him mad.

'Right, well, show her in.'

Perhaps he could give her handkerchiefs at Christmas. That might drop her a hint.

'Mr Hollis is due. His appointment's at half past.'

'That'll be all right, Aggie. I don't suppose Miss Waverley will be here long, and he's always late.'

'Very well.'

She huffs out of the office.

He knows she blames Jo for the commotion yesterday, and she hasn't forgiven him for not doing as Waverley asked and giving Jo notice.

'Good morning, Miss Waverley.' He stands as the woman strides into the room. It's been a long morning, and he could do without another fractious female on his case. 'Won't you take a seat?'

'I brought you this,' she says, ignoring the invitation. She bangs a large red ledger down in front of him. 'To show you. There's no record of any Ruth Taylor living in our district.'

'I see.' He sits, pulls the book towards him, opens it. He's not going to let her intimidate him. 'How is it arranged?'

'By household,' she huffs. 'And I've checked it all the way through.'

'And if someone has arrived or left the town since the register was drawn up?'

'They've been added, of course. Or deleted.'

He flicks through the pages. It would take a long while to be sure a particular name wasn't included.

'Could you spare it for a few hours? I'd like to look through it myself.'

'You don't trust me?'

'It's not a matter of that,' he says, although it is.

She's been so unhelpful until now, he can't imagine she would have carried out the task with the attention it deserves.

'Have to have it back by nightfall,' she snaps. 'Sooner, if the sirens go.'

'Of course.'

'You won't find anything.'

The way she says it makes him suspect that there is something to find. Or that there has been. The question is what, and why Edith Waverley should want to hide it. Her tone makes it a challenge, and as Jo said once, the code is never to refuse a dare.

'I don't suppose I will,' he tells her, but he doesn't mean it. If there's something, he'll find it.

I get myself under control eventually. Find things to do to keep busy, occupy my nerves. I sponge Nash's coat clean, hang it in the sun to dry. Drag the dogs' bodies out into the yard, cover them with sacks. Wipe the layer of oily soot from all the surfaces I can get to without interfering with Ollie's arrangements, then set and light the range. When I've finished, the kitchen is clean and warm, and I've stopped shivering. But I'm not stupid. I made sure not to touch the Aladdin stove or the glasses without a cloth. I'll talk to Nash about it later, see what he thinks. I tuck the stove in the corner, out of the way, hide the unwashed glasses on a high shelf in Ollie's larder. It's not much, but it's the best I can do. If Nash thinks we should tell the police, there might be a chance of fingerprints, or finding out what the bitter white residue might be.

Upstairs, Ollie sleeps on, the white lurcher on guard at her side. I'm preparing myself for the last job – the one I least want to tackle – when I hear the distant hum of an engine.

It comes closer, grows to a buzz then settles to a steady beat. There's a tractor coming up the track to the cottage.

I go out to the front gate. At first, it seems the grey tractor and trailer must be something to do with the farm. Then I see it's Alf who's driving. He pulls up at the gate, jumps down. I'm pleased to see him, but puzzled. Even more so when he goes round to the back of the trailer and helps someone down. Dot.

'What are you doing here?' I say, but I'm sure she can hear the relief in my voice.

'Mr Nash told us what happened. He thought you might need some help.' She starts to pull a series of bags and baskets out of the trailer. 'I brought a few things along.'

Between us, we manage to get the assorted baggage into the cottage. Amongst other things, there's a marketing basket like Ollie's that looks as if it's full of hay, and a straw shopper that seems to have some of my clothes in it.

'What's all this?'

'Ah, well, now,' she says. 'First things first. How's Miss Olivia doing?'

'She's been sleeping most of the morning. I think she's all right, but I wish she'd let us call a doctor.'

'Don't you worry about that. I'll take care of her. I'll pop upstairs and see how she's getting on. You show Alf where to bury the dogs. We don't want her seeing that.'

I'm so glad I don't have to explain. It's not a job I wanted to tackle on my own. Right on cue, Alf appears in the doorway with a spade.

'Brought me own,' he says. 'Best be about it.'

Outside, I don't know where we can bury them. There's not an inch of wasted space in the garden. In the plot beyond the yard there are rows of cabbages and overwintering onions, fruit trees and a cold frame full of seedlings, the burgeoning clump of rhubarb. And what isn't already in full cultivation has been dug over ready for planting. We can't put them here.

I look at Alf. 'I don't know what to suggest.'

'Tell you what,' he says. 'We'll borrow a corner of the field. Just beyond the hedge there. Cows aren't going to mind.'

He hops over the stile and starts to mark an oblong in the greensward.

'What do you want me to do?'

'Reckon you can bring the bodies?'

I find it heartbreaking. They weren't my dogs, but the pathetic little corpses, stiff already, the half-open eyes and mouths, the cold fur, wiry or coarse or soft as velvet, were dear to Ollie, survivors of war she'd done her best to protect. It'll be such a shock for her. I just hope she won't ask about them till she's well enough to hear the answer.

As I bring out the last body, Alf looks into my face. I'm not sure what he sees, but he gives me a half-hearted grin.

'Tell you what. Why don't you go and make us a cuppa now? This is thirsty work, and I bet you could do with one yourself.'

'All right.'

Part of me is ashamed to leave a boy to do work I can't face myself. But for the rest, I'm just glad of the excuse.

I make the tea, not hurrying. Take cups up to Dot and Ollie, who seems to be stirring from her sleep at last. Finally, I pour a mug each for Alf and myself, take them outside. He's almost done, only the turf to put back.

'What d'you reckon then?' he says, blowing on his tea to cool it. 'How did it happen?'

I shrug. 'I don't know.'

'Think it was an accident?'

'I don't know.' What else can I say?

''S all right. If you think she did it herself, I won't peach on her to the coppers.'

'Never.' It comes out fiercer than I meant. 'She wouldn't, Alf. She'd never have done anything to hurt the dogs. And she wouldn't have abandoned them either.'

'Makes sense.' He drinks his tea in two mighty swallows. 'You make a nice cuppa.'

He hands the empty mug back to me. Starts to replace the turf.

'Alf . . .'

'Yep?'

He's absorbed in his task, doesn't look at me. It makes it easier for me to say what's on my mind. Too easy, perhaps.

'What if someone did it to her?'

He looks sideways at me. 'That's what I was thinking.'

'You were?'

'Mmm.' He's putting the pieces of turf back as carefully as if they're pieces of a jigsaw. 'What if she knows too much?'

'About Ruth, you mean?'

'That an' all.' He stamps down a stray tussock of grass. Looks at me straight. 'Stuff that happens round here, it's not right. People think if you're a kid, you don't notice. Or else they think it don't matter if you do see. That photograph. I could tell you things—'

'Go on.'

'I bet I know who took it.'

It feels as if everything has come to a halt around me. As if the wind has stopped blowing, the sunshine has lost its heat. Even my heartbeat seems like hard work.

'You do?' It comes out a croak.

'Yep. That couch thing. Reckon I recognise it.'

If he can tell me who took the picture . . .

'Mrs Lester?' Dot's standing in the doorway, calling. 'Can you come?'

'Alf . . .'

'You better go,' he says. 'Tell you later.'

'Mrs Lester.' Dot's calling again, beckoning me over. I go to her.

Nash scans the register. Page after page. Names he knows. Names he doesn't. A snapshot of the town. It's like walking down the street at dusk when the lights have been lit, before the curtains are drawn. Here's Basswood House. *Abraham Nash, Frances Stewart, William Stewart.* The evacuee family that came to them in September 1939 is there too. *Freda*

Collyer, Alice Collyer, Stanley Collyer, Maisie Collyer. The names carefully crossed through, annotated. *Returned to London January 1940.*

It doesn't say what he knows, though. What he'd gone to London last autumn to find out, the day he met Jo. He'd wanted to persuade the Collyers to come back to Romsey. Never mind that the children drove Billy Stewart mad and fuelled Fan's grumbles about bed-wetting and lice. But he'd been too late. Freda, pregnant with her fourth child, had been killed in the Blitz. Maisie, the two-year-old, with her. Stanley and Alice had survived, but no one seemed to know where they'd gone. Miss Waverley didn't have that marked down in her careful accounting.

He pushes on. Page after page. Household after household. Name after name. No Ruth Taylor.

'It's about Miss Olivia. Sit down.'

'Is she worse?'

A pang of anxiety overlays my irritation at being inter-rupted.

'No, it's not that. We need to talk, deary.'

Talk ... ? With relief comes impatience. If it's just talk, surely it could have waited? But I do as she asks and sit down.

'What's it about, Dot?'

'Got a sort of a favour to ask you. And, well, it might do you a bit of good, too.'

'Go on.'

'I want to take Miss Olivia back to our place for a day or two. Take care of her. Don't think she should be all on her own out here.'

'Seems fair enough.'

And it does, though I'm not sure what it has to do with me.

'Thing is . . .' She seems uncomfortable.

'Yes?'

'Only place we've got is your room.'

'Oh.'

'I talked about it to Mr Nash.'

You what . . . ?

Dot talks through my silence. 'He thought it was a good idea.'

Did he indeed?

'He said maybe it would be good for you to keep your head down for a day or two. Out of Dr Waverley's way. We thought you could stay here at the cottage.'

'What if Dr Waverley comes here?'

She shakes her head. 'Not a chance. Him and Miss Olivia, they've been estranged for years.'

'I know, but . . . What if he comes to tell her about her father? Or if he hears she's ill?'

'Who's he going to hear it from? It won't be Alf or me, nor yet Mr Nash. And I don't suppose you'll go running off to tell him either.'

'But—'

'We thought,' she goes on, 'if we could let Miss Olivia know you'll be here, we wouldn't have to say anything about the dogs till she's a bit stronger. We can tell her you'll look after things till she's better.'

Great. What if she thinks it's my fault they died?

'Course, we'll tell her the truth in the end but . . . See, she's . . . Well, she's never been exactly strong.'

'Oh, come on, Dot. She's got to be strong as a horse to keep the garden the way she does.'

'I don't mean . . . Look, promise you won't tell anyone.'

'OK.'

I don't know what I'm promising, but I agree. Anything to stop hedging around and find out what's on her mind. Anything, so I can get back to Alf.

'It's not the first time,' she says. 'Something like this. It's in the family. She's tried . . . Well, she's tried to do away with herself before.'

I open my mouth to repeat the things I said to Nash and Alf. *She wouldn't, she was all right last night, she wouldn't hurt the dogs.* I close it again, remembering what Ollie had said yesterday when she was talking about her marriage breaking up. *After what happened* . . . I hadn't pursued it then, but perhaps I should have.

'Years ago,' Dot continues. 'She had a breakdown. Shhh.'

The creak of a floorboard. Dot holds up a warning hand, but I've no intention of speaking. We both sit listening, but there are no more sounds from upstairs.

'She had a little girl,' Dot goes on at last, almost in a whisper. 'Adele. Sweet little thing, pretty, but not altogether . . . Well, a bit young for her age, always. You know. They said it was because Miss Olivia and Dr Waverley were cousins. But they doted on her, the pair of them. Reckon she was the only thing kept them together. Then when they lost her . . .'

'Lost?' I can't help myself. 'Do you mean . . . ?'

Dot sighs. 'Adele was ten when she died. She drowned. Hushed up, see, because . . . she'd done it herself, hadn't she? No doubt about it. She'd put great stones in her pockets, gone into the pond up at Ramillies. When she heard, Miss Olivia tried to do the same. Dr Waverley wanted to have her put away, but her father wouldn't let him. But she and the doctor, well, that was the end of them. She moved out of Ramillies, came here. Dr Waverley went back to that sister of his in town. Left poor old Mr Oxley up there on his own. Terrible bad luck the old man had. All his sons gone in the war, and then his granddaughter.'

Poor Ollie. To lose a child like that. A girl of ten. What could have driven her to it? Unless Dot's *not altogether* means something more than just being a bit simple. For the first time I doubt my own judgement about what happened to Ollie last night. Maybe the welfare of the dogs wouldn't have weighed more heavily on her mind than the death of her father.

'That's terrible, Dot. Of course I understand. If you think it'll help, I'll stay here.'

Not that I've got much choice. If Dot gives Ollie my room, I'm homeless.

'Good girl. I knew you'd see sense. I brought along some of your things.' She stands up, starts to bustle about with the various bags and bundles she brought with her. 'Think you'll find everything you need. There's a pan of stew in the hay. I'll pop it in the range, it should do you all right for your tea.'

'I'll look forward to it.'

'You keep the range in, now. Keep warm. Alf can fetch in some more wood.'

'No. It's fine. But how will you get Ollie back with you?'

'Same way I got here,' she says. 'In the trailer. It's a soft ride, we can wrap her up nice and warm. There's plenty of blankets, there'll still be enough for your bed. You won't mind making it up yourself?'

Before I know it, there's a stack of my things piled on the chair, and Dot's set me to pack a similar selection of Ollie's belongings into the emptied bag. I've hardly got my breath back, it seems, before she's hustled Alf into helping Ollie downstairs, half leaning, half carrying her on his shoulder. She protests all the way, 'I can do it, I can manage,' gives me half a smile as she passes. I don't know how she feels, but it makes me much happier to see her up and conscious.

And then they're gone, and I'm left staring at a diminishing view of the trailer, Dot waving as they pass out of sight. It's barely three o'clock in the afternoon and I'm stranded here, nothing to do. Nowhere to go, if I have to keep out of sight. Not even the dog for company: Tizzy wouldn't leave Ollie's side for a moment. And there's a part of me, a paranoid voice in the back of my brain, that wonders if I've been played for a fool. Perhaps it isn't just Dr Waverley who wants me out of the way. Most frustrating of all, Alf's gone off and I still don't know who he thinks took that picture of my mother.

It's the violets in the lane that make me think of Granny. Purple or white, scented or unscented, she loved them all. We used to compete to bring her the first of the season each year. It's long past the first violets of spring this year, but I don't care. I'll take some to her grave. It's time I paid my respects.

I pick a bunch, purple and white together, surround them with dark, heart-shaped leaves. I remember to wrap the stems in wet moss so they won't wilt too soon, tie the bunch round with a twisted grass stem.

It's a bit of a hike back to town, but I've nothing better to do. And the walking helps me order my thoughts. It's good to get a bit of calm after the shocks of the morning. I'm hot when I reach the top gate of Botley Road cemetery, and I'm glad of the shade of the yews which line the path. I know where to go, but I'm not really paying attention to where I am. I'm not thinking about the last time I was here, just remembering Granny. How she was, the loving care she took of us all. The good times we had, the laughter when my grandfather wasn't around.

I come out from the shade and stop dead. It's as if thinking about my grandfather has conjured him up, because there he is, standing by her grave like a sentinel, a guard to keep intruders away.

For a moment I consider turning tail and retreating. But I've no reason to run. I've as much right as him to visit my grandmother's grave. I go forward a pace or two.

'What are you doing here?' His voice is harsh.

'I brought some violets for Granny.'

He laughs. It's not a kind sound, not the sort of laughter I've been remembering.

'She don't need your flowers.'

He steps aside, and I see beyond him. See the grave clearly for the first time. It's smothered in growing violets.

'Oh.'

I feel the way I did as a child, bringing her flowers, finding I wasn't the first. Only she's not there to make me feel better, to assure me she loves mine as much as the ones she already has.

My grandfather comes towards me.

'And you can sling your hook. I told you before, we don't need you round here.'

'I'm not a child any more. You can't make me leave.'

'Going to keep on nosy-parkering around the town, are you? What's your game, Josephine?'

'It's no game. We're trying to find out about the girl who was killed.'

'She was caught in the air raid,' he says, contemptuous. 'No mystery in that.'

'That's what someone was trying to make us think, but it isn't true. Someone killed her.'

'Little tart with her red shoes and bottle blond hair.'

He works at the hospital, he'd know about her hair. But *red shoes?* I can't believe what I've heard.

'How do you know about her shoes, Grandfather?'

'Saw her, didn't I, prancing down the street. Easter Monday afternoon. Proper little whore.'

'Why didn't you say? You knew we were trying to find out where she'd been.'

'Nothing to do with me,' he says. 'None of my business.'

'It's everyone's business, Grandfather. She was murdered.'

'So you say. Don't have to believe you, do I?'

'Where did you see her? Where was she?'

'Don't have to answer your questions, either.'

'Perhaps it was you. Perhaps you did it. Where were you that Monday night?'

'You bitch. How dare you?'

He comes at me, raising his arm in a gesture I'm all too familiar with. I stand my ground.

'You hit me, and I'll go straight to the police. Tell them you've been concealing evidence. You'll have to answer their questions.'

'I saw her once,' he says through gritted teeth. 'In the street. Coming out of Cupernham Lane. Don't know where she'd been, don't know where she was going.'

'But you noticed her shoes?'

'I noticed her shoes because she was clacking along like she was somebody. And you know what they say about girls who wear red shoes. Didn't think no more of it till they turned up in a bag someone left for the jumble.'

'You don't know where the bag came from?'

'I do not. It was left outside the hall. I'd offered to help Miss Waverley out.'

'And you didn't think to mention it when you found them?'

'Leave well alone, that's my motto. This talk about murder, it's all a load of rubbish. If Dr Waverley says she died in the air raid, that's good enough for me.'

'But, Grandfather—'

'I've answered all I'm going to.' He pushes past me. 'Do what you like with your bloody flowers, I don't care. Just . . . stay out of my way if you know what's good for you.'

25

The same day, afternoon and evening

NASH HAS BEEN ALL THE way through the register. It's taken him most of the day. He's reached the stage where the more he tries to concentrate, the more his vision blurs. Miss Waverley has been proved right, up to a point. There's no obvious listing for Ruth Taylor.

It's possible the girl was using an assumed name, in which case it's anyone's guess what he should be looking for. But against that is the fact that the nuns knew her as Ruth. It's strange that there's no entry for her at the convent. She should have been listed there after her arrival in February.

It's the first thing that makes him wonder.

As he works through the book, he takes note of every anomaly. The register has page numbers, top centre, as printed by the manufacturer, and page 13–14 is missing, a tag of paper showing where it has been razored out.

That's the second thing.

Before and after the missing leaf, the households seem to run consecutively, with nothing left out. But there are blank pages at irregular intervals throughout the book, so it's possible one could have been removed to suppress the name, the page rewritten afterwards. He makes a note of the road and the affected households, but it's a street of terraced houses that are crammed together, close to the centre of town. It doesn't seem likely Ruth could have stayed there unnoticed, though it can't be ruled out. There's always the possibility of a conspiracy of silence, solidarity against authority.

And then there's a third thing.

In places, whoever has made corrections in the register hasn't been satisfied by simply crossing out or annotating information. Here and there, the lists have been amended with strips of stamp paper, stuck on top of an offending line and overwritten. His attempts to peel one off to see what lies underneath are unsuccessful. The paper is glued down so firmly that it rips at the page beneath. All he can do is list each household where a correction like this has been made. There are eighteen in total. Plenty of avenues to explore.

When he finishes, there are three addresses which seem to him to stand out, though he forces himself to consider the whole lot dispassionately. Some of the rest, like those on the missing page, are in streets where there is little privacy. Some are in more secluded neighbourhoods, and might perhaps have harboured Ruth unseen. He won't discount them, but they're not at the top of his list. That leaves the three which are. One is the convent, where Ruth's name *doesn't* appear. The other two attract his attention for different reasons.

Common Farm is on the outskirts of Romsey, isolated from the rest of the town. The list of names here is chaotic, multiple strips of stamp paper used to cram in four names on to three lines. It's a community in itself, insular, the sort of place where people take pride in keeping themselves to themselves. They might not have felt the need to offer information if they had any. It might be worth a visit.

And last, the one which raises his suspicions most. Ramillies Hall, where a name that could be *Ruby Sugden* has been written on a pasted strip and crossed out. Next to it, someone has annotated the entry in fresh blue-black ink with a single word: *Relocated*. It makes the hair on the back of his neck bristle. Ramillies Hall, where Ruth, when she was living at the convent, nevertheless had a hideout.

Pete brings me the letter with a sheepish air. He shouldn't have it, of course. He shouldn't have brought it to me. Come to that, he shouldn't even have known where to bring it. I thought Dot said nobody would know I'm here. She must have meant some special kind of definition of a secret, particular to Romsey. It's just a pity the place isn't so keen to give up information about what I need to know.

'I clocked it this morning,' he says. 'With all that writing on the envelope, it looked like it was important. Sort of urgent, maybe, an' it's been all over the place. I thought you maybe didn't know about it to collect it yourself. So I thought, quickest thing, pinch it when the boss wasn't looking.'

I look at the envelope. I see Pete's point. It does look important with that printed origin across the top and the way it's been redirected from one address to another, following me. I should be grateful for his efforts.

'Thanks, Pete.' I put it in my pocket. I can see he's disappointed I don't open it straight away. 'If you hang on I might be able to dredge up a copper or two for your trouble.'

'Nah.' He looks embarrassed. 'We're mates now, aren't we?'

'If you like.' The thought makes me smile. It's nice to have someone on my side. 'You're not going to get into bother for taking it?'

He shakes his head. 'Who's gonna know?'

'Now there's a question.' Mates or not, I have to ask. 'Here's another one for you. How did you know I was here?'

'Easy. Took the letter round to Alf's. He told me.'

'He did?'

So much for that, then.

'He didn't want to, but after I showed him the letter he thought he'd have to. Said he wouldn't have told me if he could've brought it himself but he was on his way to work. Like I said, we thought it was important.'

'Yes, you're right, Pete, it is. It was good of you to fetch it. I just don't want to open it.'

'Oh. I should've thought.' He reddens, embarrassed. He must take telegrams that bring bad news all the time. 'Sorry.'

'Never mind.'

He makes an effort to change the subject.

'You staying here then?'

'For a little while.'

'Coo. What's happened to the dog lady then?'

I tap my nose. 'You know what they say. "Be like Dad, keep Mum."'

'An' the dogs?'

'Sorry, mate, can't tell you. Careless talk.' In this case, it might just be true. 'Look, Pete, I mean it. I'd rather you didn't tell anyone I'm here.'

He draws a finger across his throat. 'Never.'

He's so serious, I want to laugh. But I don't. Instead, I have an idea. It might be some kind of reward for him, and it would be company for me.

'Are you hungry?'

'Am I ever.'

'I've got a bowl of stew with your name on it, then. Come on in. If it won't spoil your tea.'

'Nah.'

He eats, and chatters, and I watch him and listen, but I don't take in much of what he says. It's *Boy's Own* bluster, war and Nazi spies and how he hopes the fighting won't be over before he can join up. And I hear that, and ask him how old he is, and he tells me nearly fourteen, and I think, God, four more years, surely it won't last that long? But he's chattering on, saying he thinks that by next year if he's lucky he'll look old enough to pass because his brother did and he's in the navy already. And I think of Frank's story and wish I hadn't fed Pete the stew after all. As far as I can see, the longer he stays small, the better. So when he finishes the food I've given him I don't offer him more though there's plenty, and after a while he says he'd better get home for tea and saunters off.

I watch him go with mixed feelings. It's getting dark, and though I don't mind being alone, never have, I'm conscious of how out-of-the-way this place is. I see him notice the spot where Alf buried the dogs and wonder if he'll work it out. Whether curiosity will get the better of him and he'll talk, or whether he'll keep his promise not to tell anyone I'm here. But whether he talks or not, I'm beginning to see this isn't the safest place to be. If someone did try to kill Ollie, and they come back to see if the job's been done, I'm in trouble. Because if it was about her knowing too much, I'll be in the same boat. Slap bang in the firing line, the minute I see them. Because then I'll know too.

There's part of me that's fired up by the thought. I'll *know*. But mostly, I wish I hadn't let Nash and Dot strand me here. I'm bait, a tethered goat waiting for the tiger to arrive.

I shake myself out of it. I'm being ridiculous. If I'm nervous, all I've got to do is go indoors, lock myself in. Put up the blackouts, avoid answering the door to brandy drinkers and purveyors of white powder. If I use common sense, I'll be perfectly safe inside.

Mrs R. Lester
~~Silverbank~~
~~Isle of Wight~~

~~4 Garden Row~~
~~London, S.E.1.~~

Post Restante
Romsey, Hants

THE WAR OFFICE CASUALTY BRANCH
BLUE COAT ~~HOSPITAL~~ School
LIVERPOOL

23rd March 1941

Madam,

With reference to your enquiry of 29th July 1940, which was forwarded to me, I am directed to inform you that it has been announced on the German wireless that Richard Marshall Lester, born 30th November 1894, has been interned in Germany as an enemy alien. The report did not give further information regarding his status or location. The usual practice of the German Government is not to report the address of ~~a prisoner of war~~ an internee until he has been placed in a permanent camp.

I am,

Madam,

Your obedient Servant,

F. Algar

I can't cry, that would be a hypocrite's trick. But I did love him once. It's appalling to think of him consigned to some Nazi hellhole, status unknown. And so pointedly, not a prisoner of war. What on earth does that mean?

Nash goes to the ARP post first. His quarry is there.

'Your register.'

Miss Waverley smirks, secures it under her hands as if it's holy writ.

'I hope you're satisfied.'

'I think so, yes. It makes interesting reading.'

'You didn't find the name, of course.'

'You made sure of that.'

'What d'you mean?'

The smirk has been replaced by something like outrage. Or, it would be satisfying to think, with alarm.

He smiles. 'Didn't you tell me you'd checked all through the register?'

'Yes, yes, I did.'

'So I wouldn't find anything, would I?'

'No. No, of course not.'

'I just wondered—'

'Yes?'

'Didn't you find it strange that her name doesn't appear at all? We know, for instance, that she was at the convent for several weeks. Sister Gervase identified the body, and she knew her as Ruth.'

Miss Waverley blusters about the difficulty of keeping the registers up to date, complains that people won't co-operate in telling the wardens about changes in their household. She's gone out of her way to be helpful, he ought to be grateful instead of doubting her. He lets her talk herself dry without comment, doesn't push his advantage, though he knows he has one. He keeps his suspicions about Ramillies to himself. No point in showing his hand too early.

When she runs out of steam, he lets the silence settle a moment, then says, 'I quite understand, Miss Waverley. I don't expect you to do anything further. In fact, you've helped me a great deal already. More than you realise, perhaps. I don't think it'll be long before I can say for certain where Ruth Taylor was staying when she first came to Romsey.'

'I wish you joy of it,' she says. But the expression on her face says something quite different. Confirmation, if he still needed it, that she knows more than she's telling. 'It's of no interest to me whatsoever. Now, please, I'm a busy woman. I'd be glad if you'd let me get on with my work.'

He tips his hat to her and leaves. He's almost certain he knows where to look, but it's not going to be easy. With Oxley dead, and the Waverleys so hostile, he'll have to tread lightly, work out a way to go roundabout to find the information he needs.

26

The same day, evening and night

THE KITCHEN IS WARM. COSY, with the blackouts up and one oil lamp lit. It's been a long day, full of emotion, so it's probably inevitable I should fall asleep in the armchair as soon as I've eaten my meal.

I dream I'm standing in front of a huge iron door. Around it, there's a wilderness of barren, empty plains as far as the eye can see. It's growing dark, and though I don't want to, though I could easily avoid it, I know I have to go through the door. I raise my hand, bang on the door. The sound echoes as if there is some vast edifice behind the door, invisible to me. A babble of voices begins to call to me out of the twilight, but I can't make out what they're saying. A hot wind blows out of the void, bringing the smell of burning. The echo of my knock grows like the thrumming of some monstrous church bell, threatening, sinister.

'Jo!'

I wake with a start. There's a knocking on the door, insistent, and a fug of smoke is rising from the enamel dish I've carelessly left on the range.

'Jo!'

'Who is it?' But I know, of course. It's Nash. What I don't know is why he's here at – a glance at my watch – ten o'clock in the evening.

'Bram Nash,' he says. 'Let me in.'

I go to the back door, unbolt it. Open it cautiously. Smoke rushes out, replaced by cold air coming in.

'For God's sake,' Nash says as he steps through the door. 'What happened? I was afraid ... I could smell smoke. I thought ...'

'Come in.'

I turn away, go to the range where the dish is still smoking, pick it up without thinking.

'Ow.' Drop it again, put my burned fingers to my mouth. 'I left Dot's casserole dish on the heat.'

He comes across the room. Takes my hand in his, inspects it. Frowns in the dim light.

'Get some cold water on that. Now.'

The tall jug by the washbasin is still half full. He pours water into the sink, a shallow puddle of cool liquid, pushes my hand into it.

'Five minutes,' he tells me. 'Don't take your hand out for at least five minutes.'

With my back to the room, I can only follow what he's doing by craning over my shoulder. He picks up the jug, uses a cloth to collect the hot dish from the stove. He takes them both outside, shouldering the door wide. The wind whisks into the room, sets my letter fluttering from the table onto the floor. I'm torn between retrieving it and keeping my stinging fingers in the water. I can hear him operating the pump out in the yard, and then he's back again, carrying the full jug of water. I notice that this time he shuts the door securely, pushes the bolt home.

'I'm glad you made the place secure,' he says as he pours more water into the bowl. It's so icy cold it makes me wince. 'Sensible of you. I discovered some things that made me concerned. I thought I'd better come and talk it over with you. See you were OK.'

'What things?'

'I think I know where Ruth must have been when she first came to Romsey. And I think I know who knew it.'

'Ramillies,' I say. 'She was there, wasn't she?'

He can't hide his surprise. 'I think so, yes. How did you know?'

'I've had plenty of time to puzzle over it today. I couldn't believe a stranger to Romsey would have found the summer house by chance, so she had to have been at Ramillies. And then I remembered, when I asked old Mr Oxley who took care of him, he said something about having had a girl to look after him. He said she'd left, and I got the impression it hadn't been long ago. I'm sorry.'

'What for?'

'I should have pursued it. Asked Mr Oxley about the girl. I was so fixed on finding out about Nell, I didn't think of it at the time.'

He shrugs. 'Can't be helped.'

'What made you think of Ramillies? I bet you've done better than me.'

'Up to a point, perhaps. I finally got my hands on the ARP register. Miss Waverley wasn't keen to let me see it, but I insisted she let me check it for myself. No sign of Ruth's name, of course, but there are a few places where alterations have been made. Amongst others, there's one on the record for Ramillies Hall. Someone's written in the name *Ruby Sugden* as a correction.' His voice turns musing. 'Like you, I can't believe someone who didn't know the area would find the summer house. We know Ruth was there, so the only question is, was there another girl called Ruby, or was it Ruth in disguise all along?'

'You think she might have given a false name?'

'Not for a minute. The nuns knew her by her right name. I think it was her, and someone's tried to cover it up. Which brings us to the matter of who could have made alterations to the register.'

'Miss Waverley?'

'She's one. And there's her brother, too. But the registers are kept at the ARP post, so anyone who had access there might have done it, I suppose.'

I think of the unlocked cupboard I saw there.

'That's true. It's so frustrating, Bram. I might have known for sure if I'd only asked Mr Oxley. Can I take my fingers out of the water now?'

'Another minute.'

Over my shoulder, I catch sight of him stooping to pick up the letter.

'Oh, please don't . . .' but it's too late.

He looks up. 'I'm sorry, Jo. Unforgivable of me.' He puts the letter back on the table, comes towards me. 'Couldn't help but see what it says.'

'It doesn't matter.' But of course, it does. I take my hand out of the water, turn towards him. I didn't want him to know. I didn't want anyone to know. But now the dam's breached, it feels as if I have to explain. 'I haven't loved Richard for years. But you hear things . . . You wouldn't wish them on your worst enemy.'

He reaches out, touches my face so gently that if I'd had my eyes closed, I'd hardly have known he'd done it.

'So sorry, Jo.'

Somehow the touch, the soft words, threaten my composure in a way that my brutal imaginings of the last few hours have not.

'Don't.' But when he would take his hand away, I don't let him. I grab it in icy wet fingers, crush it against my face. 'I don't want gentle,' I say. 'Bram, I can't bear it.'

It happens so fast. I'm clawing at him, dragging his face to mine for a savage kiss. I want to feel . . . something, anything. Even pain, so long as I'm not alone any more, not left in the dark with my thoughts. The dream, the empty plain, the iron door. I can't go back to that. I don't want to be shut out, help-less. Dimly, I'm aware he's not trying to fight me off, just to slow me down. His voice travels blurred through the coursing blood in my head.

'Steady, steady.'

But I can't be steady. I want everything I can take from him. I want it now, I can't wait.

There's a moment of impossible striving. When I'm afraid he will refuse. Then I feel how my urgency lights his and he's not trying to slow me any more, he's not trying to stop me and the fire eats us both.

We don't make it upstairs. We don't even get our clothes off. Only what is urgent. What is necessary. It's over so soon and I'm sated, sore, gasping for breath.

He turns half away, straightening the disarray of his clothes. There's blood on his lip where I've bitten him. He wipes it away, stares at the smear of red on his hand. There's a look of – I don't know – shame? on his face.

'I'm sorry,' I start to say.

He shakes his head. 'No, Jo.'

Another dab at his lip. He moves away, wary. To the door. His hand on the door. He reaches to draw the bolt.

He's leaving.

'Bram.'

'Lock up after me,' he says, his voice rough. 'Keep safe.'

'*Bram!*'

But he's gone. He's left in such a hurry there's his hat on the floor where it rolled in the frenzy of that first kiss I forced on him. I pick it up gently, as gently as he began, lay it down on the table. My knees fail, and I sink into the bentwood chair. Touch the hat, a fingertip stroke of the brim. I want to crush it, to tear it to shreds. I want to hug it to my breast as tender as a newborn babe. I lay my head on the table, the cool surface against my cheek. Simply look, breathe in the scent of him. I can't bring myself to move. To get up, to lock myself in as he suggested. Who cares what happens now? One more fingertip touch and it's over. That's all there is.

In the stables at Basswood House, a light burns all night. Under blackout regulations, it is carefully shielded so no one sees it, no one knows. Fan Stewart and her son sleep undisturbed in their neat quarters at the top of the house; the ARP warden fails to catch even a glimmer as he passes. Nash, in the throes of his white night, rages unseen. He has had plenty of nights without sleep before now, but none like this. There's an energy in him that burns as fierce as his forge-fire, prohibiting rest. In the morning, he knows he will be as grey as ash, but the fury that drives him is relentless. There is nothing in him that remembers how to sleep. He can't bring his mind to bear on anything. He needs to think about what he's discovered, but all he can think of is Jo.

He fingers the little silver fox he made. Was it only last week? He made it as he planned it, eager, alert. He knows it's one of the best things he's ever done, but he's tempted to hammer it flat, to break it to shreds, to put it to the fire and melt it down.

It's on his workbench, the hammer's in his hands. The fire's ready, hot. He has so little metal left, the fabric of this would give him enough to make something new.

What a fool he's been.

So determined not to get entangled.

After London, he told himself nothing significant had happened. No more than if he'd paid for his pleasure. One gaudy night would soon be forgotten.

But he was wrong.

This is payment. One night has bred its own repeat, a cobweb thread hauling him in. Not the sex, it's not so much that. It's need, that destroyer of distance and perspective, that maker of fetters of steel.

The scraps run soft in the crucible. He pours molten metal into a makeshift mould. He's never done this before, he doesn't have the tools. It's all put and take.

Wait for the blank to be cool enough to work. It takes patience for that, no more burned fingers. Then, the painstaking shaping. But the time it takes has the virtue of making him calmer. When he arrives at the moment for chisel and point, his hands are steady enough to work the fine detail.

It's morning by the time he finishes. In his cloistered space he feels the dawn as if he could see it. He stretches, eases his back from the work. The fire has burned down; he can put out the light and open the blinds, let in the day.

In daylight, he can see the thing he has made is clumsier than he would have wished. It's not his best piece. The metal is not perfectly circular, but he's pleased with the chased design of brambles. The silver is red with firescale, but it seems right like that. He won't pickle this piece to clean it. He turns it once more in his fingers, drops it over the little fox's head. In the end, he couldn't destroy it.

The ring slips down, rests on the animal's toes. Encircles it.

Contained, he thinks, in that dazed state that lack of sleep brings. Safely held in check.

27

23rd April

I SLEEP SURPRISINGLY WELL. IT'S SOME kind of fugue, I suppose. A short-term escape from thought. The dreams don't come back, but when I wake, the memory is waiting. More than memory, it's so vivid. It's etched in my brain, stamped on my body. I'm no prude about sex. If we'd both wanted it, why not? But last night, I'd practically forced him. Even seeing his hat on the table makes me want to squirm. And under the embarrassment, the shame, there's something even more disturbing. The attraction. I thought I'd buried my feelings for Bram Nash but they're there, strong as ever, waiting to pounce. I don't know how I'll ever be able to face him again. But I'll have to. I've got so much I should have told him. If nothing else, I have to let him know what Grandfather said. I meant to do it last night, but the right moment for business never came.

The range is out and it's chilly in the kitchen, but once I've got the blackout down and the door open, the sunshine leaching in makes me feel less dismal. There's only cold water to wash in, and nothing but water to drink, but that seems pretty much all I deserve. I make my ablutions, tidy the armchair where I slept. It hadn't seemed right to use Ollie's bed.

It's still early, and I can't face the prospect of a day wasted here, doing nothing, seeing no one. I've started to feel angry now, and not just with myself. What makes them so sure I'll do as I'm told? I'm cold, and I'm hungry. I've been left on the sidelines when there's work still to do. Hang Dr Waverley and his hysterics. Why should I give him the satisfaction of knowing he's driven me out? And hang Bram Nash and his scruples, too.

There's no key for the back door, so all I can do is shoot the bolt, go out through the front. The key's a monster, and I have to wrestle it out of the keyhole. I'll take it to Dot's, for Ollie, and she can do what she likes about explaining that her unwilling guest has flown. I don't know where I'll sleep tonight, but I really don't care. I sling the basket of my belongings over my shoulder, and set off for town.

At Dot's, I find breakfast is over. She's busy washing up, but she takes one look at my face and abandons the sink.

'Blimey, girl, what's wrong with you?'

I'm not cold any more, the walk's seen to that, but I'm hungrier and crosser than when I set out.

'I've had nothing to eat, and I let the range go out at the cottage. I couldn't even have a cup of tea.'

'Easily remedied,' she says, pulling the kettle over the range. 'Sit down a minute.'

It's a relief being here. I hadn't realised how anxious the isolation of the cottage had made me feel. Dot's kitchen is warm and friendly, and in what seems like moments there's a cup of tea in front of me, and she's reheating a pan of porridge.

'Just needs a bit of milk,' she says. 'That'll loosen it up.'

'How's Ollie?' I ask.

'She's doing all right. She's in the parlour with Pa. Fine pair they make, dozing in front of the fire with that dratted dog.'

'I'm glad.'

'I don't want you to disturb her. And so long as you don't go through, she won't know you're here. We still haven't told her—'

'It's all right, I won't go and upset her. Has she said anything about what happened?'

Dot shakes her head. 'Says she can't remember.' She passes me a bowl. 'You'll feel better with that inside you.'

I already feel better, but it's good to eat.

'Do you think . . . ?'

'I don't think anything,' she says. 'I leave that to you and Mr Nash. I just get on with picking up the pieces.'

Chastened, I eat my porridge in silence while she finishes the washing up. When I'm done, I take the bowl across to her.

'Dot, look, I'm . . . I didn't mean to . . . I'm sorry. I'll get out of your hair.'

She turns towards me. Smiles, though it's a bit forced.

'It's all right, Mrs Lester. Not your fault. Just, well, Miss Olivia's special to me. First job I had was looking after her. Never had a child of my own, so it's hard to see her like she was yesterday.'

There's the unexpected prick of tears behind my eyelids. What's happening to me? It's ridiculous to feel so sentimental.

'Never mind.' Dot pats my arm. 'Don't you worry. Give it a couple of days and you can come back to us. If I know her, she'll want to go back to her cottage as soon as she's feeling up to the mark. You get on and I'll put a few things ready for you. Alf can drop them over later, light the range for you and that.'

'There's no need. I can manage. But I'd like a word with Alf if he's around.'

'He's out in the shed.' There's a knock at the front door. 'Now, who's that?' She hesitates. 'You'll see yourself out?'

'Yes. Thanks for the breakfast, Dot.'

'No trouble.' She waves my thanks away as the knock comes again. 'Excuse me.' She bustles off.

I suppose it's curiosity that keeps me in the empty kitchen. Or perhaps I know who it will be, coming to Dot's front door. I need to see him, but I don't want to talk to him here, in front of Dot.

A murmur of voices. I can't hear the words, but I know it's Nash. Dot's not likely to bring him into the kitchen, but I'm not going to take the risk. I go to the outside door, stand with it ajar, ready to leave.

Dot seems to be arguing with him, but she won't get far if he's made up his mind. No, that's the parlour door opening and closing. He's come for that appointment with Ollie. Let him sort it out. I've got other things to do. I slip out into the garden before Dot comes back to the kitchen. Now to tackle Alf.

Nash takes no notice of Dot's black look. He's come to see Ollie, and see her he will. Dammit, she's his client, and she asked for him.

When he's made it clear he's not budging, Dot shows him grudgingly into the parlour.

'Miss Olivia.' Dot speaks gently. 'Wake up. Mr Nash is here to see you.'

Ollie opens her eyes. 'Oh, I'm sorry. Can't think what's wrong with me. I keep dropping off.'

'You wanted to see me,' Nash says. 'I'm here, if you feel up to it.'

'Of course.' She looks at Dot and the old man. 'I'm afraid it's rather confidential.'

'I'll go, Miss Olivia. No need to worry about Pa, he won't wake up till lunchtime. Besides, he can't hear what you're saying.'

Nash cocks his eyebrow at Ollie.

She nods. 'Thank you, Dot. If you wouldn't mind?'

He thinks it's poor grace that takes the older woman out of the room, but she does go.

'What can I do for you, Ollie? How can I help?'

'It's hazy,' she says, 'after yesterday. I can't really remember anything. And Dot's being so protective. But I seem to think you must have saved my life.'

What can he say to that? 'The Aladdin stove. It's not wise to have it burning in a closed-up room.'

'I know.' Her face is troubled. 'I thought . . . I was *sure* . . . Oh, I can't remember. Never mind. I wanted to see you, I told Jo.'

'That's right. She asked me to call. That's why I turned up yesterday morning.'

'Lucky for me that you did. I wanted to talk to you . . . She told me my father died?'

'I'm afraid so, yes. It must have been a shock.'

'She didn't know he was my father.'

'No. Not till you told her.'

'My father's will, what does it say about Ramillies?'

'You're worried you won't inherit?'

'I'm afraid I will. That he will have . . .'

She seems to shrink in on herself, and Nash wonders if she really is well enough to deal with this.

'Yes?'

'He was so old-fashioned, he hated it when I stopped living with my husband. I'm so afraid . . . he'll have used the entail to bind me to Eddie. I don't want it, Mr Nash. I don't want Ramillies. But if . . . If Eddie thinks the only way he can get it is for me to go back to him, he'll . . . He'll make my life a misery. Worse than a misery. Please, won't you tell me?'

'I'm sorry, Ollie, I can't. I don't know. Whatever testamentary provisions your father made, they weren't made with Nash, Simmons and Bing.'

'You haven't got his will?

'I'm afraid not. After my father died, your father took his business elsewhere. Your . . . Dr Waverley changed his solicitor around the same time, I believe. I heard the name Struther mentioned. It's a London firm.'

'But you could act for me? Help me?'

'Of course. I'm surprised you haven't heard from your father's solicitors already. I would have thought Dr Waverley would have informed them.'

'He may have done.' She shivers, despite the warmth of the room and her blanket. 'I don't know. I haven't seen him. I told you, if it hadn't been for Jo I wouldn't have known.'

'Please, don't distress yourself. Time enough to think about all of this when you're better. I'll act for you in whatever way I can.'

'I won't have to see Eddie?'

'Not if you don't want to. Or at least . . .' He doesn't like to tell a client outright lies. 'I promise, whatever happens, you won't have to see him alone.'

Inside the shed, there's the sound of metal on metal. Something being filed? I tap on the door.

'Alf?'

The noise stops. The door opens, just a crack, and Alf peers out.

'Mrs Lester.'

'Can I have a word?'

'Sure thing.'

He comes out, making sure I don't see inside the shed.

'Busy?' I ask.

'Never you mind.' He laughs. 'What you don't know won't hurt you.'

'That's what I want to talk about. Something you know and I don't.'

'What's that then?'

'Yesterday, at the cottage, you said you thought you knew who might have taken that photograph Pete found.'

'Yep, I did. Probably shouldn't've said anything, but I was upset about the dogs and that.'

Feeling my way cautiously, I say, 'The picture's old. It must have been taken a long time ago. But you still think . . . ?'

'I told you. I recognised the thing she was lying on.'

'And will you tell me? Who took it, Alf?'

A pause. He doesn't look at me. And then, 'He's a dirty old man, that's what he is. Takes pictures of all the kids. Line up, stand against a screen, one at a time, just in your knickers. Says it's a study. Medical records. That's bad enough, makes you feel dirty, ashamed. But there's some, you hear he gets them back in his consulting room. Gives them sweeties, dresses them up for other kinds of pictures. Dirty stuff.'

I feel as if I've swallowed a brick of ice. I know already, but I need him to say it.

'Tell me, Alf. You have to give me his name.'

'Dr Waverley!' he spits out. 'I hate him. Everyone thinks he's so good, but he's a bastard. Look what he did to her.'

He jerks his head towards the house.

I didn't think I could feel any colder, but I do.

'What do you mean?'

'Dot told me he tried to have her put away. She lives out there in that cottage hand to mouth, while he swans around like Lord Muck. Bloody bastard.'

'Yes.' It feels like an effort to speak. 'Thank you for telling me.'

He looks at me properly. Now he's said it, he seems relieved.

'You don't look so hot, missus.'

'I'm all right. Just . . . angry, Alf. Like you.'

More than angry, but I don't want him to know it. I start to move away, round the side of the house.

'What are you going to do?'

Even through the haze of my thoughts, I hear the anxiety in Alf's voice.

I don't know.

Nash is at the front gate when he sees Jo coming down the path towards him. She seems preoccupied, as if she doesn't notice him until the last minute. Or as if she's deliberately ignoring him. He stands in her way, hand on the gate.

She stops, avoids his gaze. 'Let me through.'

'If this is about last night—?'

'Not now,' she says. 'Let me pass.'

He stands firm. 'Look at me, Jo. Talk to me.'

She turns her face to him. Her pale skin is as white as milk, as marble, as snow. Her gaze is hard, an intensity of pain that shocks him. He steps back, leaves the way open.

'Jo.'

He reaches out to her, but she evades him. Stumbles out into the street.

'Things to tell you,' she says. 'Later. I'll come to the office later.'

The pain comes in waves. Like childbirth, I suppose, though I've never given birth to a child. Like a stone in the kidney, griping, a blockage that won't be dislodged, a useless warning, functionality destroyed.

Waverley took the picture.

Waverley might be . . .

Even in my own head, I can't complete the thought.

Waverley, the bastard . . .

The bastard I've been looking for?

I don't know what I'll say but I'm determined to confront him. Make him admit . . .

That photograph.

My *mother*.

How did Ruth get the photograph of my mother?

I know where Waverley lives. The doctor's house is where we used to go for summer fetes. We'd look forward to the occasion each year, a chance to see how our betters lived. But try as I might, I can't remember Waverley being there, nor his sister. I've a kind of recollection of his mother opening the fetes, a joyless woman in black with a stern face and a cut-glass accent. And now I think of it, she had red hair. Back then, Waverley would have been newly qualified, I suppose. Not so much older than Nell, but miles above her in class. Mr Oxley's nephew, taking advantage of the servants, exploiting her. Taking his dirty pictures.

Does he know about me? Does he see me and think about her? Was it the pictures that made her stay away, frightened of what people would say if they were ever revealed?

The bastard.

But I'm the one who's a bastard.

The pain convulses me. I think of what Alf said. *What you don't know won't hurt you.*

I think of Nash's face, so shocked as I passed.

What will I tell them after this?

28

The same day

NASH IS LATE AGAIN AT the office. Two days in a row, and nothing in the diary. No wonder Miss Haward looks shocked.

'Mr Hollis called, sir.'

'What did he want this time?'

'He wanted to know if the codicil was ready.'

'And is it?'

'On your desk, sir. Waiting with some other papers for your approval.'

'You didn't give him an appointment, I hope?'

'No, sir. I didn't like to, the way things have been.' She sniffs, prim and repressive. 'I told him I'd have to wait until I'd spoken to you. He was rather annoyed. I should think he'll telephone again later.'

'I'm sure he will. Tell him . . . Oh, I don't know. What about Monday? That should be all right. He can come and sign it in the morning, if he hasn't changed his mind again by then.'

'I'm afraid he won't like that. He told me this morning he was having palpitations. He's concerned he might die before he can sign.'

'The old devil's got the constitution of an ox, he'll see us all out. If he insists, you could suggest that Mr Bing might be able to see him before the weekend.'

'Very well, sir. I assume you'll want to check the insertion yourself?'

The emphasis on *sir*, her insistence on peppering every other phrase with it tells him how annoyed she is with him. But like Mr Hollis, she'll have to put up with it.

'I'll see to it, Aggie. Anything else?'

'A Superintendent Bell telephoned. He wants to speak to you. He left a number. I said I'd ask you to call him back.'

'Did he say what he wanted?'

'He offered no information at all, sir. Except that it was confidential.'

'Well, I'll be in my office, Aggie. I'm not to be disturbed unless Mrs Lester calls or comes into the office. I want to see her as soon as possible.'

'Very well, sir. Shall I get Cissie to bring you coffee?'

'Thank you.'

'And a biscuit?'

'*Aggie . . . !*'

'Sir.'

It'll be arrowroot today, for sure. He hasn't earned anything nicer.

*

The Briars is a nice house. When I was a child, its position near the hospital gave it importance, a role to play. Like the rectory close to the abbey, its incumbent was always at hand, ready for any emergency. Now, with the hospital moved to higher ground, it seems ordinary, somehow, any special significance lost.

I still don't know what I'm going to say, but my anger carries me up to the front door without a pause. I ring the bell, knock, ring again, but no one comes.

There has to be someone home. I crunch across gravel to a brick arch at the side of the house, where a gate leads through to the back. I'm expecting someone to challenge me as I pass in front of the bay windows, but nothing happens. The gate has a black iron latch, but no lock. From the garden beyond I can hear a rhythmic noise, like chopping wood. The sound of a voice, cheerfully vigorous, singing 'Onward, Christian Soldiers', is punctuated by the strokes of sound. I'm puzzled for a moment, and then it comes to me. Someone's beating a carpet.

I lift the latch, go through. The singing and the flogging beat get louder as I walk along the side of the house to the back garden. The glorious space, site of those summer garden parties, is the same as it ever was, except that today there are no stalls or coconut shies. Only a red-cheeked girl in the uniform of a maid, and a pile of rugs. There's one already hung over the washing line: bright with sumptuous colours, orange and gold. The maid, rattan carpet beater in hand, falters when she sees me, hits the rug a glancing blow. It slips from the line, slithers onto the grass below.

'Oh, bother,' she says. And then, 'What do you want? See what you've made me do.'

'I'm sorry to disturb you. I'm looking for Dr Waverley.'

'He's not here,' she says sullenly. 'Neither of them are. Went out first thing. Give me a hand, can't you? If it hadn't been for you . . .'

She's trying to get the golden rug back onto the line. I move up next to her, help her wrestle it back. It's a beautiful thing, with a long silky fringe that blows in the breeze, but it's awkward to lift.

'Ta,' the maid mutters, picking up the beater again.

'Do you know when the doctor will be back? Or Miss Waverley?'

'He's gone to London. Not coming back till tomorrer.' She hits the rug a hefty blow, and a cloud of dust rises from it. 'Dirty old thing. Picks up the dust something chronic. Only did it last week and look at it now.'

'And Miss Waverley?'

'Gone over to the big house. Measuring up, shouldn't wonder, and the poor old bloke not even cold.'

She's being remarkably indiscreet, but I don't mind taking advantage of it.

'Do you mean Mr Oxley?'

'That's right.' Another hammer blow. 'She was off up to Ramillies at first light. Couldn't wait, could she? It's all "Get the rugs done, Mary, we'll want them fresh at the Hall. Polish the silver, Mary, we'll take it up to the Hall." Says it's for the funeral, but that's all my eye. They'll have their feet under the table before sexton gets the hole filled in.'

I know Nash said the Waverleys were related to Oxley, but surely Ollie must be the heir? And now I know what happened there, I can't believe she'd ever go back to Ramillies. Or that she'd take Waverley back as her husband wherever they might be. But perhaps her father cut her out of his will.

'They're moving to Ramillies Hall?'

'It's what they seem to think.' Her words are punctuated with vicious thumps of the beater, more clouds of dust. '"Oh, Eddie, it's our birthright." Make a cat spit she would. But if she thinks I'm going with them to that ruddy . . . great . . . draughty . . . old . . . falling-down . . . dump they got another think coming.'

At the last slap of the carpet beater, the rug falls off the line again.

'Drat it,' she says. 'It'll have to do.'

'Would you like me to give you a hand?'

'Wouldn't I? Awkward bloomin' thing. If you just grab that side?'

We lift it between us, shuffle our way indoors. I catch fleeting glimpses of a scullery as we pass through, get an impression of a chilly cold kitchen that reeks of cabbage and bacon fat. Then we're through the green baize door and into the hallway beyond, an altogether different kind of space. From the flashes of brass and gloomy oil paintings I get as we struggle past, everything here is in keeping with the status of the town's most senior doctor.

'Last door on the end,' the maid pants. 'Study.'

The study's fitted up to suit a man of substance. Everywhere I look, there's the solid gleam of polished wood and metal. Oak panelling, a magnificent fireplace, fire irons that wouldn't disgrace a medieval knight's equipage. Silver-framed diplomas on the walls, testifying to the achievements of the Great Man. But I'm past being impressed by Waverley. The stink of him, stale tobacco and musty tweed, fills the room. Makes me feel sick.

Arms aching, I'm about to drop the rug onto the floor when the maid stops me.

'Doesn't go on the floor,' the maid says. 'Blimey, whatever next? Gotta put it over the ottoman.'

So we drape it to her satisfaction and all the while I'm wondering if he keeps the photographs here, or if they're in his consulting rooms up at the hospital. What wouldn't I give for a minute alone in here to search. But it's not going to happen. The maid might be indiscreet, but she's not daft enough to let me go rummaging about in her master's things.

'Fancy a cuppa?' the girl says. 'The missus won't be back for ages yet.'

I look at my watch. 'I'd better not.'

If Waverley and his sister are out, there's nothing I can do here. I might as well get the meeting with Nash over and done with. It'll only get worse, the longer I leave it.

'If you don't mind me saying,' she says, as she sees me out through the back door, 'you don't seem like one of the missus's friends. Wouldn't catch any of them helping out. Not if I was drowning.'

I smile. 'No. I'm not a friend.'

'Won't go telling on me, then?' She giggles. 'Not that I care. Soon as the funeral's over, I'm off. Got a job up Winchester way. War stuff, hush-hush. Better pay'n this and no bloody rugs. Ain't half looking forward to seeing her face when I tell her.'

'Sounds like fun.'

I'm at the gate, ready to go.

'I'll tell them you called, shall I?'

'If you like.'

I'm out through the gate now.

'Hey. You never told me your name.'

I wave, walk away.

Nash is in his office when Jo slams in.

Before he can open his mouth, she says, 'Can we start by not saying sorry to each other?'

'What?' He's startled.

'Oh, you know the drill. I'm sorry for having coerced you, you're sorry I was ever born.' Her tone is brittle enough to break them both.

'That's not—'

'These things happen. Maybe it'll happen again, maybe it won't. We're adults, if there's a spark, if sometimes there's a spark and we choose to . . . It's no one's business but ours who we fuck.'

'That's such an ugly way of putting it.'

'Ugly word for an ugly deed—'

'Shut up, Jo.' He closes the distance between them. 'We need to get this sorted out.' His gaze falls on something glittering and fine on her sleeve. He reaches to pick it off. 'What's this?'

She peers at the orange fibre.

'A hair, I suppose. One of mine. It looks the right colour.'

'This isn't a hair. Oh, I grant you, it's not far off your colour, but . . . I've seen one like this before.'

He moves to his desk, lays the thread down on the blotting pad.

'See. It's too fine for a hair. It's silk. Careful now, don't make a draught or it'll blow away.'

She pulls out a hair, lays it beside the other to compare.

'You're right, it isn't mine. I suppose it must have come off Waverley's rug.'

'What?'

'It's a long story. I was helping Waverley's maid with a rug from his study. Why does it matter?'

'Because of this.' He pulls an envelope from a drawer, opens it. Takes out a folded piece of paper. It's dated, *15th April 1941*. Underneath, *Fibre retrieved from body of unknown girl.*

It's signed with his name. He unfolds the paper, discloses what's inside. An orange–golden thread that shifts in the slightest movement of air. A perfect twin of the one on his blotting pad.

'You got this—'

'From Ruth Taylor's body.'

'It came from Waverley's rug.'

He folds the paper away, puts it back in the envelope. Picks up another blank scrap and writes on it. *23rd April. Fibre retrieved from Mrs Lester's sleeve. Possible origin, rug in Dr Waverley's study.* Signs it. Folds the filament from his blotting pad into it, puts it in a separate envelope. Sticks down the flap.

'Sign across here,' he says. 'Date it.'

She does. '*Possible* origin? You know it must have come from there.'

'To stand up in court, we'd need a proper sample. Taken by an independent witness. A policeman, for preference.'

'So you'll take it to the police?'

'I don't know, Jo. At this stage, it's just supposition.'

'You can link her body to his study, and it's supposition? What the hell does it take to convince you?'

'I'm convinced, but I'm a lawyer too. Think how this looks. He'd only have to say there were two threads on your sleeve, and we used them to fabricate evidence against him.'

'He'll get away with it.'

He hears the anguish in her voice, but feels none. Only a steely determination.

'Oh, no. Not now we know where to look. It all comes back to Waverley. We just have to get evidence he can't contest.'

She paces. 'What can we do?'

'It wants thinking through. We've got to get it right. Won't do any good if we go off at half-cock.'

There's so much going round in my head I can't make sense of it. It's hard to keep track of what Nash is saying.

Evidence found. Evidence of a murderer.

Ruth was in Waverley's study the night she died.

Evidence, conclusive evidence that that man . . .

That Dr Waverley is the man who . . .

I should tell Nash what my grandfather said about the shoes. I should tell him what Alf told me about the photograph. It's what I came to do, but now it hardly seems relevant. We know, we have the evidence.

Waverley's the man who took the photograph.

The man who . . .

He must be the one.

I don't want to think it. I don't want to admit . . .

I've found my father, and he killed Ruth.

I'm conscious Nash is laying out the sensible course. I nod and agree as he explains about chains of evidence, building a case. It's all so dreary. So horribly likely to go wrong. He talks about interviewing Baxter, Oxley's manservant, so I tell him what the maid told me, that Miss Waverley's gone to measure up at Ramillies, ready to move in.

'Has she just?' The light of battle gleams in his eye. 'We'll see about that.'

And he gives me some footling task to do, something about Ruth's ration book, and he's off up to Ramillies in Mercer's taxi before I've had time to draw breath.

After he's left, I think he's not the only one who can go on a quest. With Waverley away and his sister occupied, the field's clear for me to investigate. Forget ration books, I'm starting with Waverley's consulting room.

There's an art to theft, going unnoticed in a place you're not supposed to be. I've spent enough time in hospitals, one way or another, to know that if you look as if you're meant to be where you are, no one will challenge you. Everyone's too busy going about their own business to worry about yours.

It's quarter to three, almost visiting hour. Hair tucked into a snood to hide the telltale colour, I aim to look anonymous, official. So long as I don't bump into Grandfather, I should be all right. I know Waverley's safely out of the way, and the woman on the front desk said his secretary only works mornings. She apologised for the inconvenience, but I couldn't be happier.

I step into the corridor leading to Waverley's office. If someone asks what I'm doing, I can make an excuse about getting lost. But it's deserted, there's no one to ask me anything. For form's sake, I knock on Waverley's door.

No answer. I turn the handle and go inside.

There's a desk where Waverley's secretary must sit, a door beyond which leads to the inner sanctum. I knock on that door too, but no one answers. Not that I'm going to go in straight away. I need to make sure I can get away if I need to. There's a small window at the far side of the room. I open the sash, poke my head out. A blank wall to the right, windows that must be Waverley's inner office close by on the left. Ahead, there's nothing overlooking the window. It's only a short drop to the ground, where a narrow bank skirts the building, then there's an overgrown cutting falling thirty feet or more to a rough piece of ground beside the railway. I could go that way if I need to. I draw back, leave the window as wide as it will go.

There's a key on the inside of the outer office door and I turn it, lock myself in. Put the key safe in my pocket. Another minute gained if I need it. I take a deep breath, open the consulting room door. The room smells so strongly of Waverley's mix of cigarettes and tweed it's almost a physical presence. I half expect him to rise up out of the shadows like the Demon King.

I steel myself to go on. It's dark in here; the windows I noticed before are blocked by fixed shutters. I leave the door to the secretary's room open so I can see what I'm doing without having to put on a light.

After the institutional green-and-cream of the corridors, this room is opulent, fitted out like a grand drawing room. There's a red Turkey carpet, an impressive desk and chair. A Chinese lacquer screen cuts off one corner, shields whatever's behind it from view. The only sign that this is a consulting room is a stainless steel trolley which stands to one side of the screen, stethoscope laid ready on the top.

I try the desk first. There's only one drawer that will open. Waverley obviously doesn't think it's worth locking up this jumble of accumulated junk. Rusty paper clips, a broken leather bootlace, the stub of a lipstick. A jar of aniseed balls.

A thermometer, some surgical gloves. The gloves make me think of fingerprints. I've been careless so far, but it isn't too late. I put on a pair. Rub over the surfaces I can remember touching.

Now for the dragon in the corner.

I cross the room, pull the screen aside. I'm ready for it, expecting it, but even so my heart clutches when I see the couch behind. It's all very proper with its starched linen draw-sheet, but unmistakable. The twisty legs, the animal feet. Alf was right. It is the one from the picture of my mother.

At the foot of the couch, in the corner, there's another door. A red light bulb is fixed to the wall beside it. A notice says DARKROOM. DO NOT ENTER.

As I open the door, there's a whoosh of stale air, a chemical reek. It's pitch black inside, but a switch turns on another red light bulb hanging unshaded from the ceiling. Though it's not much bigger than a cupboard, the room's been neatly fitted out. There's a bench, a sink, a pile of stacked trays. A drying line overhead, pegs twisting at angles along its length, an array of iodine-brown bottles lined up on top of two narrow filing cabinets.

I try the drawer of the nearest one. It opens.

To start with, it doesn't seem as if Waverley's got anything to hide after all. The files crammed in these drawers are all patient records. Some of the paperwork seems to date back as far as the last war. There are photographs, but they're of wounds and amputations, stomach-churning, but not illicit.

327

My courage begins to fail. The only crime here is paper-hoarding.

I try the second cabinet. It's locked.

I take the bottles off the top, stand them on the floor. Drag the cabinet far enough out from the wall to tip it. It makes a racket, but once it's tilted, it's simple enough to reach underneath and release the lever that locks the cabinet. I ease it down, breath catching. Has anyone heard?

Far off, there's the sound of a bell, doors banging, voices. Visiting hour. With luck, the noise I made will be put down to that.

I open the top drawer. Like the other, it's crammed. Folders labelled *Board School*. Pictures of children in their underwear. These are what Alf was talking about. The children look cowed, miserable, but however exposing, the photographs seem to be official. Year by year, the pictures show each child standing against a yardstick. On the back of the photographs, there are details of age and weight, some kind of percentile calculation. The next drawer's the same. Folder after folder, records of growth and development. There's a set of pictures of faces gridded with lines and measurements. They make me feel uneasy, but their purpose, outwardly at least, is scientific.

But when I get to the bottom drawer, I hit gold. Gold Flake tins, to be precise, the kind that hold fifty cigarettes. Two neat stacks of them, the same as the one we found at the summer house. I pick up the top one, open it.

More photographs. They're anything but official. Not of my mother this time, but the subject's the same. A girl in early adolescence. Wearing, or mostly not wearing, rags. Hand and face dirty, bare feet. Traces of tears and bruises. I don't recognise her, but that doesn't make it any easier.

Tin after tin the same. Different girls, different poses, but the same intent. Inside each lid there's a bit of tape with initials. *C.H.; I.W.; L.D.*

Crouched on the floor, surrounded by open tins, I have to fight not to be sick. I pick two photographs, shove them in my pocket. Shut and stack the tins. I don't know if I've kept them in the same places. I don't care. Let him make a fuss if he dares. I slam the drawer shut, regret it at once. The echo is as loud as a gunshot. More cautiously, I wrestle the cabinet back against the wall.

My hand's on the light switch when I hear footsteps outside. Purposeful this time. A hand rattles the outer door.

'Is there anyone there?'

I hold my breath. The rattle comes again.

'It's all right, Joe. It's locked.'

Slower steps, halting.

'You sure?' My grandfather's voice. I think my heart has stopped.

'See for yourself.'

The rattle again, more determined.

'It's gotta be the pipes. You know what they're like. It'll be another airlock.'

A pause. The footsteps move off.

There's no time to tidy up. Waverley will know someone has been in here as soon as he comes inside, but that's too bad.

I switch off the light, close the door, push the screen back in place. In the secretary's office, I pause, draw breath. Everything seems quiet. I've got the key in my hand, ready to unlock the door, when I hear a muffled cough.

Grandfather. As if I can see him, I know. The old devil is lying in wait.

Lightning fast, I turn back. Drop the key into a jar on the secretary's desk. At the window, it's a struggle to squeeze through. I don't want to land on my head, and my legs scrape as I twist to drop feet first. On the ground, I stumble and lurch to the top of the slope. I should've thought to close the window behind me, but it's too late now. Someone's shouting, the door's being rattled loudly beyond. I can't go back.

I launch myself into the undergrowth, worming my way into the empty spaces beneath the bushes. Brambles tear my skin. My hands and knees shred, my hair catches on thorns as I leave dignity and my snood behind.

While it's still daylight outside, deep in the bushes it's dark. I don't think anyone will be able to see me hunkered down here. But someone's brought a torch. A light stabs through the bushes, searching into the hidden spaces. I make myself as small as possible, turn my face away from the light. Freeze as the beam searches along the slope. The hunt is up.

There are voices. One's my grandfather's.

'There's someone out there, I tell you.'

'I can't see anything.'

'There's something moving. Over there, in the bushes.'

'You're imagining it, man.'

'Listen, you fools.'

I hear it myself. Movement in the bushes beside me. I put my head down as the torch beam moves closer. There's the sudden musk reek of dog fox, the sense of a presence going past.

A shout of laughter goes up. The light withdraws.

'It's your namesake, Joe.'

'You've woken Brer Fox.'

'Come away, man. Get in out of the damp. There's a cuppa going cold inside.'

I wait a long time, cramped and stiffening. A train goes by and the fox comes back but still I wait. I'm locked into my hiding place. I'll have to move eventually, but I don't know where to go, who to go to.

29

The same day, early evening

Nash's visit to Ramillies hadn't gone well. He wasn't able to make Oxley's manservant, Baxter, understand that his master was dead. As for remembering the girl – it was hopeless. If she'd given birth in front of the old man, he wouldn't have remembered. Not unless it had happened fifty years ago.

And Edith Waverley was behaving equally strangely. He'd found her in the dining room, blinds drawn but all the lights on. She was emptying a china cabinet, making stacks of dusty cups and saucers on an even dustier table. She'd greeted him with open hostility. *What do you want now? Things to do. Uncle's funeral.* He'd taken a certain amount of satisfaction from telling her that he would be acting on behalf of Mrs Olivia Waverley in the matter of her father's will. Edith was shocked. There'd been the gleam of something desperate, almost hunted, in her eyes as she looked around the room. He might have felt sorry for her, until she snapped that Ollie was mad, unfit to live in a place like this. But it was Edith, he thought, who looked mad, clutching a precious Minton tea-cup so tightly in her hands he was surprised it didn't break.

When I finally find the courage to crawl out of the brambles, I know there's only one place I can go. I get some strange glances on the way, and I know I must look a fright with my hair dishevelled, scratches on my face and legs. And there's a tear in my skirt. But I don't care. I've got the pictures.

Nash is still in his office, though it's clear he hasn't been expecting me.

'What's happened?' he says. 'You look as if—'

'I've been dragged through a hedge backwards?' I finish for him. 'Well, I have, in a manner of speaking.'

There's nothing for it. I tell him what I've done. I've never seen him so angry.

'Do you know what you've done? These photographs – they're no use to us now. You broke into Waverley's office, stole them.'

'I didn't break in. The door wasn't locked.'

'Don't chop logic with me, Jo. What you did was illegal. They're not admissible as evidence.'

'There are hundreds of them, Bram. Girls he's frightened, humiliated. Who knows what else?'

'I know that. But you've made sure we can't bring him to justice for it. Out of context, they mean nothing. And as soon as Waverley realises someone's been in his darkroom, he'll get rid of the rest. Destroy the evidence.'

'He's away till tomorrow. Can't you get someone to go in? Sergeant Tilling? Surely he'll listen now?'

'Indecent photographs?' Nash says. 'They're wicked, Jo, disgusting, but they're not enough. Waverley wouldn't get more than his knuckles rapped for those. We want him for Ruth's death. For her murder.'

'That's Ruth,' I tell him, pointing to one of the photographs. She looks much younger than the sixteen we now know she was. 'She's pregnant in that picture, you can see it. He knew. He must have . . .'

'It's still not proof.'

'What about this one?' I say.

It's different from the others. An outdoor scene. A girl in water, floating like Millais's *Ophelia*, flowers all around. She's naked, and she can't be more than ten. I never knew her, but I know who she is. I've seen the portrait in Ollie's cottage.

'This is his daughter, Adele. His *daughter*, Bram. It's horrible. Ruth had a tin of his photographs. Who knows who was in them? What if he was afraid she'd expose him? It'd be a motive for him to kill her.'

'I don't deny it,' he says, and the heavy patience in his tone is worse than his anger. 'But we can't prove it, can we? None of it. Nothing. There's no real evidence, just our word against his.'

'You're scared!' I'm blind with rage, I don't care what I say. 'Just like the others. Scared of Mr I-am. Just like my mother was.' I slap the original photograph down on the table. 'That's her, Bram. That's Nell. My mother. It makes me sick to think it, but . . . he's probably my father.'

There's a long pause. Nash rubs his face. 'I know.'

'You . . . *know*?'

He pushes a piece of paper across the desk. It's a letter.

I acknowledge that the female infant born to Ellen Fox on 5th July 1901 is my child. In respect of this (and so long as the matter remains secret between us) I undertake to pay Mrs Rose Fox the sum of £12 per annum until she or the child shall die or the child attains independence.

It's signed by Edward Waverley.

I drop the letter back on Nash's desk. If I say anything, I'll say too much. I turn on my heel and walk out.

30

The same day, late

IN THE CANDLELIGHT, THE BARREL of the navy-issue revolver gleams. Tucked into the shed roof in its wrappings, the steam from a succession of baths doesn't seem to have damaged it.

I weigh it in my hand. Frank's gun, the one he made me take. I was frightened of it then. Now, I'm glad of it.

I know what I have to do. It's almost time.

I slide it into my bag.

Tomorrow.

It will serve.

31

24th April

I SHADOW MISS WAVERLEY FROM FIRST light, follow her as she moves from The Briars to Ramillies Hall and back to The Briars again. Watch as Mary comes storming out of the house a little while later, hat rammed skew-whiff on her head, coat dragged half over her shoulders, suitcase in hand. It looks as if she's leaving before the funeral after all.

When she's gone, I venture closer. The side gate swings free, and the back door is open. It's careless of Miss Waverley, not to have locked up after the girl. But I'm glad I won't have to break in.

There's nowhere to hide in the scullery, but a big cupboard door opens to reveal a spidery space full of mops and brooms, a pail of dirty water. Definitely below-stairs territory. I can't imagine Miss Waverley ever comes in here. I squeeze inside. And wait.

It must be almost midday before someone comes into the kitchen.

'Dratted girl. Whatever will Eddie say?' It's Miss Waverley, I recognise her voice. She's alone as far as I can make out, and talking to herself. She rattles around the room, clattering doors, drawers. 'Now, where did she put the—?'

'Edie? Where are you?'

'I'm here!' Her voice is loud, so close to the cupboard door I freeze. 'Just looking for a knife.'

'What are you doing here?'

'Trying to find something for your lunch. Stupid girl walked out on us this morning. I told her she wouldn't get a reference, but—'

'Never mind.'

It's him. It's my father's voice. It's all I can do not to shout.

'What news?' Miss Waverley says. 'What did Struther say?'

'I've hardly got in the door, my dear. Can't it wait?'

'Not for a minute. Tell me, Eddie. Don't keep me in suspense. Who gets Ramillies? Did Uncle Paul break the entail?'

'I'm afraid not, my dear. The whole estate passes to Olivia.'

'No!' It's a wail of distress. 'It's not fair, Eddie. She doesn't want it.'

'You could look on the bright side, my dear. Uncle Paul *didn't* break the entail. That means—'

'We're next in line?'

'Of course. And you may like to know, Struther tells me Olivia has made no will. At least, not with him.'

'If she were to die intestate—'

'Right.' The smile in his voice makes me feel sick. 'Such a good job I didn't divorce her.'

'She's not at the cottage, Eddie.'

'I told you not to go there again.'

'I couldn't help it. I had to know.'

'And?'

'I don't know.'

He laughs. 'Silly girl.'

'What if she won't let us live at Ramillies?'

'I don't see how she can stop us. She's my wife, we're one flesh. It's the law. And with her history, who do you think a judge would believe?'

'What about that bugger Nash? He told me he was representing her.'

'You let me worry about Nash. Now, give me that knife, my dear. I'll cut the bread. Your hands are shaking.'

'I'm worried, Eddie.'

'Don't be. When the time comes, I'll take care of Olivia.'

It's as if a cold wind has blown down my spine. A cold, gas-haunted breeze. I miss what he says next, something about sandwiches.

'There's only jam,' Miss Waverley says.

'We'll go out for dinner tonight. A small celebration.'

'I'm on duty till six.'

'I'll come and pick you up. Now, bring the tray.'

The door closes.

If I had any doubts before, they've gone. What I'm doing may not be right, but it's the only thing. I owe it to Nell, to Ollie, to Ruth. I owe it to old Mr Oxley. I don't know whether he had worked it out. That it was his nephew who was my mother's seducer. Perhaps that's why he died. The shock of it.

It's making me want to die.

Dr Waverley, my father.

My father, who takes disgusting pictures of girls. Who uses his status to frighten them, to dress them up in rags and dirt.

Who uses them, gets them pregnant. Disposes of them. Because whatever Nash says, I know. It's not just about photographs. Ruth died in this house.

My mother was lucky to survive.

Perhaps I was luckier still. I can't bear to think about what happened to his other daughter. Adele. Dressed up, humiliated, drowned.

I can't bear to think about Ruth's baby, left nameless on a doorstep to die.

The rage is hot inside me. For him, for Nell, for Ruth and Adele. Even for myself. For all the children the bastard's abused.

I don't care what Nash said. The only chance we had was to catch Waverley red-handed. Before he could dispose of the evidence. But that won't happen if he gets a look inside his filthy darkroom.

I don't care about the chain of evidence. I just want to see him locked up in a cell, his precious status ripped away. And there's only one way that can happen now.

He has to confess.

I'm going to make him admit that he seduced my mother, frightened her, drove her away. Confess that he killed Ruth and her baby.

I feel in my pocket for reassurance. The photographs?

Still there.

The revolver?

That too.

The gun isn't loaded, it never has been. But my father won't know that, any more than I did when Frank held it to my throat. It's the fact of it, unmistakable against the flesh. The threat of it. One doesn't take chances.

The kitchen door again. I tense. Miss Waverley. A rattle of crockery. Their lunch tray.

'I'll be off then,' she calls.

Footsteps come close. They're right outside. Surely she can't want anything in here? I hold my breath. My heart's beating so loud I'm afraid she'll hear. But the footsteps fade and I breathe again.

I wait, ears straining for sounds. The hop and step as Miss Waverley gets onto her bicycle. The side gate banging.

Now he's alone.

My father.

My target.

When my breathing settles, I venture out of my hiding place. Creep through the kitchen. Push the baize door open a fraction. Listen again. Nothing. I'll have to guess where he is. Begin with the study.

I take out the gun, make sure I'm holding it as if I know what I'm doing. If Waverley's at his desk, he'll be facing me when I go in, so I need to be ready.

I turn the handle, open the door. Step inside. Dr Waverley is sitting by the fire, his back towards me. He doesn't even turn.

'Did you forget something, Edie?' he says.

I'm behind him, the gun pressed into his neck, before he can wonder why his sister doesn't answer him.

'It's not Edie,' I tell him. 'Sit still, Doctor, and I'll try not to kill you by mistake.'

'Who are you? What do you want?'

His voice is steadier than mine was, when Frank ambushed me. But he's tense as a wire, I can feel it through the barrel of the gun. It's not safe for me to stand like this, vulnerable to a physical attack I can't hope to counter.

'I warn you, Doctor. Don't move, or I will shoot.'

I take the gun away from his neck. Step back far enough so he can see me and the gun, but not reach me.

'You?' he says. 'What the hell are you doing here?'

'Put your hands where I can see them.' It's a cliché, words from every gangster film I've ever seen, but I can't think of anything better. 'That's right, on the armrests of the chair.'

He does as he's told, and I feel the heady power of it. Dr Waverley, self-appointed Mr Romsey, doing what his bastard daughter tells him. Who'd have thought it?

'What do you want?' he says again. 'What's this about, Mrs Lester?'

'It's about finding out you're my father. It's about some horrible photographs. And it's about Ruth Taylor and her baby.'

'This is ridiculous. Why don't you put that gun away and sit down? We can talk it through like civilised people.'

'You wouldn't give me the time of day if I didn't have a gun. I'm not stupid, *Father*. I wouldn't trust you as far as I could throw you.'

'Look—'

'No, you look. Admit it. You seduced my mother.'

'Nell? Nothing to do with seduction. She was asking for it. Ripe for the plucking.'

'Liar.' I cock the revolver, watch him flinch. But I have to be careful. If he suspects I can't or won't shoot, I'm done for. 'You know that's not true.'

He laughs. 'If she told you anything different, she's the liar.'

'She never said a word, not even on her deathbed. She was always too scared to say anything. What did you threaten her with, you bastard?'

'Careful, my dear. It doesn't become you to throw that word around.'

'It's what you made me.'

He shrugs. 'If you say so.'

'You admit it?'

'Why not? You can call me Daddy, if you like.'

'I don't like. It disgusts me to think that you're my father. A pervert like you.'

'That's a bit rich. I was hardly more than a boy when Nell and I—'

'A boy with a camera.'

He smiles, reminiscent, as if he's enjoying himself.

'Pretty little figure, she had. You won't be offended if I say you haven't taken after her, my dear?'

My hand shakes. 'You won't be offended if I blow your head off?'

'Steady on. Just my little joke.'

'I'm not laughing.' I do my best to stay calm. 'Nor will you be if I make the photographs public. I'm not joking about that. I've seen them. Not the official ones, I mean the others, the dirty ones. The little girls in rags.' I free one hand from the gun, reach into my pocket. Bring out the pictures. Hold them carefully, well out of his reach. 'Recognise these?'

'I don't know what you're talking about,' he blusters.

But he's not enjoying himself so much now. His skin looks yellow, sagging as if the flesh beneath has suddenly shrunk.

'You haven't been to your office today, or you'd have realised. I was there, you see. Yesterday afternoon. I had to get out in a bit of a hurry, though. I didn't quite manage to put everything back where it should have been.'

'You broke into my office?'

'Not to say broke in. The door was open. I did explore a bit, of course. But it was easy to find your filthy little hoard.'

'It's . . . nothing to do with me. Someone must have—'

'There are so many, though. I bet an expert could tell if the pictures were all taken with the same camera. What do you think? Will you risk it? I bet they were, and it was yours.

346

That natty little darkroom, all kitted out so you can develop your own prints. You think no one knows, no one tells? I've only been in Romsey a week and I've heard it already. "Don't go into the darkroom with Doc Waverley, the sweets aren't worth it." I'm not very impressed by aniseed balls myself.'

'Harmless fun, nothing more. You can't prove anything.'

'You think your reputation will survive if I publish the pictures? Tell people where I got them? The one of my mother, for instance. Even though it's so old, you can see she's weeping. And this one of Ruth, you can see she's pregnant. The bruises show up really well on her. And this one. What would people say about this, do you think? Your other daughter, little Adele. Posing like Ophelia. You call that art? What did you think when she drowned herself for real?'

'Don't you dare speak to me of her. She's nothing to do with you.'

'Of course she is. She was my half-sister. It's natural to care about a sister, you must know that.'

'What are you suggesting, you bitch?'

I hadn't been suggesting anything, but it gives me pause. The look on his face is pure hatred.

'Careful,' I say. 'I'm the one holding the gun. And if you don't want to talk about Adele, we can always go back to Ruth. I know you killed her. You abandoned her baby, left it to be eaten by rats.'

'Wrong, on every count.' The voice, not Waverley's, comes from behind me.

Edith Waverley is in the doorway, a shotgun in her hands. I've been so intent on watching my father's every move, I've let myself be blindsided.

'Put the gun down, Mrs Lester.'

There's only one thing to do. I'm back at Waverley's side in a flash, the revolver pressed against his neck.

'I don't think so.'

'You won't shoot,' she says. 'But I will.'

'You want to risk it? Go on. But my father will get hurt too.'

'Your father?' She almost spits it. 'Two minutes with a whore? That's not fatherhood.'

'Nor's what he did with Adele. Did you know about that?'

'Silly child, she was going to get us all into trouble. I had to put her out of the way.'

The jolt that runs through Waverley would have got him killed if there had been a bullet in my gun. But he doesn't seem to notice his lucky escape.

'Edie,' he says. 'Edie. What are you saying?'

'I had to do it, Eddie. You must see that. It's just like this girl they're making all the fuss about. I couldn't let them tell people what you'd done.'

'You killed Adele?'

Something comes into her eyes, something horrible. A kind of cunning malevolence.

'It's no good blaming me, Eddie. I wouldn't have had to do it if you hadn't fiddled about with her. Never could help yourself, could you?'

I've been forgotten. My father and his sister stare across the room at each other. He stands, ignores my gun. Brushes me aside.

'You killed Adele.' He says it again, but this time it's not a question. He advances towards her.

She steps back, levels the gun.

'Stay back, Eddie. I warn you, I'll shoot.'

'My *daughter*. You *killed* her.'

I'm just in time to pull him away as the shotgun goes off. There's a rush of hot air as the main blast passes between Waverley and myself, the stinging of innumerable wasps in my face and shoulder. My ears ring and my arm is instantly numb. Frank's revolver drops to the floor.

Waverley's caught the edge of the shot too. There's blood running down his face.

In the doorway, Edith brings the shotgun round to bear on me. I don't know much about guns, but I know enough to understand my danger. The second barrel hasn't been fired.

'One last little mess of yours to clear up, Eddie. Should have done it years ago.'

'No.' His voice is strange, choking. 'No more killing, Edie.'

'Don't be so namby-pamby. I'm not asking you to do it. Just stand out of the way.'

'I can't do that.'

His movements are jerky as he goes towards her. He must have been more badly hurt than I thought.

'We'll tell them she broke in,' she says. 'It's the truth, after all. And she brought a gun with her. It's self-defence, pure and simple.'

He's got his hand over the shotgun, pushing it away.

'No, Edie, it's too late.'

And then he goes down, falling in slow motion, his hand on the barrel, pulling the gun with him. Miss Waverley doesn't let go. Her finger tightens on the trigger and the gun fires. There's a huge spatter of blood across the wall as his hand and arm are blown to shreds. He screams. Edith Waverley shrieks, drops to her knees beside him. She's calling his name, *Eddie, Eddie*, over and over, but he's not answering.

Now, I find I can move. Numb, I reach the table where the telephone sits. The operator comes on the line straight away.

'There's been a shooting,' I manage to say. 'The Briars. We need an ambulance, quick as you like. And then call Mr Nash.'

32

24ᵗʰ–25ᵗʰ April

Miss Edith Waverley's confession

OF COURSE I KILLED HER, the little whore. How dare she come here, threatening me? Blaming me, asking for money. You think only a man can kill? I should have killed her before, I should have killed them all. Should have started with Nell Fox, her and her bastard. Thought I'd scared her away, scared her enough with the pictures. Should have killed her then, all the sluts and their red-headed get. I wanted to kill them all. My baby, my poor little baby. Mine and Eddie's baby had red hair all over him like a monkey. Face like a little monkey. Something went wrong, something in his brain. Said it was heredity. They thought they could trick me, make me tell, but I never have. It was all Eddie's fault, Eddie and his photographs. Those foolish photographs. I told him not to keep them here, to bring her here. He should never have let her come here. When she found out what I'd done with her baby, she thought she could blackmail us. Little fool. She was stupid, stupid and greedy. She thought she could frighten me, make me pay. But she turned her back on me. So stupid, she never saw it coming. So easy, like swatting a fly. Eddie had to help me then. Too soft to kill, always so soft. He didn't want to know, didn't like to know. But he had to help me this time. Get rid of the body. I couldn't do it. It was his little weakness. None of them mattered, none of those girls, those children. I hated them all. If I couldn't have Eddie, if I couldn't have his baby, why should they? Josy Fox should never have visited Uncle Paul like that. She had him thinkin' about Eddie. Couldn't risk it. Easy, so easy. Old man like that. He'd had a little nip. Asleep, fast asleep, he didn't even struggle. Blessin' for him really, he'd been ill for too long. A mercy, to put him out of his misery. Eddie and I, we should have Ramillies. Olivia doesn't want it. Doesn't want Eddie. Silly woman, couldn't even die when I tried ... Eddie said not to worry. Poor Eddie. Not my fault, it was Fox. Who does she think she is, she's just another whore's daughter. A bastard, a vixen, vermin. Telling him ... I had to do it. He was always so soft. She was the one I wanted to kill. You have to tell him I didn't mean it, tell him I'm sorry. Eddie, oh, Eddie. The blood, the blood ...

[*At this point, Miss Waverley became overwrought. It was necessary to call the police surgeon to sedate her. She has been taken to the County Asylum for assessment. Interview suspended at 10.30 p.m., 24–4–1941*]

Dr Edward Waverley's statement, given in extremis [Incomplete]

I've always had a weakness. Nothing strange about that, young flesh is bound to call to a man. Must see it all the time in your line of work. Right from the start, years ago. At Ramillies, there was my twin. My other half. That's what they say, your other half. They talk about marriage, but we were joined closer than that. Why not? We began as one, two halves of a whole. A unit, even our names. Eddie and Edie, right from the off. No one to worry us, no one to bother us. Our mother, deep in widowhood. Didn't miss a father, never had one we knew of. Only our mother, weeping. Of course we were curious, of course we experimented. What child doesn't? There we were, the two of us. Eating together, playing together every minute of the day. Idyllic, running wild at Ramillies, until Uncle Paul got married and we had to go. Sent me away to school, cold stone buildings by the sea, wind never stopped blowing. Like a snail out of its shell. And Edie, too, lost and angry. At home, but not at home. Longing for Ramillies, for the time before everything changed. In the holidays, we clung together, homesick for what we'd lost.

We were innocent before, but school taught me what a boy can do. It was different then. Edie was more than willing. It was all the comfort we had.

We'd turned sixteen when she kindled. Didn't realise at first, hadn't thought about consequences. It was comfort, I tell you. The need for comfort, and being together.

I was at school when Mother found out. They tried to make her tell who she'd acted the slut with. They beat her, but she wouldn't say. I couldn't understand why she stopped writing, no one would tell me. Christmas came, but she wasn't there. Later she told me about the home they sent her to, the place where the child was born. It was dead, deformed. They made her look at it, told her it was her sin caused it, made her believe it.

We didn't see each other for a year. I'd had a year to look around me. To look at other girls. Young girls, young bodies. Take my pick, my fill. Girls who couldn't say no, servants. I loved them in their dirt, especially if it came from Ramillies. If they got pregnant, it was nothing to me. They were nothing to me, no better than they should be. Get rid of them, all part of the game. No one suspected I'd been Edie's lover.

But I promised her. I'd play, but I'd never leave her. She'd always be my other self. All she wanted was Ramillies. Our childhood home. Possession was all she dreamed of. It grew on her, year by year. Obsessed her.

That's why I married Olivia. My cousin, she wasn't much to look at, but she was young. Naïve. Childish about her pets. It wasn't such a hardship in the beginning, giving up my dirty girls. With her brothers dead on the Somme, Olivia held the key to Ramillies.

I had my career, my position. I had opportunities. The Hall was mine in all but name, and Edie was happy. My sister was happy even if my wife was not. It didn't matter, because Olivia disgusted me anyway. And I had a child of my own, a daughter, with the pretty red hair of the Oxleys. I had my Adele . . .

[*Here, Doctor Waverley collapsed. Despite medical intervention, he did not recover consciousness and was pronounced dead at 9.25 a.m., 25–4–1941*]

25th April. Romsey Hospital, 10 p.m.

'Sorry to disturb you,' Nash says.

'I wasn't asleep.'

The room's dim blue bulb bleaches out all the colours from the room. Like moonlight, it makes a pattern of bright and shadow he finds hard to decode. Jo's face is smeared with new bruises, the harsh black hollows of her eyes obscuring every expression.

'I'm not supposed to be here.'

'I heard them trying to tell you that.'

She sounds . . . amused? They're both speaking low. For him, it's because of the lateness of the hour, the illicit nature of his visit. For her, he doesn't know. Perhaps she feels the same.

'How are you feeling?'

'Sore.'

The dark protects him. If he's bleached to the same jigsaw pattern of moonshine and black that patches the room, he can say what he likes, anonymous, ambiguous. But it's still harder to say what he wants than he thought it would be.

'I'm sorry about yesterday. I wish I hadn't let you walk out.'

'Don't worry about it.'

'I should have done more.'

'You were right. I shouldn't have taken the law into my own hands. But I'm glad I did.'

'Yes. Jo, you know you mustn't say that to anyone but me.'

'Speaking as my solicitor?'

'As your friend, dammit.'

'I'm in pretty big trouble, aren't I?' she says, sombre. 'That policeman who interviewed me last night, Superintendent Bell. He'd have liked to throw the book at me. He would have done it, I think. If he hadn't been afraid it would finish me off.'

'Don't worry. So long as you're sensible, all he's got to charge you with is having Frank's gun.'

'Sensible?'

'Keep your mouth shut. Don't admit anything.'

'I already—'

'The state you were in, what you said can't be given in evidence. They'll have to take another statement when you've recovered.'

'They won't charge me with what happened to Waverley?'

'They can't. You never touched the shotgun, they know that now. And neither he nor his sister said anything to incriminate you.'

'I didn't want him to die, you know. I wanted him to face it, Bram. To admit it. I wanted everyone to know what he'd done to those girls. To my mother.'

'That's why you tried to save him?'

'I didn't want him to get away with it. And I couldn't just watch him bleed, could I? But if I'd had bullets for the gun . . . I don't know what I might have done. I was so angry.' Her voice breaks.

'Hush, now. No need to say any more.'

'Let me tell you. As a friend. Please? I can't stop thinking about it.'

It's so unlike her to admit weakness. For a moment he doesn't know what to say. He's touched, but now's not the moment for sentiment. It won't help her. Keep it brisk, professional.

'All right.'

'I hated him so much. My father, the idea of him. Even before I knew who he was, what he'd done. I hated him for abandoning me, for driving Nell away. And then when I knew, I started to realise it must have been him who'd killed Ruth.'

'He didn't.'

'What?'

'He didn't kill Ruth. He was the one who dumped her body, but it was Edith who killed her.'

He wonders if he should tell her anything more, the state she's in. Will it make her feel better or worse? But before he can make up his mind, she starts to speak again.

'She said . . . When she first came in, she said I was wrong. They started to argue about Adele, and then . . . She confessed?'

'In a manner of speaking. She was defiant, almost proud of what she'd done, the deaths she'd caused. Ruth and her baby—'

'That wasn't him either?'

'No. He knew, I think, and he covered it up. What she was, the things she'd done.'

'He didn't know about Adele.'

'She drowned, didn't she? The rumour was she'd killed herself.'

'Miss Waverley said . . . When she was talking to him, she said she'd got rid of Adele so the girl wouldn't give him away. He was . . . He didn't know that, I'd swear it. He was . . . shocked. More than shocked. It was what made him . . . It's horrible but . . . I think he must have really loved Adele.'

'Love? Is that what you call it?' Bile rises in his throat, the way it's been doing all day. 'Don't make excuses for him. We found the rest of the photographs, you know. In his office.' He doesn't tell her – won't ever tell her – how her grandfather tried to stop them going in, how he cursed and raved at the police, at his own, official, presence as coroner. 'And there were more at his home. Hundreds and hundreds of them altogether. So many of them, so many little girls.'

'I can't stop thinking, how did he get away with it for so long? Why didn't anybody stop him? Why didn't his sister stop him? She doesn't seem to have cared, so long as people didn't find out.'

'No, she didn't. And that's why Ruth had to die. So she wouldn't tell.'

'So what will happen? Will they hang her?'

'No.' He's suddenly weighted down with weariness. 'They'll never be able to bring charges. She's mad, Jo. They had to certify her.'

'Mad?'

'Yes. She's been committed to the County Asylum. But before she finally broke down and they had to take her away, she admitted all the killings. Including Paul Oxley's death. She said she smothered him, hoping you'd be blamed.'

A croak of sound that might be laughter, might be a sob. Might be anything, really. The dark does its work too well for him to be able to see her face. He feels an overwhelming desire to hold her, but he knows she won't welcome it.

'Jo?'

I hear his voice as if from a distance. Hear him speak my name. He sounds anxious, concerned, and I wonder what my face must be doing.

'I didn't kill him?' The relief is overwhelming. 'God . . . I thought it was me. Because I'd given him a shock.' Though this hospital room is steam heated, far too hot, I'm shivering with release. What I want now, more than anything, is the touch of a hand, a body to hold me close. 'Thank you for telling me.'

'You won't leave, will you?'

'Excuse me?'

'If you're thinking of offering me your resignation, I won't accept it.'

It's a touch of a kind, and I cling to it.

'Not even if they prosecute me?'

'They won't. You're home and dry, Jo, I promise. Home and dry.'

Epilogue

28th April

THREE DAYS LATER, SYLVIE COMES to fetch me out of hospital. I know immediately who it is from the pattering of high-heeled shoes on the linoleum floor, the waft of perfume she brings with her.

'*Chérie.*'

Her greeting is cheerful, pitched at normal volume; refreshing after the hushed churchy tones the nurses use when they speak to me. Her hug is constrained by the awkwardness of my bandages and sling, but it's comfortingly warm and real.

I've been dreading this moment, the thought of being whisked away to Tom and Sylvie's perfect black-and-white flat. Kind as it is of them, since I can't go back to Dot's because Ollie is going to stay on, I don't see myself fitting in. Everything there's so clear-cut and brightly lit. It'll be salt in the wound after the mess I've made of everything. But Sylvie's hug reminds me of the knitting hidden behind the cushions, her kindness to my mother, and I begin to think things might turn out right after all.

If it was up to me, I'd slip out the back way, but Sylvie's having none of it. She leads me to the main entrance and as we emerge into daylight, I see she's parked Tom's Morris van bang in front of the notice which says *Ambulances only*. It practically screams for attention with its glossy black paint-work embellished with bright pictures of fruit and veg, its scarlet lettering: T. FOX, GREENGROCER.

'Sylvie,' I say, 'you shouldn't have. Grandfather ... He'll take it out on you and Tom if he knows you're looking after me.'

She waves away the protest. 'What can he do, silly old fool? High time he knew we don't dance to his tune. Now, let me help you.'

Before I know it, I'm installed on the long bench seat. She tucks a cushion against my injured arm before slamming the door, taps her way round to the driver's side. The van fires up at the first push of the starter, but our progress is sedate in the extreme. Either Sylvie's cautious or the van's done for, because we chug out of the hospital grounds at what hardly seems like walking pace. The curtains in the porters' lodge twitch as we turn onto the main road. The old man in his lair, taking it all in? I look away, pretend not to notice. No need to gloat. For Grandfather, the social order's been turned on its head. Waverley, one of the town's elite, a man he'd respected for his birth, his position in life, is dead. Disgraced. Brought down by his bastard granddaughter.

We pass the turn that would take us to Ramillies. They say Ollie's told everyone she'll never set foot in the place, that some out-of-town war office is going to take it over.

On down the hill, under the bridge. It's busier here, people standing about, waiting. Black armbands on some of the men's coats. There's a procession, even slower than us, coming up from the town centre. A funeral. Sylvie pulls to a halt.

I'm filled with sudden horror. 'It isn't . . . Not Dr Waverley?'

Sylvie shakes her head. 'No, *chérie*. The old man. Mr Oxley.'

The cars draw closer. The men in the street doff their hats. As the vehicles turn, I catch a glimpse of Nash. He's there to support Ollie. I can't see Dot, but she'll be somewhere in the background, sensible and fierce, looking after her chick.

Once the procession is past, we move off. I jolt in my seat as Sylvie grinds the gears. Pain punches my shoulder, but I'll be back at work tomorrow, bandages or no. Not sure what I'll do. What Nash will let me do.

He won't let me go . . .

On the pavement, the men put their hats back on. Women gather in groups, gossiping. A couple look our way and I guess I'm part of what they're talking about. What I did, what I found out about Waverley and his sister. Some of them will never forgive me for it. Like my grandfather, or the doctor who took his time getting the pellets out of my shoulder, telling me the hospital would be lost without its chief physician. Or the ward sister who wept because he'd always been a gentleman to her. For them, I'm more to blame than the

Waverleys. I've put the town to shame. While the secrets were tucked away in the dark they could pretend everything was all right. Now it's out in the open.

But I'm not sorry. I'd do it again in a heartbeat.

'Home,' Sylvie says, as she pulls the van to a halt outside the greengrocer's shop.

I surface at the sound of her voice. It's not home, but it's close enough.

Acknowledgements

There are so many people who have supported and encouraged me as I wrote *The Unexpected Return of Josephine Fox* that I hardly know where to start. I think the first thank you should go to the judges of the Richard and Judy Search for a Bestseller Competition – I'm still blown away by knowing that you picked my book! Thank you to Rowan Lawton, my agent, who has been such a patient guide through the business aspects of getting published. Thank you to the team at Zaffre for being so welcoming to me from the very first, and for your help and advice as you steered me through all the stages of editing and preparing the novel for publication. And, of course, for coming up with a brilliant new title for the novel! I met so many of you that first day, and I can't remember everyone's name, but I thank every one of you. Special mention must go to Katherine Armstrong, my editor, whose comments and suggestions have made such a positive difference to the novel; Jennie Rothwell, Francesca Russell, Claire Johnson-Creek, Sarah Bauer, Martin Fletcher and Steve O'Gorman.

The novel has had a long gestation – it began as the creative part of my PhD study at the University of Winchester – and

I should like to thank all my colleagues there for their help and support. In particular, Professors Neil McCaw and Inga Bryden, who as my supervisory team were stuck with me; and Professor Andrew Melrose who gave me encouragement and a friendly ear even though he didn't have to!

Writing can be a lonely occupation, and I don't know how I would have survived the process without the support, encouragement and practical suggestions which came from past and present members of Chandlers Ford Writers. Thanks to John Barfield, Jo Barker, Jan Moring, Adelaide Morris and Corinne Pebody. Particular mention and special thanks to Nigel Spriggs, without whose early intervention the novel would never have got off the ground, and Anne Summerfield for reading the first finished draft of the novel and giving me such good feedback!

Finally, I want to thank all my family and friends who have given me love and laughter over the years. I can't name you all but you know who you are. I couldn't have done it without every one of you. But especially my husband, Nick, my sons Will and Phil, my daughter-in-law Kat and Danny, my grandson.

Remembering my mother and father, who I hope would forgive me for introducing murder to Romsey, and Virginia, who I wish I could tell!

Claire Gradidge on her inspiration for

The Unexpected Return of Josephine Fox

The story of *The Unexpected Return of Josephine Fox* has been living in my head for a long time. So long, in fact, that I can't really pin down one particular moment of inspiration. It might have been when I stood in a side room off the entrance hall to Southampton Civic Centre and read the memorial to the children and adults killed there in a daylight air raid in 1940 and saw that two of the victims had not been identified. Or perhaps it was when I wondered idly about the opportunities for murderers in wartime: just how easy would it have been to conceal the victim of a private killing amongst the civilian casualties of the Blitz? Each of these fed into my earliest image for the book: a murdered girl's body, dumped in the aftermath of an air raid, an unidentified victim hidden amongst a number of recognised casualties.

The setting for the story was important to me. In using Romsey for the landscape of *The Unexpected Return of Josephine Fox*, I was drawing on my memories of the town where I was born and brought up. As I remember it first,

Romsey was still suffering from the after-effects of the Second World War. Although it hadn't been a target for bombing like its near neighbour, Southampton, the economic effects of the war meant it had changed very little: my childhood years were spent in a small market town that was very much the same as the one Jo finds when she returns to her home town in 1941.

My family moved from Romsey just as it was beginning to change. Like Jo – though not with her sad history – I left when I was a teenager, and it was a long time before I went back.

Jo Fox and Bram Nash were characters who began to talk to me before ever I'd shaped their story into its current form. For Jo, exiled from her home as a fourteen year old and returning years later to investigate the mystery of her birth, I could borrow some of my own feelings: the sense of dislocation I'd felt when I returned to visit my home town; of being a ghost in a place I knew in the marrow of my bones. Of looking for familiar places and seeing them changed by time, finding familiar faces grown old or missing altogether. But although I went on to give Jo some of my childhood memories, she was very much her own person from the first.

Being a writer holds a kind of magic: you devise a plot, draw a setting, people it with characters you think you've invented. But then, if you're lucky, the characters come to life in ways you hadn't expected. Like actors who won't take direction, the best ones do what they want. Jo was like that: I soon realised she was more headstrong, bolder and braver than I'd first imagined her to be. It's her story, after all. She makes her choices, takes her chances, drives the action.

In Golden Age detective fiction – a genre I've loved since those early Romsey days – writers like Margery Allingham and Dorothy L. Sayers give their amateur sleuth a sidekick, a foil for the brilliant deductions of the investigator. But *The Unexpected Return of Josephine Fox* isn't about brilliant deductions, it's about dogged persistence and a search for the truth. And Bram Nash isn't anyone's foil. He's his own man, and he gives the story its quiet centre of authority. A loner, he bears the scars – physical and emotional – of the First World War. He's an insider, a part of Romsey society. And he's an outsider, too – apart from it all by choice and by heritage. He stands for the dead, for justice for the underdog. Faced by the indiscriminate slaughter of war, he stands for the principle that every death matters.

The research was one of the joys of writing this story. I was able to combine my interest in local history with my fascination for learning about how ordinary people lived in extraordinary times. Even if I've given my wartime inhabitants of Romsey some extra difficulties to put up with, the sense that most people carried on trying to live normal lives when chaos reigned on their doorstep is as true to the spirit of the era as I could make it.

In putting a crime at the centre of my story, I'm aware I've taken liberties with Romsey and its people. I could have given the town a fictitious name: instead, I gave it a fictitious crime. In real life, the events of this story never happened, but the places are completely real. Though I changed some names – and embellished some details – to serve my own nefarious purposes, I could take you round the town, point out the places where the events in the story happen. In fact, if you've read this far, you know I've done that already!

Questions for your reading group

- On page 22 Jo remembers:

  Smelling the clean scent of Wright's Coal Tar Soap on his skin; aware of my own stink, ashamed of it, one bath a week in water everyone's used, the must and dust of the cottage clinging.

  How important is Jo's family background, and her sense of being 'other', to this narrative? Does she feel shame for her origins or does she rise above it? What difference does this make to the way she behaves and thinks?

- On page 29 Jo says:

  'You know what it's like when you don't belong.'

  How important is the sense of belonging or not belonging to Jo's identity, and how does it affect her behaviour throughout?

- Remembering the past and one's relationship to it is a vital element of this book. As readers, how reliable do you think Jo's recollections are of years gone by and how does this affect her thinking in the present?

- Early in the novel Jo thinks:

In times like these, even strangers do it . . . Life asserts itself, as physical, as unstoppable as a sneeze.

Why do you think this book has been set during the Second World War? Is there a sense that things happen in wartime that wouldn't otherwise? How different might the story have been if set in another time?

- Nash describes him and Jo as *'ships that pass in the night'* and says:

'I'm sorry, Jo, but I don't do tomorrow.'

By the end of the book, do you think this is still the case? How has their relationship developed and where will it go in the future?

- On page 32 Jo thinks:

Stranger? Heave half a brick at 'im has always been the town's attitude.

Discuss the insularity of Romsey and its inhabitants and whether things might have turned out differently in a larger place.

- Is Nash's estimation of Jo's character right? How tough is she really?

He's sure. He knows she's not cold, but he's banking on her hardihood. That she'll do what she has to – that she won't go soft or sentimental on him. Let Aggie think what she likes, he needs Jo to be tough. It's precisely what he wants her for.

• Why does everyone think Jo's unmarried?

Why is everyone determined to make me into a spinster?

How might their attitudes to her have differed if they'd known she was married and why? Are these attitudes confined to the 1940s?

• Keeping secrets is an important theme throughout the novel. While many are uncovered, Bram Nash's feeling for Jo, and hers for him, remain hidden. Why do you think this is?

• Jo takes the law into her own hands on several occasions as she searches for the truth about her birth and Ruth's death. Do you sympathise with her actions, or do you think she was wrong to act in the way she does?

Want to read
NEW BOOKS
before anyone else?

Like getting
FREE BOOKS?

Enjoy sharing your
OPINIONS?

Discover

READERS FIRST

Read. Love. Share.

Sign up today to win your first free book:
readersfirst.co.uk